Milo March is a hard-drinking, womanizing, wisecracking, James-Bondian character. He always comes out on top through a combination of personality, bluff, bravado, luck, skill, experience, and intellect. He is a shrewd judge of human character, a crack shot, and a deeper character than I have found in most of the other spy/thriller novels I've read. But, above all, he is a con-man—and a very good one. It is Milo March himself who makes the series worth reading.

—Don Miller, *The Mystery Nook* fanzine 12

Steeger Books is proud to reissue twenty-three vintage novels and stories by M.E. Chaber, whose Milo March Mysteries deliver mile-a-minute action and breezily readable entertainment for thriller buffs.

Milo is an Insurance Investigator who takes on the tough cases. Organized crime, grand theft, arson, suspicious disappearances, murders, and millions and millions of dollars—whatever it is, Milo is just the man for the job. Or even the only man for it.

During World War II, Milo was assigned to the OSS and later the CIA. Now in the Army Reserves, with the rank of Major, he is recalled for special jobs behind the Iron Curtain. As an agent, he chops necks, trusses men like chickens to steal their uniforms, shoots point blank at secret police—yet shows compassion to an agent from the other side.

Whatever Milo does, he knows how to do it right. When the work is completed, he returns to his favorite things: women, booze, and good food, more or less in that order....

D1287445

THE MILO MARCH MYSTERIES

Hangman's Harvest

No Grave for March

The Man Inside

As Old as Cain

The Splintered Man

A Lonely Walk

The Gallows Garden

A Hearse of Another Color

So Dead the Rose

Jade for a Lady

Softly in the Night

Uneasy Lies the Dead

Six Who Ran

Wanted: Dead Men

The Day It Rained Diamonds

A Man in the Middle

Wild Midnight Falls

The Flaming Man

Green Grow the Graves

The Bonded Dead

Born to Be Hanged

Death to the Brides

The Twisted Trap: Six Milo March Stories

Death to the Brides

KENDELL FOSTER CROSSEN
Writing as
M.E. CHABER

With a Foreword by
RICHARD A. LUPOFF
and an Afterword by
KENDRA CROSSEN BURROUGHS

STEEGER BOOKS / **2021**

PUBLISHED BY STEEGER BOOKS
Visit steegerbooks.com for more books like this.

©2021 by Kendra Crossen Burroughs

First Edition

The unabridged manuscript (1975), has been edited by Kendra Crossen Burroughs and Richard A. Lupoff.

ISBN: 978-1-61827-584-4

Americans see history as a straight line and themselves standing at the cutting edge of it as representatives for all mankind. They believe ... that there is nothing they cannot accomplish, that solutions wait somewhere for all problems, like brides.

—from *Fire in the Lake: The Vietnamese and the Americans in Vietnam,* by Frances FitzGerald

CONTENTS

9 / Foreword: 1974 and All That

13 / Death to the Brides

315 / Afterword: Editing the Final Novel

325 / About the Author

1974 and All That

Kendell Foster Crossen was as versatile an author as he was prolific. In addition to hundreds of short stories, he penned some forty-five novels, several comic book series, and many radio and television scripts. He was the author of two series of novels. In the first, the Green Lama, a vigilante crime-fighter based very loosely on the popular Shadow, was featured in fourteen short novels, and would probably have continued for many more had the magazine in which his exploits appeared, *Double Detective,* not been sold to another publisher who changed its orientation from crime and mystery stories to the sex-and-sadism themes of the so-called "weird mystery" genre.

Crossen's second major series featured Milo March, a World War II veteran turned insurance investigator and de facto private eye. Milo had served in the OSS (Office of Strategic Services), forerunner of the CIA. After the war he retained his commission as a reserve officer and from time to time was recalled to duty, thereby providing Crossen with reason to insert a spy thriller into what was otherwise a fairly straightforward private eye series.

Twenty-one Milo March novels were published during

Crossen's lifetime. Crossen wrote a twenty-second Milo March novel. In this one, Milo is recalled to the Army, summoned to the White House for a meeting with the President, and dispatched to Vietnam to rescue an important American being held prisoner in Hanoi.

The novel, titled *Death to the Brides,* was completed in 1975. The years 1974–1975 were tumultuous. Diplomatic teams headed by Henry Kissinger and Le Duc Tho had reached a truce agreement in Paris in 1973. It was an open secret that this was a flimsy device to save face for the Nixon Administration. After what was referred to as "a decent interval," all concerned expected the flimsy government of South Vietnam would collapse and the country would be reunified with its capital in Hanoi.

In the meanwhile, President Nixon was besieged by critics because of the Watergate scandal. At first, Nixon dismissed the incident as "a second-rate burglary," but his attempts to cover up the crime drew him deeper and deeper into a morass that eventually cost him the Presidency.

In the midst of this complex tangle, Milo March flies to Vietnam to begin what would be his final series of exploits. But when Crossen's editor at Holt, Rinehart & Winston read the manuscript, he demanded changes that Crossen was unwilling to make. Chiefly, Nixon appears onstage, not named but clearly indicated. Crossen's portrait of the President was, to say the least, not flattering. Later in the book, without overtly taking sides, Crossen implies that the North Vietnamese and Viet Cong were not so much Communist aggressors as anti-colonial nationalists.

Author and publisher at loggerheads, the manuscript was returned and never published—until now.

The author's executor, his daughter Kendra Crossen Burroughs, asked me to apply an editorial brush to the manuscript. As ex-military, it was not difficult for me to work through the manuscript and clarify details of protocol, uniform conventions, and insignia of rank. I also interpolated a few brief lines of dialog to clarify matters in the narrative. As for the politics of the book, it would have been totally inappropriate for me to change Crossen's expressed ideas. And in fact the passage of four decades has shown that he was far more right than wrong.

As a dedicated fan of Ken Crossen in general and Milo March in particular, I recommend *Death to the Brides* as a worthy grace note to the Milo March series and to Ken Crossen's fine career.

Richard A. Lupoff

ONE

The name is March. Milo March. I have a small office on Madison Avenue in New York City. The upper half of the door is opaque glass. On it is printed: *March's Insurance Service Corp.* Another line below it announces that I am president. I am also the corporation, the only stockholder, and the only employee. Normally, if that word can be used in connection with anything I do, I am an insurance investigator. It's a living.

I unlocked the door and stepped inside. The mailman had been there and the mail was on the floor, where it landed when pushed through the slot in the door. I scooped it up and walked to my desk. I tossed the mail on top of it and hung up my coat. As I sat down, I noticed that one envelope was sticking out from the others. The return address was a box number in Washington, D.C. There was something familiar about it, but I couldn't think what it was at the moment.

I opened the drawer of the desk which contained a bottle of bourbon and a glass. I put them on top of the desk. Then, feeling prepared for anything, I picked up the letter and opened it.

I was right about it. The box number was one that I remembered, and the clincher was that the envelope was addressed to Major Milo March. I opened the envelope and pulled out the letter. The first word I saw was "Greetings." I put it down and poured myself a drink. A quick drink gave me enough false courage to read the rest of the letter.

It wasn't exactly the sort of news that thrilled me. It merely told me that I was being recalled to active duty in the United States Army Reserves.

I must confess: I have another job, but it's only part time. You might guess it has something to do with the Army. In fact, it has everything to do with the Army. I had spent several years assigned to Army Intelligence or to the CIA, usually in espionage.

They had taught me a number of things which just wouldn't look right in civilian life, so when my tour of duty was over, they asked me to enlist in the Reserves. Like a damn fool, I did. This was the sixth time I'd been recalled to active duty. The letter told me that there was a reservation on a plane for Washington and ordered me to be on it in full duty uniform. It also included the information that I would be met at the airport in Washington and that I would be paged after the plane unloaded.

I picked up the phone and dialed the number of Intercontinental Insurance, my chief employer. When the girl answered, I asked for Martin Raymond, who was a big wheel at the company. The next voice I heard was that of his secretary.

"Hi, honey," I said. "This is Milo March. Is the great man in and available?"

"He's in, but I don't know about the rest of it. The last I knew he was working on the crossword puzzle. You want to ask him for money?"

"Goodness, no. I may sometimes pound on the desk and

demand money, but I never ask for it. It would be beneath my dignity."

"Well, I've never known you to be interested in more than two things. If it's not money, then it's girls. But where does our Martin Raymond fit into that picture?"

"He doesn't," I said. "Just ring him and tell him I want to talk to him for a moment and that it's important."

"All right. I'll tell him that you don't want any money, and that will put him in a good humor for the entire day."

I held the phone and waited. I heard the click as he picked up his phone. "Milo, my boy," he said. "How are you?"

"Just fine. I only wanted to—"

"Glad to hear it. Tell me, what's a four-letter word meaning a constant irritation?"

"Boss."

There was a moment of silence, then he gave what was supposed to be a laugh. It sounded like a whinny. "That's my boy. Always pushing the big laugh meter."

"You laughed too soon, Martin. The next line is better. If you have a job for me within the next few weeks, don't call me."

"What? Why not?" He sounded as if I were picking his pocket. "You know we have you on a first-call basis. Who offered you a job?"

"It's not a job. It's more of a command. You remember the United States Army?"

"But that's impossible. You've been in the Army. Several times. Besides, it was announced that we've achieved a new peace—with honor."

"Martin," I said gently, "they didn't say whose honor. They merely ordered me to be there today. The only additional message was that there would be somebody meeting me at the airport."

"That must be unconstitutional!"

"They sneaked it through one day when you were at the club," I said wearily. "I'll call you when I get back."

"We'll miss you," he said, making it sound like a funeral speech. "And I want you to know that we at Intercontinental are proud of you. When it gets rough, you can be sure that we're back of you all the time."

"How far back, Martin?"

"What?" He sounded puzzled.

"Remember General Custer? He fought the Cheyenne at Big Horn. The main body of soldiers, led by General Terry, was back of Custer. They were so far back they didn't arrive in time. You know what happened to Custer, don't you?"

"Well ... not exactly. He was—ah—"

"Killed," I said abruptly. I hung up without waiting for an answer.

I folded the letter and envelope and put them in my pocket. Then I called my answering service and told them to take messages until they heard from me. I had a drink and then left.

I stopped at my bank and cashed a check to make sure I could hold out until I got some expense money from the Army. Then I went out and hailed a cab, giving the driver my address in the Village.

When I reached the apartment, I poured myself a fresh drink

and sat down while I thought about what I needed to take with me. Fortunately I had one service uniform which hadn't been worn since it came from the cleaners. I quickly changed into it. I put the rank insignia on my shoulder tabs, then strapped on my shoulder holster. My gun was in the drawer, and I took it out and examined it. I had cleaned it earlier that week and it looked almost new. I slipped some shells into it and put it in the holster. Next, I pinned my fruit salad on the left breast of my jacket and put it on. All that remained was the packing of a small suitcase and donning my cap. As I left, I glanced in the mirror. I would at least pass muster.

Downstairs, I flagged down a taxi and told him to take me to the airport. Then I leaned back and didn't even think of what was ahead of me.

I was at the terminal early, which I had planned. I went into a bar and tried to look like any soldier on his way from one assignment to another. A martini in front of me helped the illusion.

I finished it and went to the desk to pick up my ticket. My flight was announced as I turned away. I carried my suitcase with me and got my pick of the first seats. I put my suitcase under the seat, leaned back, and fell asleep before we left the ground.

I awakened just as we were coming down in Washington. That gave me enough of a start to be one of the first passengers out of the plane. I went straight to the nearest bar in the terminal. I ordered a martini, lit a cigarette, and waited to hear a voice from the loudspeaker. What I heard was a small, soft voice from right behind me.

"Major March?"

I turned to look. It a very pretty young woman wearing an Army uniform with three stripes on the sleeve. She was standing very stiffly behind me.

"I'm Major March," I admitted.

She snapped a salute and held it. "Sergeant Marya Cooper. Reporting for duty, sir."

"Well," I said. "I wasn't told I was being put in command of the smallest and most attractive company I've ever seen. My first order is that you sit on this stool next to me and have a drink."

"I'm sorry, sir, but I can't drink. I'm on duty."

"So am I. On duty and drinking. Didn't you ever hear of women's lib?"*

"Yes, sir."

"Do you approve of it?"

There was a slight hesitation before she answered. "Most of it, sir. The feminists have said many things which should have been said long ago."

"It was," I told her, "but nobody listened. The women were too busy over a hot stove and the men were too busy being served a few shots of whiskey and then popping Sen-Sen into their mouths to remove the odor before they went home."

She smiled then. "You don't look as if you are old enough to remember that."

---

* The "women's lib" movement was already at least six or seven years old at this point, if you trace it to the 1968 protest of the Miss America beauty pageant in Atlantic City, NJ, and the 1969 founding of the Chicago Women's Liberation Union, from which the term "women's liberation" comes.

"I'm not. But when I was young, I was advanced for my age. And I never liked anyone giving me a hard sell on anything, so I did my own research and came up with the right answers before women's lib climbed on their first platform. Are you supposed to take me somewhere?"

"Yes, sir."

"Where?"

"To your destination, sir."

"Now, here we have a nice progressive group. The Army. First they brainwash you, then they fill you with a lot of nonsense so you'll talk like a second lieutenant by the time you have three stripes. When you reach that point, you're afraid to go to the bathroom because it might damage national security. Well, let's go, Sergeant."

"Yes, sir." She turned and strode away.

I followed her, and she stopped when she reached a big black Cadillac. "This is it," she said.

"I crossed behind the car to reach the right front door. As I went, I noticed that directly above the license plate there were three silver stars. I opened the door and slid in beside her. "Do you drive for General Roberts?"

"No, sir."

"Are the three stars meant to indicate the importance of General Roberts?"

"No, sir. This car belongs to General Baxter, who has borrowed you from General Roberts. I am General Baxter's secretary, and I sometimes drive it to pick up someone who's important to him."

"Sounds like a nice fringe benefit for you. I have a car just like it, except that it doesn't sport three stars and it *is* bullet-proof."

"Why?"

"It makes me more secure when there are generals standing behind my back. Who and what is your general?"

"General Baxter is in command of Army Intelligence."

"That makes him a kissing cousin of General Roberts. They remind me of two old ladies arguing about which one gets to borrow a cup of sugar."

She glanced at me and there was a smile on her face. "You know, I don't think you're so tough. I think you're a pussy-cat."

"That's more like it. Where did you ever get the idea that I was tough?"

"From General Baxter. And I read reports on a couple of your missions."

"General Baxter and I never met," I said, "so how can he make such a statement about me? And the reports are pure fiction."

"I thought that was your advantage in taking on the new assignment with such a detached manner."

"It's some advantage, but I have one that's more important."

"What?"

"He needs me. He wouldn't be borrowing me if he didn't. When you want something badly enough, you pay the going price. These are the rules of the game that they recognize and accept. Both sides do this."

"Do you accept those rules?" she asked.

"Partly. No more than that."

"What do you accept and what do you reject?"

"I accept those rules," I said, "as guidelines for the men who plan the mission. When it comes to being assigned to the mission, the only rules I accept are my own. The same thing is true of other agents—or they don't survive."

"Men like you?"

"More or less. Each man assigned to a mission has a double solution to provide. First, he must accomplish what he is asked to do. Second, he must survive and not be captured. If he fails in the second, then he has wasted part of the assets of the group that sends him out. In one way, the second solution is more important. If he is killed, it is almost certain that it will be far more difficult for an agent who may be ordered to follow him on the first mission. Perhaps impossible."

"Where do they find men like that?"

"Anywhere," I said, "from right underfoot to a far-flung corner of the world. The world has many such men. They seemingly obey all the rules, but they invent the game as they go along. Generals like Baxter and Roberts know this and will pay the price."

She swung the car to the side of the street and came to a stop in front of a large hotel. "We made a reservation for you in this hotel," she said. "I'll pick you up in the morning and take you to General Baxter. May I ask you one more question before you get out?"

"Sure."

"You make it sound more complicated than I thought. Can you simplify it for me?"

"No, but I can explain it a little better. When someone, like

General Baxter, decides to send a man into another country on an Intelligence mission, he knows that he is sending one man to connive and even fight, if necessary, against an entire country. If he wins anything, it will be a victory that will long be remembered. People in small, dark offices all over the world will laugh. Some will laugh with joy and some will laugh through tears. In other offices, there will be someone who pins up a picture of the agent—if he's been careless. There may be a line suggesting that anyone who sees him should fire first and explain later."

"Are you making that up?"

"No."

"Do you know where your present assignment will take you?"

"I can guess," I said. "I'm sure you know, but I don't want to hear it from you. I'd rather depend on my guess."

"Where?" she asked doggedly.

"The only place that fits everything I've heard from you."

"But it's dangerous."

I smiled at her. "So is climbing into a tub to take a bath. Or crossing the street. Or being in the Army, for that matter."

"Where?" she repeated, her voice sounding strained.

"Vietnam."

"But we're at peace with them."

"Sure," I said. "It's called peace with honor,* but it does overlook a few things. We still have thousands of men there.

---

* "Peace with honor" was the key phrase of President Richard Nixon's January 1973 speech announcing the treaty to end the Vietnam War. It signified the withdrawal of U.S. troops without the appearance of defeat. (All footnotes were added by the editor.)

They may not be flying the American bombers that have been sent to South Vietnam, but we're training the men who fly them. And once in a while, one of our pilots may make a flight just to help an old buddy get some sleep. We also have a lot of military and civilian advisors to answer questions. Plus military guards around to keep an eye on American civilians—and anything that interests them. You see, we are keeping the letter of the peace treaty but not the meaning of it."

"And what part will you play in it?"

"A small part. Just a walk-on. You're a smart girl. Figure it out when you go to bed. Now, how about having dinner with me tonight?"

She shook her head, smiling. "I don't think General Baxter would approve."

"How about coming in and having a drink with me?"

"Sorry, sir. I'm still on duty."

"All right. Dinner tomorrow night or lunch tomorrow?"

She laughed softly. "We'll talk about it tomorrow. I'll pick you up here at eight o'clock."

"Okay," I said with a sigh.

I got out of the car and walked inside. I checked in at the desk and followed a bellman into the elevator and then into a room. As soon as he was gone, I looked around. My appreciation of General Baxter went up several degrees. It was a suite instead of a mere room. I decided it wouldn't be polite to complain about it.

After hanging up my jacket and tie and putting the gun in a dresser drawer, I phoned room service. I ordered a bottle of bourbon, some ice, a glass, and a rare steak dinner. Then

I left a wake-up call for the morning. I turned on the television set and waited.

When the waiter arrived, I signed the check and added a tip. As soon as he left, I took off the rest of my clothes, poured some bourbon, and was ready to tackle the steak and the bourbon at the same time. I was afraid I might not last through the food and the drink. I was right about that.

TWO

The television was still on when I awakened, but that didn't surprise me until I realized *The Today Show* was what I was watching. I had slept through the entire night. It wasn't even time for my wake-up call. I looked at my watch and saw I could just make it. I went into the bathroom. I shaved and took a fast shower. The phone rang just as I returned to the other room. I had the operator switch me to room service and ordered two scrambled eggs, an English muffin, ice cubes, and coffee. I went back to put on some clothes and turn off the television.

The knock came on the door and I opened it. The waiter entered with my breakfast. I signed the check and added his tip. I was back by the small table by the time he was gone. I splashed some bourbon into a glass and sat down. The bourbon was just the thing I needed.

I finished dressing and sat down to wait. I had finished about half the bourbon when the phone rang. I picked up the receiver and answered. It was the desk clerk. Sergeant Cooper was downstairs. I finished the drink, buckled on my gun, put on my jacket and cap, and left the room.

She was waiting outside in the car. I opened the door and slid in next to her. "Good morning," I said.

"Good morning, Major March. Did you have a good sleep?"

"Fine. I awakened about forty-five minutes ago. Just time to shave and shower and have breakfast with a drink."

"How did you spend the evening?" she asked. "Chasing strange girls through the staid halls of the hotel?"

"Not me. I turned on the television set and ordered a steak dinner, a bottle of bourbon, and ice from room service. I enjoyed all three. That's known as clean living. Then I went to sleep without bothering to turn off the television or the lights. I slept the sleep of an innocent."

"That must have taken some doing. I went back to the office, read some of the reports on you, went home, turned on my record player, and went to sleep."

"If you read some of those reports, that should have been enough to put you to sleep."

"On the contrary, it was interesting. It made me understand a lot of things that you said last night. And what you said about men like you. I had never thought of your work as being one man at war against an entire country. The fact that you're successful at it explains why you get away with breaking regulations and still manage to collect all of that fruit salad. And I also know you have more that can't be given you, because the ribbons provide information that would be a security risk for you. Tell me, sir, do you also collect women the way you collect medals?"

"I do not collect women," I said. "I like women. I enjoy talking with women. I get pleasure from looking at women. I get even more pleasure from making love with them. Does that answer your question?"

"I think so," she said. There was something in her voice that sounded like a smile. "I imagine that both activities require a certain amount of intelligence work, but I'm afraid the Army doesn't issue medals in the second area."

"Please," I said. "You're touching on a tender spot. I have always felt I was a failure because I've never been given a good-conduct medal."

"I'll leave a note for General Baxter. In the meantime, relax. We'll be there in five minutes. Don't forget that he's taking you to meet someone. You might call it a command performance. Then you may have some personal plans for the day."

"I do. Suppose we have dinner tonight?"

"We'll discuss that later. Anything else?"

"Since I don't know what day I'll be leaving Washington, I'd like to get some money and buy additional military clothes."

"I already have a voucher for you, and I'll drive you to the store. Is that all right, Major March?"

"If you can't call me General, then just call me Milo. Isn't that the Pentagon?"

"Yes. We're driving right inside of it." She proceeded to do just that, ending up on a huge platform. It immediately took us up several floors. She drove off and pulled into a parking space with General Baxter's name on it.

We walked down a long corridor, went through a door, and then walked down a shorter hallway. We stopped beside a small enclosure that contained a desk, two chairs, and a large filing cabinet.

"This is my office," she said. "I'll tell him you're here." She picked up the phone and spoke softly into it, then replaced the phone and looked up at me. "Go right in. He's waiting for you. Just be yourself. He may frown sometimes, but inside he'll be friendly. Good luck."

I nodded and stepped to the door, which was only a couple of feet away. I opened the door and there he was: a tall, trim man with gray hair and a curious expression on his face.

I stopped and saluted him. "Major Milo March reporting for active duty, sir," I said.

"At ease, Major." He motioned me toward a chair in front of his desk. I went over and sat down. "Cigarette?" he asked. I took my lighter and held it to his cigarette. Then I pulled out one of my own brand and lit it.

"I'm sorry we never met before," he said. "Normally, we should have, but I'm afraid that General Roberts likes to keep his men under cover even at home. Actually, you were originally assigned to us, but the General borrowed you and then decided that possession was the better part of a contract."

"That sounds like him. General Roberts and I have known each other for a long time and have had our differences of opinion since our first meeting."

He smiled. "Having read your files, I think I can understand that. I must admit that I'm impressed by your files, but I can see that a commanding officer might take a dim view of your attitude. You have broken almost every military regulation I can think of, and many reports give the impression that you were lucky in being able to accomplish your mission and return safely. I do not accept this theory. The agent who depends on luck seldom accomplishes anything and seldom returns. I got a feeling from the reports that you went into every situation with an exact knowledge of how you would reach your destination, the best way of accomplishing your mission, and at least an idea of how you would get back."

"Fortune favors the bold," I said.*

He was staring at me. "Is that idea of your own creation, Major?"

"I'm sorry to say it isn't, sir. Some Roman fellow named Publius Vergilius Maro said it. *Audentes Fortuna iuvat.* The Goddess of Luck helps those who dare. It's been kicking around for a long time."

"Good grief, March, do you know everything?"

"Hardly, sir. I'm afraid I've got a mind like a vacuum cleaner. It picks up all sorts of things. Some of them are just dust and scraps, but others turn out to be pretty worthwhile, like the line from Virgil."

He nodded, smiling. "You know, I've often thought that poets and philosophers should be required reading for intelligence agents. Has Sergeant Cooper told you where you will be going on this mission?"

"No, sir, but I'm sure I have guessed where it will be."

"Let's hear it."

"Vietnam."

"Why do you think so, Major?"

"It's the only logical place. Vietnam."

His eyebrows lifted quizzically. "Why there?"

"We have peace there, but it doesn't mean a damn thing. We still have a hell of a lot of men there. Sure, I know they're not supposed to be fighting, but I'd like to have a bundle of

---

* This is a Latin proverb *("Audentes Fortuna iuvat")* that appears in Virgil's *Aeneid.*

money for every Vietnamese, from North and South, that Americans have killed. Soldiers and civilians."

"I think that's true," he said, "but where the hell do you get your information?"

"I do know something of what has happened and is happening in Vietnam. I was there five years ago and then I was there again a little more than a year ago. I also have personal friends all over that area who give me information when I want it."

"I thought you must have been there about a year ago. One of my men got some unexpected help in Vietnam about that time. I thought it looked like your work, but I checked on the records and you were supposed to be in Cambodia. Who assigned you to Vietnam?"

"I did," I said. "I was sent to Cambodia by the CIA, but that job was pretty much under control. A friend of mine told me that an Army Intelligence man needed some help near Saigon, so I went there."

"Is that the only time you have made your own orders and then followed them?"

"Not exactly."

"Has anyone briefed you on your present assignment?"

"No, sir."

"I will do so," he said. "Later. First I'm taking you to meet someone. I very much doubt you'll get any information or pleasure from the meeting, but I have no alternative. You do have my permission to answer any and all questions as you see fit."

"I've never met such a nice-talking general in my life. May I ask where we're going?"

"The White House. All roads in Washington lead there. Let's go." He stood up and led the way out of the office. "We're ready to go, Sergeant."

"So am I, sir," she said.

He nodded and led the way. Sergeant Cooper slid in under the wheel. I held the back door open for the General. I hesitated only a minute and then climbed in next to him. I would rather have sat up front with her, but that might be breaking too many records in one day. I knew I'd been right when I noticed the tug of a smile on his lips. It gave me another clue to him. He was a man who liked to make bets with himself, and he had just won the bet.

In minutes we were there and she turned into the White House grounds. After winding around a few short curves, we pulled into a parking area labeled "Army." The General looked at his watch as we got out. "I don't think this will take long, Sergeant," he said. "But you can turn off the motor. We don't want him to think we're wasting energy. Come on, March."

As I fell into step with him, I noticed the little smile was busy once more. Maybe he wouldn't be so bad to work for after all. We entered what seemed to be a side door and walked down a long hallway. There was no sound except that of our feet on the floor.

"We check in here first," he said, stopping in front of a door. "You are about to meet another general."

"How lucky can I get? The worst that can happen is that I get blinded by the lights reflecting from stars."

"He is Brigadier General Manchester, presently the chief

aide of this part of the White House. In civilian clothes and on temporary leave from the Army. He's our last sentry post." He tapped on the door and a voice answered from the other side. General Baxter opened the door.

"Good morning, General Manchester," he said. "This is Major March, temporarily working with me."

"Good morning, Major March," the man said. He studied me for a few seconds, then his gaze returned to Baxter's face. "He's expecting you. Go on in. I'll let him know that you're on the way." He reached under his desk, and I suspected there was a button there.

We turned and stepped across the corridor. General Baxter looked at me with a strange smile on his face. "This is your big moment, Major."

"I can hardly wait," I said as he opened the door.

Although I had guessed who we were going to see, I would have recognized him the minute I saw him. His face reminded me slightly of Bob Hope's. The big difference was that if it had been Hope, I would have probably laughed when he spoke. Nothing like that happened. He stared at me with an expression that must have been like that of a slave buyer being offered the first item on the block.

"I'm glad to see you, Major March. I've heard so much about you that I feel as if I've known you for a long time. I suppose you have your game plan ready?"

"I beg your pardon, sir?" I said.

"Your game plan," he said impatiently. "I know you must be a team player, and I'm sure you give your players all of your instruction before you get on the field."

I took a quick glance at General Baxter. The small grin was again tugging at the corners of his mouth. I shrugged and turned back to the man at the desk.

"I'm afraid, sir," I said dryly, "that you are confusing my mission with this week's football game. It's true that I'm in charge of the action, but I'm also the only player on my team. It does, however, bear one resemblance to a football match: if anyone throws you a forward pass, you'd better make sure you catch it and get rid of it without waiting to admire it."

His smile stiffened as he picked up something and came around the table. "I know your record, Major, and it's one to be proud of. I have the honor of giving you one of the rewards that is due you." He reached up and fumbled with one of my shoulders. He moved around and did the same thing with my other shoulder. He tossed something on the desk but continued to fumble. I glanced down at the desk and saw my bronze oak leaves. Then I looked at one of my shoulders and got a glimpse of a pair of silver eagles.

"Congratulations, Colonel March," he said as he moved back in front of me. I automatically stood at attention and started to salute him. "That's not necessary," he added. "In this office, I'm just one of the fellows. Now we'll do that once more for the record."

"What record?" General Baxter asked quietly.

"It's a regular procedure here. Whenever I give any sort of award to a man, we have it photographed and sent out to all the newspapers. The friendly ones, at least. The photographer is in the next room. I'll get him right over here."

"There are to be no pictures of Colonel March," the General

said. "There are at least a dozen countries looking for photographs of our men. The minute they find one of Colonel March, he'll be a dead hero within days. This *is* a matter of national security, sir."

"I agree with General Baxter," I said. "If your photographer comes in here with a camera, he'll leave with a broken camera. Now, if you'd like to take back these pieces of silver on my shoulders, you're welcome to them. I've seen the defoliation you've ordered in Vietnam. I don't care to be the victim of another such order."

His mouth tightened with anger. "All right. I thought you were a real man."

"You wouldn't know one if you saw him. You're a small man in a big job. Why don't you go back to warming the bench for some small-town football team?"

He pushed some papers on his desk, and I noticed his hands were shaking. "Get out," he said. "Keep your damn promotion. Maybe we'll see if you still have it after a court-martial."

"At your service, sir. General, let's go out and get some fresh air."

"A good idea, Colonel," General Baxter said. "Let's consider that we achieved peace with honor. Go ahead, March. I'll cover your back."

I opened the door and stepped outside. He joined me and we walked down the hallway and outdoors. Sergeant Cooper was out of the car and had the door opened by the time we reached it. "Straight back to the Pentagon," Baxter told her. He glanced at me. "There should be someone there waiting to see you."

"What is this, Show and Tell day?" I asked. "Well, it can't be too bad if he's coming to see me. It's better than being dragged in and being told to perform."

"What performance do you mean?" the Sergeant asked.

General Baxter told her about our visit. He did embellish it slightly, but she seemed to enjoy it. "You must be very brave, Colonel," she said over her shoulder. Speaking of which, I could tell she was looking at mine.

"Pardon me, sir," she said, "but weren't you just a major?"

I grinned. "That's right."

"And now you're a bird colonel? You didn't get a promotion. You skipped right over lieutenant colonel to full colonel!"

"The Commander-in-Chief giveth," I said. "And speaking of bravery, there is a Chinese proverb: 'He who is too brave may not live long enough to prove it.' "

"I suppose you speak Chinese?" she asked.

"Shih. Pu ts'ui."

"What's that mean?"

"Yes. Of course I do."

"And Vietnamese?"

"Mot thu tieng thi khong bao gio du." *

"He does," General Baxter said, ending that conversation. We were already in the Pentagon and soon pulled into the General's parking place. "Colonel Locke," he continued, "is waiting for us in my office. Our talk with him shouldn't take long. Sergeant Cooper has a voucher for you and she will get it cashed. She'll wait for us to finish with Locke, then she

---

* One language is never enough.

will send you to look at a photograph of a man. I want you to memorize his features. Sergeant Cooper will take you to do your shopping."

"Thank you, sir."

By this time we had reached his office. There was a girl wearing the stripes of a corporal sitting at Sergeant Cooper's desk. She looked up and seemed relieved at the sight of us.

"Sorry we're a little late," Sergeant Cooper said. "Did Colonel Locke arrive?"

"Yes. He's inside waiting, but he seemed a little impatient when I told him to go in. He had a dog with him and insisted it had to go with him."

Sergeant Cooper smiled at me. "By this time he's probably tried to find his own files so he could read the reports. He's the only other person whose files read like those of another colonel we know."

"I've never had a dog in my life," I declared indignantly.

"You should have asked for one at the office where you went this morning. He usually has several dogs who help to rescue him when the heat is too much."

"I didn't know you were talking about two-legged dogs," I said.

The General cleared his throat. I guessed it was a signal and wheeled around to face him. "We'd better go, General, before the plantation hands get too restless."

He smiled as he opened the door. I followed him into the offices.

There was a man sitting near the desk. He wore civilian clothes, but I recognized his face. There was a dog lying on the floor next to the man's feet. I remembered one of them. The man was Kim Locke, but the dog was unfamiliar, and the minute he saw me he stood at attention. He was small and muscular with a black and tan coat. He could have passed for a fierce Doberman pinscher who'd been put through a mad scientist's shrinking machine.

"Colonel Locke," the General said, "you remember Colonel March?"

"Sure," he said. "How are you, Milo?"

"All right, I guess," I said, "although I do feel a little like a pig starting up the first ramp in the slaughterhouse."

"Why don't you sit down, March," the General said. "Then I'll tell you both why you're here."

Locke and I looked at each other and shrugged. I sat down and the dog made a small noise in his throat.

"It's all right, fella," I said. "I'm a friend." I looked inquiringly at Locke. "What happened to Dante?"*

Locke looked pained. "Dante has gone to his reward, I'm sorry to report. But he lived to a ripe old age, staying with my family after retirement. He was buried with honors," Locke added proudly. "Now, this is one of the new dogs I've been training. Before you ask why he's so little, I'll tell you: it's because sometimes a working dog has to navigate small, confined spaces or conceal himself easily. He is extremely agile and a master escape artist. He can open doors and climb

* Kim Locke of the CIA and his dog Dante, a Hungarian puli (lifespan 12–16 years), made their debut in a magazine story, "The Red Candle" *(Bluebook,* December 1953), written by Crossen under the pen name Christopher Monig. They next appeared in two novels: *The Big Dive* (1959) and *The Gentle Assassin* (1964). *The Tortured Path* (1957) features Kim Locke without the dog. See further comments in the Bonus Material.

fences. He was so smart and quick as a pup that I decided to name him in honor of his predecessor. So … Dante the Second, meet Major March."

The dog approached me slowly. His body language said, *Is this guy all right? I'd better check him out!* He sniffed at my ankle, then stretched out between us. He looked at me again and wagged his tail. I guess I'd passed the smell test.

"As you both know," the General said, "Colonel Locke was assigned to this mission. Unfortunately, his last mission was a little rough. Our doctor insisted that he be given a leave before going on another assignment. You, Colonel March, weren't on a mission and you are familiar with the territory. Locke and I discussed it, and he agreed with me that you would be a perfect replacement."

"Thanks a lot, Colonel," I said.

He smiled. "Anything for an old buddy."

"He also made a suggestion," Baxter replied. "He will loan you his dog for the job."

That surprised me. "I assumed he was a one-man dog, like most working dogs."

"He is, but I think you may be an exception. He came to you readily a minute ago. Don't make the mistake of under-selling Dante. I think he already knows that you're going to work with him. And he'll be worth more than any three men you could take with you."

"You're probably right," I agreed. "The question is, will he obey me?"

"It won't take long. Call me this afternoon and we'll talk about it. Sergeant Cooper will give you my phone number.

Dante, I'll see you later. Take good care of Milo." With that he was gone.

"You made a good choice, March," the General said. "I've never seen the dog work, but the reports indicate that he may accomplish even more than Colonel Locke claims for him. He may be of help to you. The way it looks, this will be one where you're playing it by ear."

"When do I ever get any other kind?"

He smiled. "That's one of the reasons you were picked. As a result of the overall picture, I'm going to tell you only what I want you to accomplish. The rest will be up to you."

"Thanks," I said, and I meant it. "When I get detailed instructions, I feel bad when I have to change so many of them."

"The only thing I do insist on," he continued, "is results. You probably know the present situation in Vietnam better than we do. Things are a mess there. In the last year, hundreds of villages, and their inhabitants, have been destroyed. More, you can be sure, than were wasted by the soldiers from the North. Some of our men have been involved in the theft of medical supplies, television sets, radios, and anything that can be sold in Europe. Then there are the profits from prostitution and drugs. Our helicopters bring back wounded and dead from the battlefields—but for a price. Much of this money goes to local men who have strong political connections. But some does go to our men. Most of the places that are destroyed are leveled by American machines known as Rome plows. And we believe that three small armies are in charge of almost all of these activities."

"Three armies? Who does the third army belong to?"

"A small group of Americans who don't see any reason why a bunch of men whom they call 'gooks' should make all of that profit. Or why the Vietnamese from the North should be cutting in either. I believe there are three command posts in South Vietnam. One run by the South, one by the North, and one by Americans who have shown no desire to be discharged and returned home. I want to know more about this whole situation."

"Is that all?" I asked dryly.

"Not quite. We want you to penetrate into the interior of North Vietnam."

"I see," I said, drawing a deep breath. "Is that my other mission?"

"Yes. There was a man in Saigon several months ago. He worked in our Embassy. He was also one of my men. His name is Martin Rigsby. It is his picture you will be shown when you leave this office."

"How does he figure in this mission?"

"He *is* the mission. He was one of our men. He was at the Embassy as a civilian employee, and it made a good cover. He went up into the highlands with a small military group looking for a number of men who were reported missing in action and probably dead. We had permission from the North Vietnamese. Rigsby was supposedly there because he could identify several of the men. Not a very good reason, but the only one we had. He and two soldiers disappeared and were not found. We believe that he was captured, possibly killed. But we have no evidence that he is either a prisoner or dead."

"And you expect me to find him?"

"Yes, but that's not all of it. If he's alive and a prisoner in Hanoi, we expect you to bring him back alive."

"And that's all?" I asked lightly. "You know, while you were talking, I thought I felt the Tooth Fairy's hand under my pillow. And I think I felt a cold wind on the back of my neck. When do I leave?"

"That depends on when Colonel Locke tells me that you and Dante have rehearsed enough."

"Do I have a cover when I reach Saigon?" I asked.

"Yes. You'll be the new military attaché to our embassy. As soon as I know when you'll leave, I'll phone them and tell them to put their present attaché on a plane for here at once. And I'll tell them when you'll be there."

"Gee," I said, "that's just like a movie I saw once."

"You'll report to General Lawson at the embassy. He'll be expecting you. And that's the best cover we can give you. Now get out of here."

"Yes, sir. Come on, Dante. We're not wanted around here."

Dante was at the door before I reached it. "You see," I called over my shoulder, "he can't wait to get out either. We'll see you around."

"You'd better. Good luck, Milo."

"Sure. I think I'll need it."

"Don't forget that you're supposed to look at some photographs on the way out. And Sergeant Cooper has new identification for you."

Dante and I left his office and stopped at Sergeant Cooper's desk. She looked up as I stopped beside her. "You're to look at pictures," she said. "Go down that way to the third area that looks just like this, even the furniture. There is, however, a long table crowded in there, too. There's a corporal at the desk. Her name is Marcia Wild and she's very pretty.* Be sure to look at the photographs she has there. I'll be down to get you soon and we'll go shopping."

"Come along," I said to Dante. "You can protect me from the pretty lady."

I walked away and he followed at my heels. We soon found the right place. I knew it was the destination, for there was a corporal at the desk and she was pretty. Then I realized that she had said something to me. She said it again. "May I help you, Colonel?" she asked.

"I've been led to believe so," I said. "I was told you have some photographs to show me. I trust they're not too spicy."

Her cheeks were slightly pink as she gestured over her shoulder. "They're in that large envelope on the table," she said.

I walked around her and she caught her first sight of Dante. She almost jumped out of the chair but caught herself in time. "What's that?" she asked in a tight voice.

"A dog," I said mildly. "His name is Dante and he's a min pin."

She held her hand down and Dante sniffed her fingers. He seemed to approve, or at least he didn't snap one of them off. "I never heard of a min pin," she said.

"A miniature pinscher. I got a little briefing from Colonel Locke. They're not miniaturized Dobermans; they're a breed

* While this character is not indispensable to the plot, it was very sweet of the author to add a pretty lady with his wife's maiden name, Marcia Wild. She was his fourth and last wife, also called Marcelia.

of their own. But they look a lot like Dobies. Smart, brave, and loyal. Make one your friend and you're lucky. He'll never betray you."

By now Dante and Corporal Wild had decided to fall in love. The mutt jumped into her lap and proceeded to settle down like a long-time chum.

"Unfortunately, Army brass takes a dim view of mere dogs holding rank. If it weren't for that, he'd be at least a four-star general. As it is, I think his only rating is a mere K-9. Come on, Dante, before the lady realizes she didn't salute you." He jumped off her lap and followed me over to the table, and I sat down in front of the envelope and took the pictures out.

There were several photographs, all of the same man but from different angles. He was about my age. He had an interesting face but not an unusual one. My overall impression of the man was that he would almost disappear against any normal background. I had just finished memorizing his features when there was an almost inaudible sound from Dante. I looked around and noticed that Sergeant Cooper was standing next to the Corporal. I put the photographs into the envelope and stood up.

"Let's go, Dante," I said.

We walked up and stopped beside Sergeant Cooper. There was a smile on her lips when she looked at me. "Are you ready?" she asked.

"Yes."

"Then let's go."

"Okay," I said. I looked at the Corporal. "Thank you, Corporal Wild. The photographs were very exciting."

Her cheeks turned pink again. "You're welcome, Colonel March," she said, but her heart wasn't in it.

We turned and left, the Sergeant and me with Dante at our heels. She didn't say anything until we were in the car. Then she turned to me and the smile was fully grown. "What did you say to Corporal Wild to upset her?"

"Nothing important. She told me that the photographs I was supposed to see were on the table. I merely told her that I hoped they weren't too spicy. Then she saw Dante and that upset her, so I told her he held no rank and that was all."

She was laughing. "You shouldn't have. Corporal Wild is a lovely, sweet girl. You should watch your language with her."

"I'm not a language watcher. There are other things more interesting to watch. Where are we going?"

"Shopping, as planned. Then I'll have lunch with you. I've already made a reservation ... at my apartment."

THREE

Shopping used up about two hours, but I got everything I needed, including a .38 automatic. I could pick up the duty uniforms the next day, by which time they'd be altered to fit. Everything else was stuffed into two large shopping bags. I had also bought an extra suitcase, which I hoped was large enough to hold everything I would be taking. We drove straight to her apartment and I carried everything upstairs. Then I went back downstairs with Dante and waited until he had paid his respects to all the bushes and trees.

"There's a martini on the table," Marya called out as we entered. "I'll be right out." A door slammed somewhere in the apartment, so I guessed she was in the bathroom.

Dante stretched out on the floor and I looked around for the martini. It was on a coffee table in the living room. I took off my jacket and sat down. It was a good martini. I lit a cigarette and sipped the drink while I waited.

She came out a few minutes later, wearing a red robe that fit better than her uniform did. She went to the kitchen and came back with another glass and the pitcher of martinis. "Do you like my robe?" she asked.

"What's not to like?" I wanted to know. "If I'm asked, I'll recommend that the Army make that the official uniform for women who sign up. There's only one thing wrong with it."

"What's that?"

"You'll have the advantage. They will only have General Issue material under their uniform."

"I never thought of that," she said. "Are you ready for lunch?"

"Not just yet. I'm supposed to phone Colonel Locke. Do you have his number?"

"I knew you were supposed to call him, so I copied it on a card. It's beside the phone. Help yourself. I'll be back in a minute or so."

She walked across the room and entered the bedroom. I went over to the phone and dialed the number. He answered after the second ring.

"This is Milo March," I said. "You wanted me to call you."

"Yeah. How's everything going?"

"Fine," I said, "if you're referring to my shopping. If you had anything else in mind, I'm not sure. Dante keeps upstaging me."

He laughed. "He'll do it every time if you let him get away with it. Want to come over to my place tonight?"

"What for? To tell me how patriotic you are to give up a night with the girls?"

"Not unless you're going to give up your night with the girls."

"All right," I said. "Why do you want me to come over?"

"To work. With Dante."

"All right. What time?"

"About eight. There's a new housing area going up on the edge of the city. We have permission to work out there tonight. That's good. It'll make it possible for us to work all night."

"What the hell is good about that?" I wanted to know.

"It should give us enough of a start so we can finish some-time tomorrow. That means that you can leave for Saigon the next morning, which should make the General happy. And it may even make you happy."

"And you?" I had some suspicion about the fact that what he had claimed would take a week could now be done in one night and one day.

"In a way, I guess," he admitted. "I have a special date for tomorrow night and I'd hate to have to change it."

"I may just make it impossible for you to keep that date. Is the use of firearms permissible in that new housing area? I'll see you later." I slammed down the receiver.

"What was that all about?" Marya asked. I looked around and she was standing in the doorway to the bedroom. She was dressed in her uniform again.

"What's that all about?" I repeated. "You just took that uniform off. Now it's back on. Why?"

"That was Colonel Locke, wasn't it? I heard your last few words and I guessed that he delivered some bad news."

"You could call it that. He said that we'll work all night tonight and maybe all day tomorrow. That's so I can have the pleasure and honor of leaving for Saigon the following morn-ing. I don't know what I'd do without him, but I'd like to try."

She laughed. "I thought it was something like that when I heard your remarks. You wouldn't really shoot him, would you?"

"Not in a vital spot, but I'd guarantee he wouldn't dance when he takes his date out tomorrow night. Now, where are you going?"

"Right now," she said, "I'm going to sit down and help you partake of your favorite tranquilizer." She refilled our glasses and picked her own up. "Let's drink a toast to Dante."

I laughed. "He probably knows what you said. The trouble with Kim is that he starts thinking he's smarter than his dog is." I lifted my glass and emptied it. She refilled it.

"Now," she said, "what was this all about?"

"Earlier today, in the General's office, Kim thought I would have to work with Dante for about a week. Now he's either just made a date for tomorrow night or just remembered that he has one for then, so I'm supposed to be at his place at eight o'clock this evening. The idea is that we will work all night—or at least I will—and probably all day tomorrow so I can leave early the following morning. He will report to General Baxter this afternoon. Before eight, I'm sure. Now, what's the explanation of the uniform? I thought you were going to cook when I got hungry."

"I will, but you're not hungry yet. I heard the tone of your voice when you were talking on the phone and thought it might be something like this. So, with your permission, I have an idea for regrouping and thinking up a new plan."

"What is your game plan—chief?"

"You think you will have to work all night and maybe all day tomorrow. You might even have to work part of the second night. Then, with only two or three hours' sleep, you have to gather all your things and be on a plane early the next morning. My suggestion is that you go into the bedroom and get some sleep. In the meantime, I'll go to your hotel and have you checked out. I'll gather up your things and bring them back here. Then I'll wake you in plenty of time for you to have breakfast, and I'll take you to Colonel Locke's place. How's that?"

"That," I said, "is great, but I had hardly thought of it that way. I had been thinking that whenever I got the order to board that plane, we would have had a little more time together."

"We'll get as much as we can. I want it too. I want to talk to you, but there won't be enough time to do all the talking and listening that I want. But it'll have to do."

I thought about it for a minute. "You mean you're inviting me to move in here?"

"Why shouldn't I?" she asked defiantly. "You won't be here very much in one day and two nights, and we won't have to dash back and forth between here and the hotel and to the Pentagon and to Colonel Locke's apartment, and we'll probably have to do last-minute shopping for things we forgot today."

I poured another drink into my glass. "All right. If you're sure that—"

"I'm sure," she said. "I'll go to the hotel now. You be sure that you go to sleep."

"How can I, when you just stay there running off at the mouth?"

She opened the door. "Good-bye." The door slammed and she was gone. I looked at the pitcher. There wasn't much fluid left in it, but there were several cubes left. I went into the kitchen and came back with the bottle of gin. I returned to the kitchen, found a dish and filled it with water, and took it to Dante. Then I poured some straight gin over several ice cubes and went to work.

I finished the drink, then went into the bedroom. I said good night to Dante, closed the door, got undressed, and climbed into the bed. It felt good. That's about all I had time to do. I drifted into sleep.

Sometime later I slowly surfaced from sleep and groped at remembering where I was. Just as I was about to have it all straight, I moved slightly and realized that someone was lying next to me. I opened my eyes and turned my head. It was Marya. Her eyes were closed and her breathing was gentle. I reached over and touched her body and she inched closer to me. I put my left arm under her head and pulled her gently to me.

Later, I was lying half asleep with my arms still around her. "You know," I said, "I've left wake-up calls in hotels all over the world, but I've just discovered what I've been missing all of these years. There's just one thing that bothers me."

"What?"

"I don't remember the exact wording in the code of military conduct, but you didn't salute me before you climbed into bed. Maybe I should have worn my silver eagles."

She laughed. "My only experience with saluting has been under more restricted circumstances. When I first came in, I thought I saw you standing at attention. Then I thought you ordered 'at ease,' so I forgot about saluting."

I leaned over and kissed her lightly on the lips.

"Flattery," she said, "will get you nowhere. Besides, it's time to get up. You have to have your belated breakfast. Then you'll have enough time to relax for a while before going to meet Colonel Locke." She swung her legs out of the bed and stood up. She brushed the hair out of her eyes and walked to the wall closet.

She was a lovely sight, reminding me of a line in a poem I had once read. Unconsciously, I spoke the words: " 'She walks in beauty, like the night ...' "

She was halfway into the red robe as she turned to face me. "What happened to the tough Intelligence agent I recently met? That had to be Keats or Byron."

"Byron," I admitted. "There are three more lines that should be included with that one:

'She walks in beauty, like the night
of cloudless climes and starry skies;
And all that's best of dark and bright
meet in her aspect and her eyes....'

"I hadn't remembered it in a long time until I saw you walk across the room."

"That's sweet of you, Milo." She shrugged into the red robe. "Wait and I'll get your robe from your suitcase." She walked into the living room, and I followed her. She bent down and took my robe from the suitcase. When she turned around, I was there. She smiled and held the robe for me.

"I think Dante is annoyed with us." He was staring up, but

at the sound of his name, his tail managed a few faint movements.

"I think he's trying to tell us that we overlooked his lunch," I said.

"I forgot all about it," she said. "I have some Canadian bacon in the kitchen. I'll cook up several slices for him." She hurried into the kitchen, and I went over and sat down.

There was the clatter of pans from the kitchen, then the frying of meat. Dante caught the smell of the latter. He came over and rubbed his head against my leg to show that he appreciated the fact that he was going to get some attention at long last.

Marya soon came from the kitchen with a bowl of meat for him. He wagged his tail at her and went to work on it. She went back to the kitchen and returned with a bucket of ice cubes, two glasses, and a bottle of vermouth. The gin was still on the table. She poured from both bottles into the pitcher, added the ice, and stirred. Then she filled our glasses.

"Did you get some sleep?"

"Sure. As much as I need."

She took a big swallow of the martini. "Milo?" she said, her voice sounding subdued.

"Yes?"

She was looking at her drink. "This afternoon. Did I make a mistake?"

"Not that I know of, Marya. What kind of mistake?"

"When I came back from the hotel. I was aggressive. Men don't like it when women are aggressive."

I lit a cigarette and passed it to her, then lit one for myself.

"Honey," I said, "you sound like something out of the last century. Besides, I never believed it. We were both aggressive. You were initially aggressive and I was receptively aggressive. And, finally, we were both receptive. I think it was a beautiful thought, no matter who had it."

"I'm glad. I mean I'm glad I was aggressive. But immediately afterwards, I was afraid, and it was too late to be afraid."

"Don't be afraid of having thoughts and desires of your own. Just be reassured by the fact that you have them. That makes you normal. If it turns out to be a warm, pleasant experience, you're way ahead of the game. What you feel inside of you is City Hall. Don't fight it."

She glanced at the small clock on the table and made a startled sound in her throat. "I almost forgot *our* lunch. It'll take only a few more minutes." She vanished into the kitchen.

There were noises from that direction, but I couldn't hear anything that was a clue. Finally, I poured another martini for myself and waited. After a short time, she returned with two plates. She put the plates down and stood back to wait for me to react.

"Eggs Benedict," I said. "Did you make these?"

She nodded and continued to wait. So I cut off a bite and put it in my mouth. It was good. I said so.

"I hoped you'd like it. I worked hard enough on it."

"Worked?"

She nodded. "I learned that you liked them before I even met you. I'd never tasted them. I'd read some of the reports on you, and I was curious. I'd heard that you could tell a lot about people by knowing what they liked to eat. So I found a recipe and tried making them. For several days, all I had to eat was Eggs Benedict. Finally, one day, I discovered that I loved them. I invited a friend over and made them. She loved them. So all I had to do was wait until you showed up."

"Sounds like a plot."

"In a way, I suppose it was," she said. "I read all of the March reports, some of them twice. I decided that you were the only person who could help me with something I want to do very badly. Will you?"

"Depends on what it is. Or do I have to make a blind answer?"

"No. I'll tell you. To begin with, there are many things I don't like about the Army—but there are some things I do like. I've been lucky, but I don't want to spend the rest of my life as a sergeant or pounding a typewriter and driving a beautiful car to run boring errands for someone."

"Thanks for the classification. But you might run into someone with the wrong lifestyle or who would never be home."

She laughed. "I wasn't suggesting that you make a proposal of marriage. I know what I want to do, but I don't know how to accomplish it. Will you help me?"

"I'll try," I said. I glanced at my watch. "And we don't have much time. What is it you've set your little heart on doing and what kind of help do you need?"

"I want to be an Intelligence agent."

I almost choked on my eggs. "Why didn't you choose something that's difficult?"

"You don't think I could do it? You don't think I'm intelligent enough?"

"Frankly," I said, "I never thought there was any connection between *intelligence* and Intelligence. I do think that it's going to be difficult to get the Army to admit that you, or any other woman, is intelligent enough to be an agent. That's your big hurdle."

She nodded. "I know. I think I have enough intelligence for the job. I'm not so sure about the violent aspects, but I could learn. I'm stronger and quicker than I look."

"I don't doubt you, Marya. But there are other obstacles that you haven't thought of. First, you'll have to go to an officer-training school."

"General Baxter has already promised he will send me to school as soon as I know what I want to do."

"That doesn't mean much. And don't forget that the word 'agent' covers a multitude of sins. I'm an agent. So is some poor person who's buried in the records room. And the real trouble starts once you become an agent. You may never get an assignment in the field, which is what you want."

"Because I'm a woman?"

"There are two reasons, but the answer is yes in both cases. There will be a lot of objections to your assignment to Intelligence. There will be a lot of men who don't want a woman working next to them unless it's in a bed. Then there's a smaller group that will join them if the subject comes up of giving you a mission in the field. They are the ones who don't care if a male agent is raped while on duty, but if it happens to a female agent, they will feel as guilty as if they did the deed themselves. Bad publicity for the Army, you know."

"You're saying that they'll find a way to keep me out."

"No. I'm only saying they will try."

"But you'll help me?"

"I'll help all I can," I said. "There are, however, more things involved than you can possibly imagine. The most important lessons are never taught in any school. You have to learn them on your own in an actual situation. I'll teach you all that I know."

"Before you leave for Saigon?"

"When I get back from Vietnam."

"You mean if—" She stopped with her mouth open. "I mean, if you have the time," she finished quickly.

"Sure," I said easily. "When or if. It all counts on twenty."

"But I don't have twenty years," she said. "I'm sorry, Milo. I shouldn't have said that. I know you can't make any plans until the General tells you what time you're leaving Washington. And I don't suppose he can tell you until he hears from Colonel Locke. And Colonel Locke's opinion partly depends on the girl he has a date with tomorrow night. And that's the Army."

"Sorry, honey. I told you I will do all I can to help you, and I meant it. But I can't be of much help if I have to face charges for refusing to carry out orders."

"I know that, Milo." She looked at her watch, then picked up the bourbon and poured some in my glass. "You might as well have one for the road. It's almost time for me to drive you to Colonel Locke's apartment. I don't suppose he ever thought of picking you up."

"Don't worry about it," I said. "I'll take a taxi. Do you know his address?"

"I wrote it down on the back of the card where I put the phone number. And you won't take a taxi—I'll drive you there. I'll get dressed now." She stood up and walked across the room. She stopped at the door and looked back. "I must be slipping. I should have started this schedule earlier and it might have developed into something.... I'll only be a minute and then you can get dressed." She stepped inside and closed the door.

I took a drink and looked down at Dante. He was staring at me. "It's all right, Dante," I said. "We're going to make a visit and then it'll be back to the drawing board for us."

He wagged his tail and stood up.

FOUR

She pulled the car over to the curb and stopped in front of an attractive apartment house. She turned off the motor. Then she turned to look at me. There was a sad look in her eyes.

"Don't look like that," I said. "I won't be gone long. And when I return, I'll give you all the help I can."

"I know," she said. "But tonight my apartment will feel empty—and very soon it will be empty. That is what I was thinking, and I was wishing we'd been more aware of the time this evening…. How do you like the building where Colonel Locke lives while in Washington?"

"It's too good for him. He must have been around when he was able to spoon up some of that Watergate gravy."

"No," she said strongly. "He may cut some corners when he reports his expenses on a mission, but he'd never touch a mess like that."

"I was only kidding," I said. "I know he wouldn't touch it. But why are you so defensive on his behalf?"

"He's one of the family. And I guess I feel like the Den Mother."

"Just don't get any of those motherly feelings when you're around me. I guess Dante and I better go see him and get to work."

"Wait a minute," she said. She picked up her bag and

fumbled around for a minute. Then she reached over and dropped something in my hand.

"What's this?" I asked.

"The spare key to my apartment. If you should be lucky enough to finish anytime tonight, you can come up and let yourself in without waking me up."

"If that's an order, I refuse to obey it."

She laughed. "I'm going to bed right after I get back to the apartment. But the key also serves another purpose. If you work all night but manage to be finished sometime during the day, I may not be home when you get there. I have to do some shopping, probably during the afternoon. You can go there and get in with the key, and it'll be a nice surprise to find you there. Oh, I'll also bring home your two new uniforms."

"Then we'll go out to dinner," I said.

"No, we won't. I still have a lot of talking to do."

"Okay." I opened the door. "I'll see you when we both get there."

She leaned over and kissed me lightly on the lips. "Don't let him pull rank on you and work you too hard."

I got out of the car and Dante followed me. I shut the door and waved to her. As I walked up to the building, I looked for Dante and saw he was busy with the shrubbery. He saw me looking at him and wagged his tail. I guess he knew he was home.

When Dante was ready, we entered the building. I pressed the button under Kim's name and a moment later the door buzzed and we went inside. There was an elevator and we took it to the third floor. Kim had the door to his apartment open and was there waiting for us.

"It's about time you got here," Kim said.

"It's my time. Besides, I wanted to give you enough time if one of your girlfriends had just dropped in." I looked around for Dante. He was standing in the hallway watching both of us. I decided I might as well show off a little—or at least try to. "Come on, Dante. Let's go in." He trotted through the door.

Kim Locke and I followed him inside. There was a large, square coffee table in the center of the room, with a couch on one side and a couple of chairs on the opposite. Kim dropped into one chair and I sat down on the couch. Dante sat on the floor, his gaze going back and forth between us. I decided to take another chance. "It's all right, Dante, he's a friend," I said, "if you're careless about words."

Dante walked over and sniffed at Kim's ankles. Then he went back and sat down on the floor. It was then I noticed what was on the coffee table. A quart of bourbon, two glasses, and a bucket of ice. I leaned over and poured myself a drink.

"Care for a cigarette?" he asked wryly.

"No, thanks. I'll smoke one of my own." I took one out of my pack and lit it. "I thought we were going to go to work."

"I thought so, too, but now I'm not so certain. You come to Washington and suddenly you have my mission. You help yourself to my liquor. You borrow my dog and now it looks as if you're trying to make that a permanent transaction. Where is it all going to end?"

"Is that why you never introduce me to any of your girls? Afraid I'll steal some of them?"

He poured himself a drink and looked at me over the rim of the glass. "No, I'd be ashamed of what I was doing to them.

They're all nice girls and not accustomed to animals like you."

"I understand that," I said. "It would be coming up in the world too fast. Give them the bends." I picked up my drink and finished it. "If we're going to work, let's get started."

"I never knew you to be so anxious to go to work, Milo. There must be a girl somewhere in the background. How are you making out with the Washington belles this time?"

"I don't know. Gallup hasn't released his latest survey figures yet."

He laughed. "Okay. I'll be back in a minute." He walked out of the room.

Dante was sitting on the floor looking at me. "We're going soon, Dante," I said. "Just as soon as your old buddy returns." He stretched out on the floor and closed his eyes. I was thinking I should follow his example as I reached and poured another drink.

Kim was back sooner than I expected. He had changed to heavier clothes and was carrying two small duffel or airline bags. "Looks like it's going to be a small trip," I said. "Or are they for booze?"

"This one," he said, tossing one of the bags to me, "is for Dante. Sometimes it's smarter to carry him than to let him saunter along the street with you. He might as well learn now that it will be you stashing him away. All you have to do is open it and call him. He'll come right over and jump in. Then you zip it shut, leaving just enough space to give him air."

"Okay. What's the other one for?"

"Some tools for tonight. Finish your drink and let's go."

I put the bag on the floor and opened it. It looked like a perfect size for Dante. I glanced at him and his tail was wagging. "Okay, Dante," I said. "Your carriage awaits you." He bounded across the floor and leaped into the bag. I zipped it almost closed, leaving about two inches to let fresh air in.

"You mean," I asked, "that he even understands complicated words like that?"

"Not exactly, but he understands what the bag is for and he also gets the meaning, mostly by the tone of your voice. Don't ever underestimate him. It's easy to do."

He led the way and we left the apartment. "He understands at least seventy-five commands in more languages than you and I speak. He also understands as many body movements, or more. And he sees, hears, and smells more things than you possible can. He's one of the smartest dogs I've known, and probably the bravest."

"He's already made a believer out of me," I admitted. "You'd better not let the Army know how smart he is. They're liable to promote him and fire you and me."

"Well," he said, "you can't have everything. The car's right down there. In front of that building."

"There's one thing I want to do," I said as we drove off. "I'd like to stop off and get a couple of hamburgers. For Dante. He had some Canadian bacon not long ago, but if we're going to work all night, he might appreciate a snack later."

"There's a place on the way."

A few minutes later we came to a small drive-in and I bought the hamburgers. Then we drove on. I could tell we were getting to the edge of the city by the time we reached the housing project. There were only a few streetlights and they were dimly lit, but I could see the shells of the new houses that were going up. They were ghostly, with the open eyes of what would be windows and doors before long.

"Are you sure you have permission for us to mess around here?" I asked.

"I'm certain. There's a night watchman on duty here all night. He gave us permission. And he'll be on hand if anyone questions us. He has a little shack, over where you can see that light. You and Dante stay in the car and I'll tell him we're going to work. It won't take long." He brought the car to a stop and got out. I could see the dim light through a small window, maybe a hundred yards away.

I leaned back against the seat and lit a cigarette. "You might as well rest while you can, Dante. And this is only the beginning." There was a soft, throaty acknowledgment from the bag, so I guessed he'd gotten the idea.

I was on my fourth cigarette when Kim came back. "We can go to work anywhere around here," he said. "Let's try it right over there. Just enough light without there being too much. Don't let Dante out yet."

I opened the door and got out, picking up the bag with Dante in it. We walked over to what would eventually be a row of houses. The light was so dim I could barely see the outlines of the structures.

"First," Kim Locke said, "while Dante can't see us, I'll show you the most important signs and movements for him. You can use language with them, but it's not necessary. Try to memorize them as I go along."

He ran rapidly through them. He bent over and held his hand below his knee, the palm parallel with the ground. That meant for Dante to lie down and keep quiet. The hand in the same position but with one finger pointing indicated a direction for Dante to watch. A swinging arm, with hand and pointing finger stretched out, would tell Dante where to attack. A semicircling arm would send him dashing back and forth, creating confusion. A movement of my fingers, next to my leg, sufficed for Dante to dash into the darkness, then circle around behind a man and nip his ankles. It was enough to give me time to get my gun up for a shot.

There were literally dozens of such commands and an equal number of warnings of danger that Dante would give me. It was hard to believe how much he could understand and do.

I don't know how long we spent on the amount of communication that could pass between the dog and me. We must have spent several hours at it without a break. I knew that I was tired, and Dante's tongue was hanging out when Kim called a stop.

"Let's go sit in the car while we catch our breath," Kim said. "Or would you rather run through that once more to make sure you remember all of the signals?"

"What for?" I said. "I remember them."

We walked to the car, with Dante staying at my heels. I lifted him and put him down in between my feet. Then I got one of the hamburgers, broke it up into small pieces, and placed it on a napkin in front of him. He wagged his tail and started eating.

"It's time Dante had some refreshments," I said.

"He won't even talk to me when you're through with him. But I did think of bringing some refreshments for us. Hold this." He put a paper cup in my hand and then pulled a bottle from the bag he'd brought. He poured from it into the cup. "It's just cool enough to properly chill this." He poured into another cup and lifted it. "Cheers."

I lifted the cup and took a drink. Bourbon. I finished the drink and held out the cup for another pouring. In the meantime, I was thinking about Kim Locke, as I knew him. There had to be something back of this whole thing, and it seemed to me that it was more complicated than the date he had mentioned.

"What time is it?" I asked.

"It's later than I thought," he said after looking at his watch. There was, however, no surprise in his voice. "It'll be daylight in about another hour."

"What does that mean? That we go back to work?"

"Not exactly," he said. He poured two more drinks and lit a cigarette. "You know, I want to tell you that it surprised me how quickly you picked up the signals to give Dante. And I'm even more surprised by the way he reacts to you. I've never seen him respond to anyone as he has to you. You know what I think?"

"My mind-reading has grown a little rusty lately," I said dryly. "I think it may be because there was a scarcity of minds. What do you think, Colonel?"

"I was worried that we couldn't get in enough work to be finished by tonight—since it's already tomorrow. I've changed my mind now. I'm certain that there is enough communication between you and Dante that there is no need for you to know every command. I think that you'll know what to do if there's a sudden need to give him an order. Suppose you were given official permission to visit briefly with a man in prison. You want to give him some information or you want to pick the lock of the door without being overheard or observed. There is a guard on a platform off to one side and slightly higher than the cellblock. The guard is armed with a rifle and there is a floodlight shining on the cell, you, and Dante. What order would you give Dante and how would you give it?"

"I wouldn't," I said. "I'd leave it to Dante. I'm sure he would create a distraction, probably by barking at the guard. I suspect the guard would find it amusing rather than dangerous, but he'd shift the rifle to bear on Dante before he'd start laughing."

"You're right. Dante will always bark if anyone points a gun in his direction."

"Okay," I said. "Now, what's this about changing your mind? I always knew you had a dirty mind, but I didn't know you changed it often."

"Very funny," he said. "I did think we'd have to work all night and all day, but I think you can handle anything without another class. In a few minutes I'll drive you back to my apartment and call General Baxter. He'll be happy about the news. You'd better check with him today, and tomorrow morning you'll be on your way."

"I'll drink to that," I said, holding out the cup. "But you don't have to drive me to the hotel. I want to do a couple of things on the way, so you can drop me where I can get a taxi."

"That's easy. There's an all-night taxi stand very near here."

It was getting light as we finished our drinks. He started the car and drove off. I leaned over and put Dante in his traveling bag. I sat back against the seat and lit a cigarette. There was one cab at the stand when we arrived. The driver seemed half asleep.

"Well," Kim said, holding out his hand, "good luck, Milo. I wish I were going with you." He sounded almost sincere. He leaned over. "Take good care of him, Dante." Dante's tail thumped against the side of the bag.

I shook hands with Kim. "Thanks. But don't say 'Good luck' too often. The Lady Luck requires wooing, not nagging."

"Okay," he said, laughing. "Anyway, happy landing. Give my best to the girls of Saigon."

"If I gave them your best, I might get my arm blown off by a grenade. I'll see you around, Kim." I got out of the car and picked up Dante. The cab driver awakened as I opened the door and I gave him the address. Looking out the window, I was just in time to see Kim throw up his arm as he drove off. I smiled to myself and settled back against the cushion.

It was only a short drive to Marya's apartment building. I paid off the driver and carried Dante upstairs. I used the key and opened the door. The apartment looked empty, but the bedroom door was closed, so I guessed it wasn't. I let Dante out of the bag. He made sure that he knew where he was and then stretched out on the floor. I took my shoes off, left them next to him, and went into the bathroom. The only thing I could think of wanting at that moment was a shower to take some of the tiredness out of my muscles.

Finally, I was so water-logged that I turned off the shower and stepped out of the stall and began drying myself. I was almost finished when I heard the door open.

"Milo," she said sleepily, "are you really back so early?"

"I think so," I said.

"I brought your robe, or are you just going to fall into bed?"

"Bring it in. And no."

When I turned around, she was holding out the robe. She was wearing her red robe. "Did anyone ever tell you that you're a beautiful hunk of man?"

"Not that I remember. Usually they just tell me I'm a big hunk. And you are a beautiful lady. I can say that because I have a good memory and I don't need x-ray vision."

"All right," she said. "Will Canadian bacon and scrambled eggs be all right for you?"

"Perfect. You might give Dante a scrambled egg, and you'll find a bag with a cold hamburger in it in the pocket of my jacket. You can break it into small bits and mix with his egg. I'll be right in."

She gave me a smile and left. I finished drying myself and put on the robe. I walked into the living room, took cigarettes and my lighter from a pocket, and continued on to the table in the dining area. There was a bottle of bourbon, a glass, and a bucket of ice on the table. I lit a cigarette and poured a drink. "Aren't you having a drink?"

"Not before breakfast," she said. "It will be ready in two minutes."

"Why aren't you working today?"

"It was General Baxter's idea. He suggested that I take a

couple of days off and that if you had anything you needed to do before leaving for Saigon, I should drive you. That includes taking you to your plane. Once you're airborne, my brief vacation is over. When will that be, Milo?"

"Very early tomorrow morning, I expect. I have to call General Baxter this afternoon. That gives Locke enough time to call him this morning."

She came in with Dante's food and put it on the floor in front of him, along with a bowl of fresh water. She went back to the kitchen and returned with our plates. She sat in the chair opposite me and picked up the bottle of bourbon. "I'll have just enough of a drink to make a toast." She lifted the bottle. "To … everything."

I lifted my glass and drank with her. "Rightfully," I said, "we should break the glasses, but I don't want you breaking that bottle. It's still half full."

She laughed. "Now tell me what happened. I thought you were going to work straight through until tonight."

"That was Locke's idea. He's a good agent but he's a bastard to work with. He likes to give all the orders, he likes to do all the planning, and he hates to make a mistake—unless it's a mistake that makes the project and him look better. He knew damn well it wouldn't take as long as he said it would. But he flattered me by saying that it amazed him how quickly I learned to work with Dante, bragged about how much communication there was between Dante and me, and then admitted he had made a mistake in the time it would take. He made it clear that the best time for me to check with the General would be this afternoon. So he makes his call early and takes credit for saving twenty-four hours on the schedule he had already sold to the General. Like I said, a bastard."

She laughed. "You wouldn't do anything like that?"

"No," I said firmly. "I don't even make any plans until I've already started the mission. It's better that way. Now, let's drop it."

"Okay." She looked at me silently for a minute. "Tell me something, Milo. What do you want out of life?"

"When I'm working on an assignment, all I ask for is one more day. If I get that, I may live for many thousands of days."

"Do you feel that way when you're working on your civilian job?"

"Let's change the subject," I said. "Did you get any sleep?"

"Yes. I went to bed early and slept until you arrived. Milo, do you know how many ribbons you've earned that haven't yet been given to you?"

"No, and I don't care. The ribbons aren't worth a damn when you go to bed on a cold night. They'll never replace a good woman."

"Have you ever found a good woman?"

"Many of them," I said honestly.

"How come you were never married?"

I smiled at her. "But I was. A good many years ago. On the same day we were married, we adopted a little boy from Spain who didn't know a word of English. At least, not one he could use in mixed company."

"What happened?"

"We agreed to divorce a couple of years later and that she would have custody of the boy. He's already a young man by now. I haven't heard from either one of them, so I imagine they're doing all right."*

"Why haven't they heard from you?"

"It would be a cruel thing to do. Can you imagine a man trying to explain all of these sudden mysterious trips? Or trying to answer questions about what I did in the Army? It would be impossible. We're having a conversation that has only questions and no answers. Have you planned anything for today?"

"I do have to go out and do some shopping later. That will give you the chance to grab a nap."

"There's plenty of time for naps. Where are you going and at what time?"

"I have to shop for the kitchen," she said. "Breakfast used up the last of the supplies. I thought I'd go about one o'clock. Why?"

"I want to do a little shopping myself. Mine won't take long, so if you'll drop me near where you're going, I'll find a watch store and then walk to where you are."

"There's a Chinese shopping area about a block from where I'm going. There's a jewelry and watch store there. I'll drop you off."

"Perfect," I said. "I'll tell you what I'll do. I'll take a nap

---

* In *No Grave for March* (1953), Milo helps a young woman named Greta escape from East Germany to America. In *The Man Inside* (1954), Milo meets a ten-year-old Madrid street urchin who assists him in his case. In *As Old as Cain* (1954), Milo and Greta are married in Denver, but as soon as the wedding is over Milo must fly to New York because Ernesto has just arrived as a stowaway on an ocean liner from Spain, claiming to be Milo March's assistant. In order to make Ernesto legal, Milo and Greta adopt him. In *The Gallows Garden* (1959) it is mentioned in passing that Milo and Greta have divorced. There is no way Milo, with his occupation and habits, can be a husband or family man, a fact that Milo discusses with his girlfriend Mei Hsu in *Born to Be Hanged* (1973).

if you'll wake me up in time to call General Baxter and get dressed before we go."

"It's a deal," she said.

I pulled over the bourbon and poured another drink. I lit a cigarette and leaned back, sipping from the glass and watching her clean off the table. By the time I'd finished the drink, I was relaxed and sleepy. "If anyone is looking for Agent March," I said, "tell them that I am, in the words of our Leader, inoperative." I went over and kissed her on the cheek and walked to the bedroom. I just threw myself across the bed and I think I was asleep by the time I hit it.

It seemed that I had barely closed my eyes when Marya was waking me up. One hand was on my shoulder and shaking me gently. "Milo," she said softly, "it's time to get up." My eyes opened and slowly focused on her.

She must have seen the expression in my eyes. She laughed softly and moved away. "It's twelve-thirty. This is a good time to call General Baxter. He usually goes to lunch at one. Then you can get dressed and we'll go shopping."

"Dante might need a walk."

"Already done. He did everything a good boy should." She smoothed her skirt and walked out of the bedroom.

Muttering to myself, I followed. "Do you remember the General's number?"

"There's a phone book beside the phone. Look under B."

It looked more like a notebook, but I found the number and dialed it.

"Colonel March calling General Baxter," I said when a girl answered. Then I waited.

"Good morning, Colonel," he said finally. "How'd it go last night?"

"All right, I guess. Dante seemed to be satisfied."

"Colonel Locke had nothing but praise for you."

"I knew it would go like that, sir. As one betting man to another, I wouldn't mind making a small wager that he also said that he'd made a mistake by underestimating Dante and me."

"He did say that. He also agreed with me that there was no reason why you can't leave for Saigon tomorrow morning. Be at the field a little before six. A Major Lazar will be the pilot."

"I'll be there, sir."

"Good. If there's any question from the embassy or headquarters, remember to tell them to call me, and I'll make sure you don't have to deal with any interference. Happy landings, Colonel."

"Thank you, sir. And happy peace in our time to you, too." I hung up.

Marya came out of the bedroom. She'd put on her uniform while I was on the phone. "Get dressed," she said. "This is a good time to do our shopping."

"I never saw a sergeant who didn't enjoy giving orders," I answered. "But I'll do it. Otherwise you might get spoiled, because I won't be around to take orders after tomorrow."

She made a face as I walked past her to the bedroom. It didn't take me long to get into my uniform. I went back to the living room. Sure enough, she was standing by the door. "You took long enough," she said lightly.

"That's not the way to talk to a man who is on the verge of being reinserted."

"What does that mean?"

"Sent back to the battle area. Dante, stay here. We'll be back soon." He stretched out on the floor and wagged his tail to say good-bye.

It was a short drive to where I wanted to go. Both sides of the street were lined with Chinese stores. She stopped the car in front of a jewelry store.

"I'll be in the supermarket. It's down the street, less than a block. What's wrong with your watch?"

"Probably nothing, but I want to be sure it's not losing or gaining. I'll see you over a barrel of hot sugar."

She waved as I got out of the car. I went into the store. There was a man behind the counter, but no customers in sight.

"Good afternoon," he said as I approached. His English sounded as if he'd gone to Harvard. "May I help you?"

"You may try. I want something in jade. I think a pendant."

"We have a wide variety of choices in jade, ranging from American jade to the best of Chinese jade. If you can give me some idea of what you want, I'm sure I will have it."

"The best jade will be a little more than I can go," I said, "but show me something not too far below it."

He bowed and walked to the rear of the store. When he returned he was carrying something in his hands. When he reached me, he carefully placed it on the piece of black velvet in front of me. He stepped back and watched me.

It was a beautiful piece of jade, a deep green with flashes of light from it that seemed to tell me that I possessed it. "It is lovely," I said. I rubbed my fingers across the surface. "I can tell it's old. How much is it?"

"It is expensive," he said. "It is, however, quite old, which does increase its value. It is one of the three best jades we have. It is worth what we charge."

"I'm sure of it," I said. I rubbed my fingers over it again. *"Han yu?"* I asked.

"You know it?"

"Shih. Pu ts'ui."

He stared at me with interest. "It sounds like you speak my language better than I do your language. What is your name, Colonel?"

"Colonel Milo March."

"Have you been to China?"

I nodded. "China, as well as Hong Kong, Singapore, and South Vietnam."

"You have friends in Hong Kong?"

"A few."

"Did your friends ever give you a Chinese name?"

"Yes."

"Was it, by any chance," he asked, "K'uai Pai Ti Ti?"

I smiled. "Quick White Younger Brother. So I was called by Tang Lok Hee, whom I've known for many years."

"It is a small world," he said. "You wished to know the cost of the pendant." He named a price was so low it was ridiculous.

"That is too low."

"It is the price."

We argued for several minutes. "It is foolish," he said finally. "We fight over this like two birds quarreling over a worm. You pay me fifty dollars more than I asked. I have known your name for several years and I do this only out of respect for you. My brother and I also own a store in Hong Kong."

I knew it was futile to argue further, so I counted out the money. "Now," I said, "out of respect for you and your brother, I would like to buy one more thing from you, but I insist it must be the price which is written on a tag connected to it."

"What is that?"

"I think it's a pin. In the center there is the Chinese character for happiness. Around the character there seem to be tiny moons. May I see it?"

"Please." He lifted out the tray and put it in front of me. "While you're looking at this one, I will bring another which you may like better." He moved down toward the back of the store and vanished.

I glanced at the small tag on the brooch. As I guessed, it was much cheaper. But it was made of gold, or was gold plated, and there were no gems on it. I put it down and looked at other items displayed on the counter.

"Here it is," he said, returning. He placed a small square of velvet in front of me, and there was a duplicate of the pin I had been looking at. Not quite a duplicate. The one he had brought had the same Chinese character in gold, but the objects around it were small balls of jade. It made the original look like something you might find in a five-and-dime. I reached down and turned over the price tag. On it was written the same price that was on the other tag.

He must have noticed. "The one I brought is an item which hasn't moved as well as the others. We have put a sale price on it."

I knew he was lying, but there was no point in mentioning it. He would only give me an endless number of reasons for the price. It is not easy to argue with a Chinese.

"I'll take it, too," I said.

"It is a most excellent gift," he said with a smile. "With the jade moons around it, the meaning is Heavenly Happiness. You would like them gift-wrapped?"

I counted out the money for the second purchase. "Thank you," I said. I glanced at my watch. "Although I do not have much time."

He smiled at me and went to the rear of the store again. He wasn't long. He reappeared in front of me with the two brightly wrapped packages. "Thank you, Colonel March. It was our pleasure to have served you."

"I think it was mostly my pleasure," I said. I picked up the two packages and put them in my pockets.

"There is," he said, "a small favor you might do for the Brothers Shan. In your travels if you should ever happen to encounter Tang Lok Hee, your elder brother, will you tell him that we send our best wishes?"

"I'll be glad to do so. Once more, thank you."

"It is I who thank you, Colonel March."

Upon that happy note, I left him. The shopping market was as near as Marya had said. She had almost finished when I arrived. I helped her to carry the things out to the car. "It feels like you are going to feed the entire Army."

She laughed as we got into the car. "Your watch is all right now?"

"It's fine. I, however, am a little tired. We had to spend the customary time in flowery Chinese compliments over which one of us was the most honored. That's the chief trouble with the Chinese language. Let me rest my jaws until we get home." I leaned back and closed my eyes.

We were soon back to her apartment building. I carried the groceries and she unlocked the door for us. Dante was overjoyed to see us, but he confined his welcome to his tail. I spoke to him but continued into the kitchen with the bags and put them on the small work table. I took the rest of the bags from her and got some ice out of the refrigerator.

"I'm going to change because I have to cook for dinner."

"Not yet. I want a drink first and it's not dinnertime yet. Join me."

"All right. For just one drink. I'll bring the glasses."

We went back to the dining area. I put the bucket of ice on the table and went over to make a fuss over Dante. As soon as he'd had enough I went back to the table. Marya had poured both the drinks. I raised my glass for a toast.

"To the future lady spook."

"What's that?" she asked, the glass halfway to her lips.

"An Intelligence agent."

We drank and put the glasses down. "Now," I said, "I've changed my mind. I would like it if you changed into the red robe. No questions. I'll tell you the reason when you come back." She smiled and went to the bedroom.

As soon as the door was closed, I moved over to the telephone. I dialed the number of the direct line to General Baxter. When the girl answered I gave her my name and asked for the General.

"Hello, Colonel March," he said a moment later. "Anything wrong?"

"Only one thing, sir. I'll be on the plane in the morning. But I did quite a bit of additional shopping and I'm afraid I'll need extra expense money when I reach Saigon."

"I expected that," he said dryly. "I'll phone General Lawson and tell him to have two thousand dollars ready for you when you report. That way, you can't spend it here and miss the plane."

"I wouldn't think of it, sir," I said gravely. "I'll see you when I get back."

"You'd better, Colonel." He hung up and I went back to the table, and then she was back. She looked great in the red robe. But, then, she looked great out of it, too.

"What's this all about? First you ask me to put on this robe, then you were asking General Baxter for more expense money. He just gave you two thousand dollars. What happened to it?"

"I'm a big tipper," I said. I reached into my pocket and pulled out the smaller package and slid it across. "Open it and see."

She picked it up and looked at it. "What's this for?"

"The Tooth Fairy left it. She didn't have time to put it under your pillow. Now close your mouth and open the package."

She opened the box and took out the smaller pendant. She held it up and looked at it for a long moment. Finally she tore her gaze from it and looked at me. Her eyes were soft and warm. "Why?"

"Because I want you to have it. It's only the appetizer. Open this one, too." I took out the second package and put it in front of her. This time she wasn't so slow. She lifted the larger pendant and held it in front of her face.

"Milo! How could you?"

"It was very easy. After I had my watch adjusted, I walked down the street and spotted a Chinese five-and-ten. Clever, these Orientals. And you might call my reaction purely Occidental."

She laughed. "Don't be silly. But they must have been expensive!"

"All right," I sighed, "but you've spoiled the whole thing. I might as well tell you the truth. There was a small Chinese restaurant. I went in and had a cup of tea and some fortune cookies. That's where I found them." I poured myself a fresh drink.

"Milo March, you're impossible. They are beautiful. Do they also mean something other than mere beauty?"

"Pu ts'ui! If you notice, the smaller object has a Chinese character in the center. It is the word for happiness. You will notice there are several round objects circling it. They represent clouds or moons."

"What kinds of stones are those?"

"Han yu. When those are added, then the meaning is 'Heavenly Happiness.' "

"What's *han yu?"*

"Don't get squeamish about it. It's jade that has been buried with the dead. This is done so that members of the family may carry objects of beauty and value with them on the long journey into the hereafter."

"They dug these up so that they could be sold?"

"Not immediately. After they were in the burial ground for one or two thousand years, it was logically assumed they were no longer necessary for the welfare of their ancestors and could be used for others. Some was undoubtedly sold to bring happiness and well-being to the less fortunate who were still alive."

"And this one?" she asked, holding up the larger pendant.

"That is also *han yu*, but a larger piece. It was included in a tomb to make sure that the spirits would remember the words of Confucius. Speaking about jade, he said: 'It is warm, liquid, strong, and firm like politeness. Like the truth, it gives out a bright rainbow.' "

"They are beautiful," she said, "and you are beautiful for wanting me to have them. But you spent your expense money to buy them."

"Now that you mention it, I believe I did. And that shows that you don't know your General Baxter as well as you think you do. He knows that I, and every other agent, is underpaid. So he tries to give them as much extra money as he can. He knows that once I'm out of Saigon, I won't have any expenses that can be handled by money. So, in honor of the General, why don't you get all dressed up tonight, put on your jade pendant, and I'll take you out to dinner?"

"Normally, I would love to. But I have another idea that will make me happier. Let's stay here. I'll cook dinner for you. Then we'll sit around listening to music and talk—but not about how you can help me. When we feel like it, we'll go to sleep."

"That's all?"

She smiled. "We'll set the alarm for four in the morning. I'll make a special breakfast for you and drive you to the airfield. How does that sound?"

"It sounds like a palace full of *ke yu*. I accept."

"What is *ke yu?*"

"Ancient jade that has been passed down from generation to generation. It is the most valuable of all."

She stood up and came around the table and kissed me. She picked up the bottle of bourbon and poured two fresh drinks. Then she went back to her chair, picked up the large pendant, and put it around her neck. She raised her glass.

"One more day," she said softly.

From the floor, Dante made a gentle noise in his throat. I was sure it was his approval.

FIVE

We were up early the following morning and sat down to breakfast before five o'clock. Marya had outdone herself. There were Eggs Benedict for us and Dante had a stack of Canadian bacon. It was also a quiet breakfast. Neither of us had much to say at the moment.

I had a brandy with my coffee and then I had a double brandy while Marya stacked the dishes in the kitchen. By that time, the slight hangover I had was gone. I made sure that I had everything in my large suitcase, checked in the mirror to make sure I was militarily correct, and I was ready. We went downstairs, let Dante visit his favorite bushes, and got in the car.

It was a short and silent ride to the field. I picked up Dante as soon as we were in the terminal and put him in the bag. He must have guessed we were going to work because he seemed happy to be zipped in.

"Damn," Marya said after we had taken a few steps. "I was hoping I could go with you to the plane, but I guess he'll stop me."

I glanced in the direction she was looking and saw an immaculate young Air Force major standing in the center of the terminal. There were two enlisted men waiting near him.

"Don't worry about it," I told her. "I'll see that you get in.

Just take Dante." I transferred the bag to her. We reached the major and stopped.

"Colonel March?" he asked. "We're ready to take off whenever you are." He saluted.

I returned the salute. "I'm not sure that I'm really ready, but it might as well be now. I have a bit of a head from last night, but just waiting around won't help."

He smiled. "We call that a touch of Washington smog," he said. "The enlisted men will take your luggage."

"They'll take this one," I said, placing the big suitcase on the floor. "You'll forgive me, Major, but I want the small one to be carried by Sergeant Cooper. He's used to her carrying him around."

The major looked surprised. "He?"

"Maybe they forgot that you are taking two passengers. He's a small dog who is often worth more than two or three men. He also has a security rating that is as high as my own. If you still have any doubts, you can phone General Baxter at the Pentagon."

He smiled. "I'll take your word for it, Colonel. Incidentally, I am Major Lazar. Let's go."

The Major and the two enlisted men led the way across the field to where a B-47 waited, its jet engines warming up. I winked at Marya as we followed him.

When we reached the plane, the two soldiers were already loading my one suitcase and making it look like hard work. Then I saw that Major Lazar was standing on the steps directing the loading of the suitcase. Three men making it look like hard work. I got the message.

So did Marya. She handed Dante to me, then stretched up to kiss me on the mouth. When she'd finished, she had a handkerchief ready and was soon wiping the lipstick from my mouth. "When you return," she said, "I will be right here waiting when your plane comes down. One more day, Milo." She turned away and marched toward the terminal, her back held as stiffly as a ramrod. There, I told myself, went a girl with guts.

I strolled over to where the men were still pretending to struggle with my suitcase. "Need a hand, Major Lazar?" I asked.

"Not at all," the major said briskly. "We were just being careful in case there were any breakables in it." At that moment, the suitcase vanished inside the plane. The two soldiers came down the steps and backed off, turning until they faced us. They both saluted.

"Dismissed," Major Lazar said as we both returned the salute. He looked at me and smiled. "After you, Colonel."

I went up the steps and entered the plane. It had been a jet bomber but had been converted for passengers. There were seats on both sides, and each seat was provided with a desk. I guessed it served as a flying bus for top brass.

"You're the only passenger," the Major said. "Take any seat you want. This baby climbs fast, so buckle in. I'll be back to see you as soon as we reach our flight level."

"I've never seen one of these planes in the flesh," I said. "Didn't know they'd even been used in the war. Didn't you flyboys go right from the B-29 to the 52?"

He grinned. "Mainly, that's true. But Uncle Sam bought

a bunch of these babies and now he's using them as flying limousines for the brass. You must be a VIP, Colonel, to rate a private ride in a B-47."

He disappeared into the cockpit. I strapped myself into a seat and let Dante out of the duffel bag.

Major Lazar reappeared once we had straightened out on our flight pattern. He was carrying what looked like a small gift-wrapped box, a bottle of whiskey, and two glasses. "This," he said, putting the box in front of me, "was delivered to the plane from the Pentagon just before you arrived. Do you mind if I join you in a drink?"

"Of course not. But I will be better if you join me in two drinks."

"Loud and clear," he said. "Wait until I get some ice." He went to the rear of the plane and was soon back. There were some ice cubes in both glasses. He added generous amounts of whiskey to them, picked up one glass, and sat down in the seat in front of me. He lifted his glass.

"Happy landing," he said. We touched glasses and drank. He had a smile on his face again when he looked at me. "Know where you're going?"

I nodded. "Saigon."

"Been there before?"

"Yes. Twice."

He lit a cigarette. "Captain Elliott and I have been flying this superbus for some time now. Most of the time it's transporting big brass and one or two politicians. The brass want to survey the field and return to be booked on lecture tours or to write a book. At the worst, it'll still look good on the record.

The politicians want to go because when they return home they'll sound like experts and big brave men. We have flown a few single-passenger flights before this one. My guess would be they were spooks. I mean for real. I know that we never received any order to bring any of them back. And they all looked as if they didn't expect to come back. If I'm stepping over any lines, I'll apologize and shut up, sir."

I laughed. "You sound as if you're thinking about writing a book yourself. What's your first name, Major?"

"Michael."

"Okay. Mine is Milo. I'll listen to your theory, whatever it is. And we'll both forget about such things as oak leaves and eagles. That way, I can suggest that you give us fresh drinks without feeling that I'm pulling rank on you."

"Fair enough." He stood up. "I'll get the drinks at once— Milo."

"Good show," I said as he picked up the glasses and left. He was soon back and pouring from the bottle. When he set the bottle back on the desk, I raised my glass. "Now I have a toast. To … another day."

"I've heard that expression somewhere," he said.

"It's been somewhere, Mike. Now, what's the theory you started on before?"

"Well … I guess it starts with you. I've been in the service long enough to become a major the hard way. I've seen a big cross-section of military men—and women—from privates to generals. They all seem to fit into a mold. I had it all figured out once, but this morning you came into the picture. It wasn't the same picture."

"Did I say or do anything that offended you?"

"Not at all. You didn't say or do anything that could have been taken as being out of line. But you were different."

"I don't feel any different," I said. "I like women and booze and gambling; sometimes I even like to fight."

"Begging your pardon, Milo, I don't think that's really the explanation. It does prove to me that you are different. I'll give you a couple of examples. This morning, for the first time since I started my military career in the air force, I encountered a high-ranking officer who was to be taken to Saigon, and he arrived carrying a small dog in an airline bag. Actually, the dog was being carried by a very pretty sergeant. And that was not the most unusual thing about it."

"What was that?"

"The sergeant and you both seemed perfectly confident that no one would question her presence on the field. Noncommissioned officers are supposed to have a pass to come beyond the terminal gate. Even I didn't question it. I also have never seen a salute like yours. It's a perfectly normal and regulation salute, but different. Most senior officers draw themselves up at full attention and the end result is that they look like a statue."

"Maybe that's the way they feel," I said lightly.

"Perhaps, but you don't feel that way or look it. No one can fault you on the salute, but you're completely relaxed from head to feet. You're just paying your dues in the club."

"It might be because I'm not a part of the regular Army. I'm in Army Reserves, subject to recall for temporary service at any time and on short notice. Three days ago, I was a civilian in New York City."

"And going to Saigon," he said. "I am told that we are no longer at war with the Viet Cong and the only soldiers we have in the South are instructors, advisors, and attachés. You don't look as if you fit into that category. As I said, you're different." He stood up. "It's time that I relieved Captain Elliott. I also feel that I have already ventured into an area in which I have no clearance. You'll find more ice cubes in the rear of the plane, plus bread and sandwich meats and hot coffee. It's on top of a cabinet. There's space in the bottom of the cabinet where you will find more breakable supplies if you run out. We will be in Saigon in about eighteen hours."

"I think I'll sleep most of the way. Dante and I had very little sleep the last couple of days. Thanks for everything, Major."

"Compliments of the Defense Department, sir. If there's anything else you want, come up and ask. We might have it." He turned and went forward.

I walked to the rear of the plane. I picked up some ham and a dish of water for Dante and ice cubes for myself and went back to the seat. Dante attacked his rations while I made a fresh drink for myself. Then I opened the package. It contained a small tiger made out of bamboo and it was a work of art. There was a small card with a handwritten message. "To the best bamboo tiger of all. One more day. Marya."

I finished half of my drink, then leaned against the back of the seat and went to sleep.

It was almost four hours later when I awakened. I glanced out the window but there was nothing to see but solid black. I hadn't expected anything better, so I poured half a drink and lit a cigarette. When I'd finished them, I went back to sleep.

This time I was awakened by Dante nudging my leg with his nose. I opened my eyes to see Major Lazar stepping out of the compartment. My watch showed that I'd slept another four hours.

"Good morning, Major Lazar—or whatever time of day it is."

"Good morning, Colonel March," he answered. "Mind if I join you for a bit of the ambrosia?" I noticed he'd brought another bottle with him.

"Glad to have you."

He picked up the two glasses and walked past me. He returned with the ice and poured the two drinks. He lifted his glass. "One more day, Colonel."

We drank to that. When we put the glasses down, I noticed that his expression revealed that he was still curious. "Someone meeting you in Saigon?" he asked.

I lit a cigarette and nodded. "I'm supposed to be met by a car and a driver from the Embassy. And just so your curiosity won't interfere with flying this plane, I'm their new military attaché."

"They called you back to active duty for that? Some of the active officers must have been reading the news about the advances the North has been making."

"The thought did occur to me, but it doesn't make any difference. It all counts on twenty."

"Is that what you're aiming for? Twenty years and retirement?"

"I already have the first twenty," I said. "Now I'm working on the second twenty. How near are the Viet Cong to Saigon?"

"Close enough that they could be dropping shells into the city, but they are only dropping them on the cities around. You might call it a ring of fire."

"Well, at least it won't be dull," I said. "I think I'll go back to sleep. I'll see you in Saigon, Major. Good night."

This time, as he left, he took the remnants of his drink with him. "Have a good sleep," he called over his shoulder.

"Happy landings," I said as he went through the door.

I waited until he was gone, then went back to the buffet. I got some more ice cubes, a couple of slices of turkey, and additional water for Dante. I gave him the turkey and his water. He seemed ready for it.

I lit a cigarette and considered the information the Major had given me. It was a couple of days since I had read a newspaper. I wasn't too surprised, however, at the positions of the two armies. The fact that the Viet Cong was shelling all around the city but not hitting it wasn't a big surprise. If they could continue it long enough, Saigon would come apart at the seams. The government would probably collapse before the army did, and the rest would only be a mopping-up action. I was sure that many of the government heads would leave before that happened, and South Vietnam would lose the war just as we had—only with more finality.

I lit another cigarette and considered what that would mean to my project. It would undoubtedly make it tougher in one way, but it might also mean that it might be a little easier. I finished my drink and leaned back. But there couldn't be a more complete answer until I was on the scene. I was still mulling this over, but had decided there was little more I could do at the moment, when I felt myself drifting back to sleep. I didn't try to fight it.

This time I didn't awaken until the plane hit the runway. I sat up and stretched and then lit a cigarette. Dante was watching me to see what the next move would be. "We finally made it, Dante," I told him. I opened the bag. "Time for you to go back to your little home away from home." He wagged his tail and jumped into the bag. I pulled the zipper on the bag and stood up. Just then the door from the cockpit opened and the two pilots stepped out.

"Well, how do you feel now?" the Major asked.

"I'm breathing," I said, "which puts me ahead of the game."

He laughed. "Where's the dog?"

"In his private baggage car." I stepped across and picked up my suitcase. "I'm ready anytime you are. Why don't you and the captain join me in a drink?"

"We'd be delighted," he said. "Will you recognize your driver when you see him?"

"No. But I imagine he's an NCO and will have enough sense to approach every colonel he sees. Let's go."

The Major nodded at the Captain, who opened the door. Someone had already pushed the steps up to the plane. "After you, Colonel," the Major said. "The Colonel has invited us for a bit of tiffin, Captain Elliott."

"I didn't know the Army was so generous," the Captain said. "Maybe I should apply for a transfer."

"Why not? We're one big happy family." I went down the steps and stopped, looking around. We were at the official Saigon airport, but I was surprised to notice there were quite a few people standing around. Probably to greet incoming passengers or to say good-bye to ones that were leaving. I imagined there were more of the latter.

We crossed the field and as we neared the edge of it, I saw a sad-faced master sergeant coming toward us. He glanced at all three of us but finally settled on me. "Colonel March?" he asked hopefully.

"Yes."

"I'm your driver," he said. He didn't sound too enthusiastic about it.

"Where are we going, Major?" I asked.

"There's an officer's club about fifty feet from here."

"I'll meet you there." I turned back to the Sergeant. "You can put the suitcase in the car. I'll take the small bag with me. Are you a drinking man, Sergeant?"

"Yes, sir. But not here, sir. There isn't an NCO bar and I wouldn't recommend any of the local bars unless you want to try for another Purple Heart the hard way."

"No thanks. I have enough Purple Hearts. I'll buy these two men a drink and meet you back at the car. Where is it?"

"Right over there, sir." He pointed to a drab-looking Dodge sedan. It didn't look like an old model, but it was certainly battered enough to be one.

"I'll be right back," I said. I followed the two officers and entered the bar for officers only just a few steps behind them.

The bar was empty except for the bartender. He had the look of a lifer NCO, probably a sergeant first class or maybe a master sergeant putting in his last years in the service and hoping to stay alive to collect his pension. He had already gotten a start on getting drunk for the day. The two pilots who had brought me to Saigon were already bellied up to the bar, along with a lieutenant who looked as if he'd been there for a while. I took the stool next to the Major and ordered three drinks for us. The bartender was having trouble focusing on us but he finally succeeded.

As for the other customer putting away liquid fuel, he swiveled around and looked at me and my two compadres. "I don't understand it," he said indistinctly. "I'm always outranked. Don't understand it. I can't be the only lieutenant in the goddam army. When I got promoted from second to first, I figured I was a real officer at last. But now all I meet are captains and majors and—"

I cut him off.

"At ease, Loot," I said. "The others are probably still in the sack. They just don't have the stamina that you have."

His face brightened as he thought about it. "Yeah, that must be it. Never thought of that."

"Give the lieutenant a drink on me," I told the bartender.

The Lieutenant stared solemnly at me as he was being served. "Thank you—Colonel," he finally said. "You're a gentleman and a scholar—by act of Congress."

He concentrated on his drink and I talked to the two pilots until I'd finished my drink. Then I promised to look them up later if I could, picked up Dante, and left. The Sergeant was waiting beside his car, but he didn't look any happier.

"Ready, sir?" he asked.

"I guess so. What are the orders of the day, Sergeant?"

"This is the car I'm driving. My orders are to take you to

your hotel, then drive you to the Embassy. I'm to be your driver for the length of time you'll be in Saigon."

I was about to answer when I saw a sudden movement from a group of people who were on the field staring in our direction. One man, in ragged clothing, stepped forward and swung his right arm. Something round and dark came flying through the air. The man turned away and started to run down the field.

The round object hit the concrete and bounced, then rolled straight at us. I put Dante down and ran to meet the object. I scooped it up and threw it as hard as I could in the direction of the running man. By this time, I was certain the object was a hand grenade. I turned back to the car. "Sergeant," I yelled, "get down!"

I dropped to one knee next to Dante. At that moment, the grenade exploded. The running man staggered briefly but continued to run. He must have been hit by one piece of metal but not fatally wounded. I had heard several pieces hit near us, but I saw that no one had been hit. Then I glanced at the spectators. They were still standing in a group, staring at us, but no one moved.

That was my welcome to Saigon.

SIX

I stood up and looked around. No one was moving, so it must have been a one-man attack. I looked at the Sergeant. He had moved to the front of his car and lifted the hood. I bent over and let Dante out of the bag. He surveyed the scene, then trotted off to take care of his morning business. I waited for him by the car. When he returned, I picked him up and opened the door of the car. I threw Dante's bag into the back seat, climbed in the front, and put the dog between my feet.

The Sergeant closed the hood of the car and came around to slide in behind the wheel. "It looks like they neglected to put a bomb in the motor."

"They need an area around here where people can check things like that," I said. "It must be messy to clean up after they go off."

"Yes, sir." He started the motor and drove out of the parking area. "I've been in this hellhole for a year. If you'll pardon me for saying so, sir, you're the first damned top brass I've ever seen who could move as fast as you did a few minutes ago."

"It's an old family tradition, Sergeant—to stay alive as long as possible. Let's keep going, unless you think somebody wants to try for seconds. In the meantime, what's our immediate schedule?"

"You're staying at the Hotel Caravelle, sir. My orders are

to take you there, then wait until you're ready to go to the Embassy and be officially checked in. After that, I am subject to your orders. May I ask you a question, sir?"

"Sure."

"What's the dog bit?"

"That's Dante. He is, as you have noted, a dog. He is a miniature pinscher and a certified military working dog. He is also my friend—probably my best friend—and sometimes he does my thinking for me. Dante, stand up and say hello to the man. He's a friend."

He stood up and wagged his tail, then looked at me. I made a motion with my hand and he stretched out again. I felt like a proud papa whose kindergartner was the brightest kid in the class.

"I'll be damned," the Sergeant said. "I never saw anything like that."

"What's your name, Sergeant?"

"Farrow, sir. Sergeant Dan Farrow."

"Career man?"

"Yes sir," he said. "I've put in fifteen years and I'm shooting for twenty-two. Then I'll retire, maybe open a little saloon back in my hometown. If I make it."

"You'll make it," I said. "I've done more than my twenty years and I'm still going."

"Yes, sir. May I ask, are you regular Army?"

"Not entirely. I served my four-year stretch and then got out but signed up for the Reserves. They've recalled me quite a number of times."

"Yes, sir." He sounded puzzled, but I didn't pick up on

it. We drove through the rest of Saigon without talking and finally arrived at the hotel.

"I'm still trying to fight off jet fatigue," I said as he parked. "I don't even know what time it is here. I do know that I'm hungry. What about you?"

"I can get a bite, sir, while you're in the Embassy."

"Can you, now? Well, you're coming in and having whatever the hell meal it is with me. And that's an order."

"Yes, sir."

I put Dante back in his bag and we got out and walked to the hotel. "I'll sign in," I said as we reached the lobby, "and take my friend up to the room. Then I'll meet you in the dining room. Order whatever you'd like to drink and a double martini for me. I'll be right down."

"Yes, sir," he said, but his heart wasn't in it.

I walked to the desk and signed the register. By that time a bellman was there and he took charge of my key and my suitcase. I carried Dante. The room turned out to be a little more than that. There was a small kitchen and dining area, a large bathroom, a small living room with a bar, and a large bedroom. I tipped the bellman and he left.

As soon as he was gone, I went over and stared out the window. It looked out on the river and beyond that I could see the South China Sea. It was a beautiful view, but what was more beautiful was that I was on the eighth floor and there was no fire escape outside the window.

I went back and let Dante out of the bag. He sniffed all over the place, then found a spot on the carpet that he liked and stretched out there.

I opened the suitcase and took out the Colt Python and my shoulder holster. I put on the holster, slipped the gun into it, and then put the jacket back on. It was a good fit. I looked down at Dante.

"I'll be back soon," I told him. "Go to sleep. You may need it."

When I arrived at the restaurant, the Sergeant was the only customer in it. He sat at the table, looking uncomfortable, but there was a glass in front of him that looked like it contained a double bourbon. He glanced up as I sat down. "I ordered the double martini for you, but the waiter said he'd keep it on ice until you arrived."

"Fine." I looked around and saw the waiter coming in our direction. He was carrying a tray on which there was a huge martini glass and a pitcher of martinis. All was well.

The waiter served me my drink and departed. I lifted the glass to the Sergeant. "Here's to another day."

"Yeah," he said, and we drank. I noticed he took two big swallows of his drink, then put the glass on the table and stared at me for at least two minutes. I lit a cigarette and waited. "Do I have permission to speak, Colonel?"

"Certainly. You always have my permission to speak. When the rest of the brass isn't around, you can forget the sir and the colonel bit. My name is Milo and you're Dan."

"I don't like it, sir."

"Why?"

"I told you I have fifteen years in. I want to coast for the last five. Two more months here and I have a good chance of being transferred to West Germany or back to the States.

I've got the stripes and now all I need is the time. That's why I'm assigned as a driver to the Embassy. But you worry me, if you'll permit me to say so, sir."

"I permit you to say anything. Why do I worry you?"

"I was told that you are to be the new military aide at the Embassy."

"That's right."

"In fifteen years, I've seen a lot of military attachés, but I've never seen one like you."

I smiled. "I'm sorry, Dan, but I don't understand what you're trying to say."

"You understand," he said gloomily. "That bothers me, too."

"How?"

"You understand. Especially if you've been in the Army for twenty years. I've never seen a military attaché that didn't throw his rank around. I've never seen one that would tell an NCO to order drinks on him. I've never seen one who would have lunch with me. And I've never seen one, even here, who was greeted with a grenade on his arrival. So, do you mind if I say that you're unusual? I can't prove it, but I suspect you're the only colonel who ever scooped up a thrown grenade and got rid of it before it went off. It makes me curious, you might say."

"I played a good game of baseball when I was younger," I murmured.

"I'll bet," he said. "It's so trivial I hate to mention it, but you're the first officer I ever saw arrive here with a dog. There must be something special about you, and if I'm going to drive you around this stinking place, I'd like to know what it is so I can duck, too."

"I don't blame you a bit. I promise I will always warn you in plenty of time to duck. Now, let's order some food, soldier." I motioned to the waiter. I ordered two more drinks and the food.

"Well," I said when we had finished, "I suppose we should go to the Embassy. I imagine that they expect me."

He smiled. "About two hours ago."

"Civilians never understand priorities. Let's go."

I paid the bill and we walked out to the car. He looked at me as we got in. "Where's the little dog?"

"Taking a short furlough up in the room. I thought I should let the Embassy people get accustomed to me before I spring Dante on them."

"That's probably a good strategy. You've been here before?"

"Two years ago."

He started the motor, but he didn't say anything until we turned into the street. "I thought you were a little too cool for a new hand. You must've been through it before."

"You mean that things still get pretty lively around here?" I asked.

"I hear it's increased. All I know is that there are usually a few scrambles every night."

"What causes them? Viet Cong?"

"That's what I hear. They've got guys all over the place, and they also have a lot of sympathizers. There's no way of telling them apart."

I lit a cigarette and looked at him. "If there's so many of them around, they must be pretty well organized."

"I guess so. I hear that the president keeps his bags packed and his personal plane on the alert all the time. A lot of his own people are against him because they think he sold them down the river when he agreed to a peace treaty with North Vietnam. There are rumors all over Saigon that he got several million dollars to sign the treaty."*

"It's a little more than a rumor. The UPI ran a story from Saigon stating that he received seven million dollars for signing. They quoted a South Vietnamese source for the story. Then the UPI ran another story, from 'a reliable American source' stating that he was paid five million dollars early in 1972 and another two million later. They also had a quote from the general who delivered the two checks. The general, however, refused to be named. The result was what has been called 'peace with honor.' Keep that in mind if you decide to run for office when you get back to running that saloon in your hometown."

"I'll think about it," he said dryly as we reached the Embassy. He parked the car and said he'd wait for me. I walked up to the ornate door where another sergeant stood. He saluted me.

"I am Colonel March," I said, returning the salute. "I am the new military attaché, reporting for duty."

"May I see your orders, sir?"

I took them out and handed them to him. He looked them over carefully and handed them back, then opened the door. "All right, sir. If you'll see the receptionist inside, he'll tell you where to report. Mr. Harrison. On the second floor, I believe."

---

* President Nguyen Van Thieu.

"Thank you, Sergeant." I stepped inside and stopped to look.

There was a desk for a receptionist but there was no one there. Papers covered the desk, so I assumed that he had stepped away for a few minutes. There was a curving stairway up to the second floor. I went up it, then moved along a corridor until I came to a door with a brass plaque on it. Howard Harrison was the name on it. I knocked and opened the door.

A young man wearing what looked like a Brooks Brothers suit glanced up as I entered.

"The receptionist is downstairs," he said coldly.

"His desk is," I said. "Are you Mr. Harrison?"

"Yes. Whom did you wish to see?"

"You, I guess. I am Colonel Milo March, your new military aide."

"A bit late, aren't you?"

"It depends on your point of view," I said dryly. "My orders were to report today. They don't say what time today. But to be even more explicit, my orders were to establish quarters in Saigon, then report here and request that you notify General Lawson that I have arrived. When you do that, you might also tell the General that he is to see that I receive two thousand dollars as expense money and that he is to phone General Baxter in Washington for verification. My tour of duty starts tomorrow. In the meantime, I'm at the Hotel Caravelle. I believe that is all, young man."

"I had no idea that we were also supposed to run errands and deliver messages for you, Colonel March." There was a resigned tone in his voice. "We've had quite a number of officers attached to the Embassy in the past two years, and I've never been quite sure what their duties were. They've always had considerable freedom as far as we're concerned. What they did with their time has always been a complete mystery to me."

I smiled at him. "You mean you think they spent all of their time chasing the local girls?"

His expression grew even more sour. "That was not what I had in mind. But you seem to be special even among the peculiar sort we've had before. We have received a special message from the State Department telling us to make no demands on your time unless it is absolutely necessary. And we have already received a report that someone threw a grenade at you shortly after you arrived today. Why?"

"Just my natural charm, I imagine. Don't forget my message for General Lawson."

He looked as if he intended to say something else, but his mouth looked as if he'd just bitten into a lemon, so I left before he could reach a decision. I did, however, close the door gently. I walked back down the stairs. There was a young man sitting at the desk.

"Colonel March?" he asked as I headed for the door.

"Yes," I said. I turned to look at him.

"Mr. Harrison said you had just been there. He wanted me to tell you that you forgot to give him your orders and that he hadn't signed them."

"Imagine that! Tell him that I also have to sign in with the general here, so that may take care of it. If not, tell Mr. Harrison that I'll give him my orders the next time I drop in." I turned and walked outdoors.

Sergeant Farrow was relaxing in the car, smoking a cigarette, but he straightened up as I approached. I climbed in beside him.

"How did it go, Colonel?" he asked.

"The way it always goes. If there's anything worse than Army brass, it's civilian brass. Let's get out in some fresh air."

"There isn't any, sir. Where do you want to go?"

"A shopping center, and I don't mean the kind that has army and navy stores all over the place. I want to buy some secondhand clothes. A place where the natives go."

He hesitated. "I wouldn't do that if I were you, Colonel. It'll be easy to spot you, and old Charlie will figure you're a spy and really fair game."

"I suppose that 'Charlie' still means the same,* but don't worry. I'll make out all right. God looks after fools and drunkards. I've been accused of being both. Let's get going."

He shrugged and started the car. "Why do you want secondhand clothes?"

"Just say I'm eccentric and like old clothes. Especially old Chinese clothes. Age is an object of worship in China.... How's the supply of girls around town? The same as it has been for a long time?"

"I guess so. I wouldn't know. I'm married, sir, and my wife is here with me."

I laughed. "I didn't mean you personally, Dan. But you and I aren't the only soldiers in town. And ... since when are soldiers in a war zone allowed to have their wives with them?"

---

* In World War II, "Charlie" referred to the Japanese. In Vietnam, it meant the Viet Cong.

He laughed. "This isn't a war zone. The diplomats in Paris worked that all out. 'Peace with honor' and all that jazz."

"Okay." I'd have to settle for that. "I just hope she's safe."

"So far so good, sir. So far so good. And as for the unmarried men … well, war is war."

I didn't say anything about the contradiction. I just waited for him to continue, and after a minute he did.

"Yeah. I guess it's about the same. Most of the girls in Saigon are Chinese or Vietnamese. As I hear it, about half of them are pros and the other half are young girls who are Viet Cong or young girls who do it because their families don't have enough food. The pros are mostly sick and so are some of the poor girls. The Viet Cong girls are dangerous—a lot of them have been caught with grenades under their clothes. A guy tries to grab a free feel and he really gets a bang out of it when she pulls the pin."

"It must shake the girl up a little, too."

"Yeah, but the Viet Cong figure they're expendable. Then I also hear there's a ring of pros who are beautiful and clean but they are expensive. About the only Americans who see them are visiting Congressmen and businessmen, maybe a few reporters. And I suppose there are guys who grab whatever they can find in the fields when they're on duty. You ever been up in the hills out there, Colonel?"

"Not for that purpose, but I've been there."

"I figured that was how you got a lot of that fruit salad on your chest. You don't get some of those by sitting at a desk. And they don't come off of Christmas trees."

I leaned back in the seat and lit a cigarette. I enjoyed talking with the Sergeant, but I doubted I would get any valuable information from him.

He swung the car to the curb and stopped. "I can't get any closer than this, but there's an old store down there in the middle of the block. You can recognize it because there's always a few old clothes hanging in front of it."

"Okay. I won't be long." I got out and started in the direction he had pointed.

Some sections in Saigon, like this one, were interesting. The sidewalk is often merely an extension of the store, and in some cases it's the entire store. There were barbers working on the sidewalk, and I passed a dentist who was pulling a tooth while admiring citizens watched. Vendors were cooking food over charcoal in their carts. Then I found the secondhand clothing store and went in.

The clothes were clean, but some were a little on the ragged side. I bought a shirt, pants, a coat, shoes, and a hat with a broad enough brim to conceal most of my face at night. On my way back, I stopped at one of the vendors and bought some cooked pork for Dante.

I put the clothes in the back seat and climbed in beside Dan Farrow. "Back to the hotel," I said. "I've finished my shopping for the day."

He started the car and pulled away from the curb. I noticed he was watching the rearview mirror, but I didn't say anything. I waited.

"I think we're being followed," he said finally.

"Yes?"

"I thought somebody was following us from the Embassy,

but I couldn't be sure. Then the same car, or one like it, parked when we did. Now they're following us again. Two men in it."

"What kind of car?"

"An old Renault."

"Left-hand or right-hand drive?"

He checked the mirror. "Right."

"What do you think it is?" I asked. "Local cops, our own Security men, or something else?"

"The last. Want me to lose them? This old boat will go faster than that heap."

"No," I said. "If it's somebody really after us, he'll only try again. Is there a street that will seem to lead to the hotel but will get us off the main streets?"

"Two or three of them."

"Pick the quickest one."

"Okay. There's one two blocks from here."

"If they are Viet Cong, what are they apt to try? Automatic rifles?"

"They have very few of those, if any. They usually use grenades."

"Good," I said. "They've already had one shot at me with a grenade. This time, they may make the mistake of being too careful. Relax, Dan, and remember it all counts on your twenty years."

"Sure," he said. He made a right turn into a broad, quiet street. "They're starting to pick up speed."

"Let them." I unbuttoned my jacket and took out the Colt Python. I checked it and pushed the safety catch off. I held it in my lap. "Get over on the left side, so they'll have to pass us on the right."

He obeyed. "They're no more than fifty yards behind us and they're speeding up."

"Turn your rearview mirror so I can see slightly back over my right shoulder without looking around. And try to look like a sitting duck."

"Look, hell. That's the way I feel."

I smiled. "Didn't they ever tell you that noncoms are supposed to have confidence in their commissioned officers?"

"Yeah, but I never had a commissioned officer who made jokes at a time like this. Are you sure that when you pull the trigger on that gun, a little white cloth doesn't come out with BANG! Printed on it?"

"Come to think of it, I don't think I ever asked. Careless of me." I was watching as he moved the rearview mirror. Finally, it looked about right. "That's it. Now just concentrate on driving and listen carefully to the next thing I say."

It was only a few seconds before the Renault came into sight in the mirror. The driver was hunched over the steering wheel as though he were entered in the Grand Prix. The other man was staring grimly at our car as though he were putting a curse on us. He probably was. I kept my gaze on the mirror and resisted the urge to look around.

The nose of their car came up even with the rear of our car. The man on my side of their car lifted a round object, which was obviously a grenade, and used his teeth to pull the pin. The Renault surged forward.

SEVEN

As the two cars slowly drew even, I counted and watched the mirror. I wasn't conscious of anything except the seconds, the view in the mirror, and the gun in my hand. I only hoped that the man with the grenade was as expert as he should be.

When the time was right, I turned to look out the window and lifted the gun. The Renault was even with us and the man had his hand in the right position to lob the grenade into the front seat of our car. I steadied my hand on the door and gently squeezed the trigger. The man's face dissolved in a spray of red and his right arm dropped.

"Stop on a dime," I snapped, "and get down as low as you can."

The tires screeched as he stopped on the brakes. I slid down in the seat and braced my legs. As the car swerved and came to a halt, there was a loud explosion, followed by a crash and the breaking of metal and glass. I straightened up and looked.

The Renault had rammed into a tree and turned over. It was already on fire, but I didn't see anyone moving inside the car.

"Turn around," I said, "and get the hell out of here."

The Sergeant started the motor and backed up into the center of the road. He turned and headed back the way we had come. I turned to look through the rear window. There was nothing to see but the burning Renault.

"Get to the nearest main street leading to the hotel," I said. "Then slow down to normal speed. Also, straighten the mirror."

He reached up and adjusted the mirror. Within two minutes we reached a main thoroughfare. He slowed down and I heard him let out a deep sigh. "Anybody see it?"

"I don't think so. Even if they did, all they could have seen was the Renault crash into the tree. The explosion could have been their gas tank. Relax, Dan."

"Yeah. I know it counts on my next five years, but by that time I may be eligible for old age benefits. Like I said, in my fifteen years I never saw a colonel like you. I never saw one who could shoot like that, and I never saw one with that kind of nerve."

"It's known as self-preservation," I said lightly. "The idea was to leave the grenade in his lap. That way, no one could accuse me of stealing it."

"That wasn't a government-issue gun you were using either."

"No," I said. "It's a Colt Python with a two-inch barrel. A fine gun."

"Who the hell are you?" he said suddenly.

"Colonel Milo March, Military Attaché to the United States Embassy in South Vietnam."

"Okay," he said in a resigned voice. "But after that little scramble, I'm in your corner. To hell with who you are."

We drove on and reached the hotel in a few minutes. He pulled up near the entrance and stopped. "I'll wait for you," he said.

"No, you might as well go home to your wife. Call me in the morning and I'll tell you what the schedule is."

"I've been kidded by experts," he said stubbornly, "so don't try it. You're planning on going out tonight. You'll be better off if I'm driving you. I know the city like the back of my hand."

"Look, Dan," I said, "I appreciate it that you want to go with me tonight. But it's no good. I'm sure that the Viet Cong agents know this car when they see it. Besides, all I'm going to do tonight is go see an old friend—if he's still alive. For his sake, I'd rather that no one knows that an Army officer is going to see him tonight. I won't be in any danger. I might be if you drive me. More important, I think my friend might be."

"You're not giving me the business … Milo?"

"I swear it. I want to see an old friend, and it's much better if I go in civilian clothes and take a pedicab. I speak Chinese well enough to pass as Chinese and I will be wearing clothes that will make it difficult for anyone to realize I am not. Go home to your wife and call me in the morning. I'm also taking Dante with me, and he'll be better protection than two men would be."

"You're sure?"

"Positive, Dan. I'll see you tomorrow."

He looked uncertain as I got out of the car, but he drove away when I closed the door. I had taken my packages before we reached the hotel, so I went straight up to my room. Dante was glad to see me—especially when I put the pork in front of him. I added a dish of fresh water to it. While he was busy with it, I took off my jacket and the shoulder holster. Removing the spent shell from the gun, I put in a fresh one. I tucked it inside my shirt. "Let's take a walk, Dante." He was ready.

While I was walking him, I cased the rear entrance to the hotel. It looked ideal. When Dante finally decided he was satisfied, we went back upstairs. I called Room Service and asked them to send up a bottle of Canadian Club and a bucket of ice, and left word for them to give me a wake-up call in about three hours. I put the gun on the table next to my bed and stretched out. There was a knock on the door almost immediately.

I got up and took the gun with me as I went to the door. I opened it and let the waiter in. I shoved the gun into a back pocket while he put the tray down on the stand. I signed the check, adding his tip, and he left. I poured myself a drink and lit a cigarette. I replaced the gun on the table and stretched out on the bed. I was asleep almost immediately.

A knock on the door awakened me. I lifted my left arm and looked at my watch. I'd been asleep for two hours. There was another knock on the door. I thought about it for a minute and decided it couldn't be anyone who was employed by the hotel. And it couldn't be anyone who had an official reason for seeing me. They would have called downstairs. That left one other possibility. Someone who wanted to learn if I was inside. In that case he might pick the lock and come in. I picked up the gun and waited.

There wasn't another knock. Instead I saw a piece of white paper shoved beneath the door. I sat up and waited. There wasn't a sound from the other side. Finally I got up and went over to pick up the paper. There was a written message on it: *Poches was here.*

That was all. I certainly didn't know anyone name Poches. Besides, it sounded like a code name. I knew that Intelligence was not stupid enough to do a thing like that, so it must have been a CIA agent who was still wet behind the ears. I cursed, then crumpled it up, dropped it into the ashtray, and set it on fire.

It wouldn't be long before it would be time to leave, so I poured a drink and sipped it. When the drink was finished I stood up and undressed. I went into the bathroom and shaved. Then I got dressed in the clothes I'd bought. I had deliberately picked things that were slightly too large. I strapped on the shoulder holster and slipped the gun into it. Then I put on the coat and hat and looked at myself in the mirror.

Everything was perfect. Nobody would even guess there was a gun under the coat. The brim of the hat made it impossible for anyone to know whether I was Asian or Western. Dante was watching me closely to make sure that he wasn't going to be left out.

"It's all right," I said. "You're coming along." I brought out his bag and zipped it up after he jumped in. I opened the door and checked the corridor. There was no one around. I slipped out, carrying Dante. I passed the elevators and found the door that opened on the street. I stepped out, closing the door behind me. There were a few people on the street, but not many. They were all Asians. There were almost no cars on the street. Most of them vanished, I knew, as soon as it was dark. Many pedestrians did the same.

I walked about a block before I saw a pedicab. I waved to him and he came to where I stood.

"Do you speak Chinese?" I asked him in that language.

"*Shih,*" he said, nodding.

"I have not been in Saigon for two years," I said in the same language. "Would you know if Tang Lok Hee still has his boat on the river?"

"*Shih.* You wish to go there?"

"Please," I said. I stepped in and sat down, putting Dante next to me on the seat.

It was a pleasant ride. I looked impoverished enough not to attract any special attention. Anyone who looked even vaguely prosperous would be lucky to reach his destination. The color of your skin made no difference; the cut of your clothes did.

We arrived at the river without any trouble. Dozens of boats and sampans were moored in the river, and dozens of boatmen were waiting for possible fares to the boats that were floating restaurants. I paid off the pedicab driver and, when he had pedaled away, found a boatman to take me out to Tang Lok Hee's boat. In reaching the deck, I had to lift my head so that the hat didn't completely cover my features. I was met by a waiter.

"Do you wish a table?" he asked in English.

"Yes," I said. I looked around. The deck was covered with tables and festooned with Chinese lanterns. There were quite a few people already seated at tables. A large number of them were American officers, although there were a few Chinese.

"You are alone, sir?" the waiter asked.

"At the moment," I said, switching to Chinese. "If it is not too much, I would like a table removed from the other guests.

I would also like a bottle of Lor Mai Tsao, and would you be so kind as to tell Tang Lok Hee that his younger brother Milo March would be highly honored to share a drink with him?"

"It will be a pleasure, March *hsien*," he said, reverting to his own language. He must have signaled another waiter, for I was no more than seated when a waiter appeared with a squat bottle of Chinese whiskey and two glasses. He put them on the table and then he, too, vanished. I put the bag on the floor and opened the zipper. Dante jumped out and curled up next to my feet.

I left the bottle unopened and waited. I looked at the floating platform that was secured to the side of the boat. It was lit by hurricane lamps, and there were cooks and their assistants who were busy netting fish and assorted seafood, which would be shown to the customer while it was still alive.

"My humble place is honored by the presence of my Younger Brother," a voice said.

I looked around. There was Tang Lok Hee, a heavyset man with light, classical features. He must have been over sixty but he looked no more than forty. I stood up and we embraced. "You do too much honor to my presence. Will you favor me by sharing a drink?"

"It is I who am favored by the gods, K'uai Pai Ti Ti," he answered.

We both sat down. I opened the bottle and poured two drinks. We drank and talked. I asked about his children and his grandchildren, and he asked about my health. All of it was the polite preamble that older Chinese love so much. It is almost a ritual.

"And how is your little dog? I heard that there was such an animal with you when you arrived in Saigon. I trust he is well."

"He enjoys good health," I said. "Dante, come out and pay your respects to my Elder Brother." I wasn't sure how much Chinese Dante understood but was fairly sure he'd understand enough to appear.

He did. He came out from under the table, looked up at Tang Lok Hee, and wagged his tail.

"He is a splendid animal and his understanding of Cantonese is amazing." He finished his drink and I refilled our glasses. "But I have failed in my duties," he continued. "I have not asked about my brother or his reasons for being here." It was a signal that protocol was satisfied and we could get down to business.

"But, first," I said, "I bring you greetings from my country."

"From so far?"

"Yes. The Brothers Shan."

"Ah! I knew them well when they were in Hong Kong. I trust they are doing well."

"Very well. They also recognized and remembered the name which you gave me years ago. It earned me a discount on what I purchased."

"Good, good! In the *I Ching** it is written that 'those above can ensure their position only by giving generously to those below.' "

"Like the grenade I caught this morning at the airport? I'm sure that wasn't a gift from the Brothers Shan."

---

* The famous ancient oracle and book of wisdom; its title translates as "The Book of Changes."

"I heard of the incident," he said. "It is how I learned that my Younger Brother was once again in Saigon. I know of only one man in the world who could get the grenade and return it in the required time. I alerted everyone on my boat to watch for you. But there are many such incidents these days."

"Many?"

"*Shih*. Even this afternoon there were two men driving along a quiet street in a residential area when a grenade blew up in their car. One of the men had already been shot in the face, possibly just as he was about to throw the grenade." He stopped and lit a cigarette. There was a twinkle in his eyes when he spoke again. "It was said that there were two men in American uniforms on the street at that time, but they quickly turned around and drove away."

"Where did you hear that?"

"One of my people lives on the street. I was curious about it, but now that you are here I am no longer curious."

"These are hard times in Saigon," I said.

"It is true. Worse than when you were here the last time. Why do you now return?"

"To look for someone. Did you hear of a man named Martin Rigsby who was attached to our Embassy here?"

"I've heard of him, but I did not know him. He is a prisoner in Hanoi. He was in civilian clothes, so was arrested as a spy. I believe he is still in prison there, although he has never been on any list of prisoners. I imagine they are saving him for a time when this is all over. The publicity may be of greater value to them and to the Russians."

"When do you think it will be over?"

"In the sense of what the people of Vietnam have experienced in several years, it may never be over. But it will soon be over for South Vietnam. I expect to leave shortly myself."

"Where will you go?"

He shrugged. "Where can I go? Either Hong Kong or Macao. I do not like living so close to the red dragon, but I have no choice. Maybe Macao. They have a large tourist trade and could use another floating restaurant. But we should return to you. What are your plans?"

"As usual, I have none. But I intend to get to Hanoi as an American officer who has come to plead for the release of Rigsby on the grounds that he is not an American agent but a civilian who was captured while he was on an errand of mercy. I will plead for his wife and children, and point out that such a show of mercy on their part will win them world-wide publicity that will benefit them."

"You are still a gambler," he said, shaking his head. "How do you expect to accomplish all of this?"

"I will have to make contacts here who will offer to help me. If I can find the right person, they will offer to help because they will be sure that once I'm there, they will throw me in the same cell with Rigsby and plan on a spectacular display of two after we signed a peace treaty. They can't refuse bait like that."

"I suppose not," he said sadly. "Unfortunately, there is no way I can help you to get out of Saigon or Hanoi. But I can get information from any part of Vietnam. Some of it may take a little time. If it is things about the city of Saigon, I may already have such information or can get it almost immediately. I know there is no chance of changing your mind, so I can tell you who is the most likely person to volunteer to escort you to Hanoi."

"Who?"

"Her name is Le Thuy Duong. She operates, and has operated for fifteen years, a restaurant in Saigon known as K'uai Pai Ti Ti. It is the best restaurant in the city and features the best in French, Chinese, Vietnamese, and American cooking."

" 'Quick White Younger Brother,' " I translated. "Is that her idea of a joke?"

"I'm sure it is, but not one aimed at you. It is possible that it is a name aimed at her customers and bears a slightly different meaning. You will recognize her meaning when you hear her pronounce the words. None of your men know our language well enough to recognize the difference between the two words. One meaning expresses love, the other expresses hate and scorn."

"What else do you know about her?" I asked.

"Almost everything. Her food is enough to attract a large number of your high officers and equally high numbers of your politicians who visit Saigon, as well as the wealthy local rulers of South Vietnam—or what is left of it. They come for the food, but they also come for other wares."

"Comes the wind from that direction?"

"Very much so. It is a great wind, before which strong trees bend. Many have sued for the favors of Madame Le, but it is said that none have won them. She has many beautiful, young, and clean girls who can be obtained—for a price. And I have left out one fact of the lady."

"What?"

"She is a beautiful lady, far more beautiful than any of her girls. In the old days, she would have belonged to the emperor."

"That is interesting," I observed.

"I knew that my Younger Brother would so think. I have told you not for the reason of attracting you, but to warn you. She is dangerous."

"If I have to die for my country, I can't think of a better way to go. After I have accomplished my mission."

"It would only be expected of you, I am sure. It is also said that it is Madame Le who issues orders to the Viet Cong in this area. She also holds the rank of major in the army to the north."

"At least, I outrank her," I said dryly. "Is that all about her?"

"The most important part," he said. "She only ran the restaurant for her first five years there, but she has owned it for the last ten years."

"Old?"

"No more than thirty-five. I believe the money to buy the restaurant came from Hanoi, but it is in her name."

"You have done well," I said.

"How do you think I survived all of these years in Hong Kong and in Saigon? I will tell you something of what I know. Within an hour after you arrived in Saigon, I knew it. I knew about the grenade. I also knew about the two men who tried to kill you this afternoon on the quiet street. I also know that you were visited in your hotel shortly before you started for here. He was an American agent. Is that not so?"

"I think so. I didn't answer the door, but he left a name beneath the door. I recognized it as a code name. As I said, you have done well."

He spread his hands. "If a humble servant such as myself knows all this, is it not to be thought that others know about it? Even the Viet Cong does not try to kill every American officer who comes here. Now, my friend, I must go attend to business. Don't forget, I may leave Saigon within a few weeks. If you should want to get a message to me, send it by pedicab."

"I may do that."

We both stood up and looked at each other. "Do not try to pay for the dinner. You are my guest."

"You honor me too much," I protested politely.

"I cannot do less for a younger brother whom I may never see again. May the path of your journey be covered with rose petals."

We embraced again and he walked away. I sat down and had another drink. Then I ordered dinner.

When I'd finished, I left a tip for the waiter and went with Dante. The waiter met me at the rail of the ship. "The master's car is waiting to take you to your hotel. You will be met as your boat reaches the shore."

"Thank you," I said. I went down the steps to where the boat that had brought me to the ship was waiting. I stepped into it and was rowed to the shore. A small man in a black uniform was waiting as I stepped from the boat. "March *hsien*," he said, "the car is right over here."

The car was a Mercedes. Dante and I got into the rear and the chauffeur drove us away. I waited until we were near the hotel. "Do not go to the front entrance," I said in Chinese. "Drive to the side near the rear of the hotel. It is better if I go in that way."

"I understand, March *hsien*."

A few minutes later, he pulled to a stop in front of the door I had used in leaving the hotel. I opened the door and got out. The street was deserted, so I pulled back the zipper and let Dante out. He crossed the sidewalk to investigate small bushes there. I turned back to the chauffeur.

"Go with the gods," he said.

"Thank you."

"It is nothing. You are my master's younger brother and it is an honor to serve you."

"It is I who am honored," I said, turning back to Dante. The chauffeur drove away as soon as my back was turned.

Dante followed as I went to the door and opened it. We entered and started up the stairs, which had once been meant as a fire escape. I might have been caught completely unaware if it hadn't been for Dante. We had just reached the third floor when Dante made a sound deep in his throat. It meant danger. I looked up just in time to see a black-clad figure leap from the middle of the steps. There was a wicked-looking knife in his right hand.

"*Yang kuei-tzu!*" he shouted as he jumped.*

---

* "Foreign devil," an insulting term applied to all foreigners.

EIGHT

I was getting tired of this. I'd been in Saigon less than twelve hours and this was the third time someone had tried to take me. I waited until he was almost on top of me, then stepped quickly to one side. As he landed, I hit him—just hard enough to turn him around so that he almost faced me.

I grabbed his wrist with my right hand and his elbow with my left. While he was still off balance, I threw all of my weight on his arm and at the same time brought my knee up to meet it. There was a sharp snap as his arm broke. His breath came out in a thin whistle of pain, and the knife clattered on the steps. I let go of him and deliberately hit him on the throat. I picked up the knife and put it in my pocket. Then I looked at him.

His face was pale and had a pinched look, but he was still conscious, holding the broken arm with his other hand.

"Do you speak Chinese?" I asked him in that language.

He nodded.

"Viet Cong?"

He nodded again.

"You," I said, "are the son of a dog and you have covered your ancestors with the shit of dogs." I sent a mental note of apology to Dante. "Who sent you to attack me?"

He spat on the floor. "No one sent me, foreign devil," he said through clenched teeth. "I came on my own."

"You are not only the son of a dog, but the truth is a stranger to your mouth."

"Kill me," he said sullenly. "My ancestors will rejoice at what I tried to do when I join them."

"Your ancestors would spit on you. I won't kill you, because your life is not worthy of my attention. You are like a child with a firecracker. If it makes a loud noise, you are pleased. If it doesn't, you weep."

He stared at me with hatred.

"Go," I told him. I made a move as if to hit him on the arm again. He turned and scurried through the door. When I was sure he was gone, I went on up the stairs. When I reached my floor, I opened the door a crack and looked out. There was no one in sight. With Dante following, I hurried to my room and went in. Dante jumped on the bed and looked at me, pleased with the whole adventure.

"All right, so you told me he was there," I said. "But he wasn't jumping at *you*."

He showed me his teeth, which I suspected was his way of smiling. Ignoring him, I undressed and slipped into a pair of Army pants. I put the knife under some clothes in the dresser drawer. Then I phoned downstairs and ordered some ice, cigarettes, and any English newspapers they might have.

It wasn't long before there was a knock on the door. I opened it and a waiter came in with everything I'd ordered—plus a folded piece of paper. I pointed to it and asked the waiter what it was, and he said the desk had given it to him. I added a tip to the check and gave it to the waiter. I mixed a drink while the waiter was leaving.

Then I opened the message. It merely stated that Dan Farrow had called and left his phone number.

I took a sip of my drink and picked up the phone. I asked the operator to call the number that was on the slip. The phone on the other end rang three times and then a woman answered.

"Is Dan there?" I asked.

"Who's calling?" She sounded nervous.

"Tell him it's Milo."

"Just a minute," she said. She sounded relieved. I guessed that he had told her something about me, but I hoped he hadn't told her too much.

"Hello," he said a minute later. "Everything all right?"

"Yeah. How are the bugs around here?"

"Pretty safe, I think. I understand they're checked pretty often."

"Well, I had a more or less pleasant evening, and in other ways it was good. You can sleep a little late in the morning, if you want to."

"What do you mean?"

"Pick me up about eleven," I said. "Tell them at the desk to call me and then wait in the car. Don't be surprised if I send Dante out first."

"The dog?"

"He's smarter than both of us put together. I don't think there is any reason to worry, but we won't take any chances. Somebody tried for me again last night."

"What happened?"

"I'll tell you in the morning. Have a drink and sleep well."

I replaced the receiver. Then I picked it up again and ordered some breakfast from room service. I got partly dressed and started on a drink. By the time the waiter arrived, I was fully awake. He brought the newspapers with the food.

I saved some of my breakfast for Dante and I got dressed in my military finery. I checked my gun and the holster. I checked the time. It was eleven o'clock. Dante had finished his scrambled eggs and was watching me carefully.

"Don't nag," I told him. "You're coming with me." He followed me through the door and into the elevator. We kept going when we reached the lobby, not even stopping at the desk.

"Colonel March," the clerk called. I turned and looked at him. "Your driver is waiting out front for you."

"Thank you," I said, and we continued out of the hotel. I stopped and looked down at Dante. "All right, Dante, look it over."

He trotted away at once. To the casual observer he would have seemed to be taking his usual visits to trees and shrubbery, but he covered a lot of territory. If anyone was hiding on the grounds, Dante would spot him. He finally came back to me, looked up, and wagged his tail. That meant that it was all clear.

We crossed over to the car. I let Dante into the back seat, then got in front with Dan. "Good morning, Dan," I said.

"Good morning." He started the car. "What was that all about?"

"He was just checking to see if any of our little friends were hiding among the bushes. They're not."

"I guess you're right about how smart he is."

"You can bet money on it. Do you know a restaurant in Saigon called K'uai Pai Ti Ti?"

"I've heard of it. It's too rich for most of us. I've heard it's run by a good-looking broad and that it's possible to make connections with the best-looking and most expensive whores. I wouldn't know."

"That's where I want to go."

He shrugged. "Okay. Are you looking for a whore?"

"Yes—but not in the way you mean. And the less you know about it, the better for you."

"Yeah," he said gloomily. "I was beginning to get that idea myself."

After a few minutes' drive to the other side of Saigon, he pulled into the parking lot of a large, luxurious, Oriental-type building. "This is it. You want me to wait?"

"For the time being," I said. "I may change it later. Then, again, we may have to try another time. In the meantime, go in and have lunch on me."

"I just had breakfast. I'll stay here and watch the car."

"Okay." I got out and opened the car door for Dante. I let him investigate all the bushes, then we went inside. It was a very attractive restaurant. There were a few sidelong glances, but no one objected to Dante as we were led to a table. A waiter appeared and I ordered a dry martini. Dante curled up at my feet.

There were several American army, air force, and marine officers among the guests, and the rest seemed to be prosperous Vietnamese and Chinese businessmen. There were also a number of beautiful Vietnamese girls who strolled through the room, turning and posing like models, and occasionally one would stop and join the men at their tables. The Beautiful People of Saigon.

I had another martini and then picked up the menu the waiter had placed on the table. The dishes offered were either Vietnamese or Chinese. I figured "When in Rome…," so I ordered a Vietnamese meal. I decided to start with a cup of *pho bo*, beef and noodle soup. I realized that I'd worked up a good appetite—having to fight for your life and win can do that to you—so instead of one main course I ordered three. *Banh xeo*—sizzling crepes, sugarcane prawns, and lemongrass chicken skewers. I knew these would come with a side order of pickled vegetable salad with *nuac cham* dipping sauce. For dessert there would be *che chuoi*, banana coconut tapioca pudding, and *ban dua caramen*, miniature coconut crème caramels. I planned to top that all off with a tall glass of *ca phe*, Vietnamese coffee.

I caught the waiter's eye and he came over. I gave him my order and he nodded approvingly. Well, maybe I'd made a friend for Uncle Sam. Before he left to place my order with the chef, I asked him to bring me chopsticks.

He came back shortly to set the table, and I thought I finally saw an opening. The chopsticks were brown ivory.

"Boy," I called, switching to Chinese, "I want to see the manager."

I thought he'd resent being called "boy." He didn't make an issue of it, but he looked startled. "There is something wrong?" he asked in the same language.

"There is much that is wrong. I wish to see the manager at once."

He stared at me for a minute and then scurried away.

She was there within two minutes. A stunning woman, she was a few inches over five feet, perfectly formed, and didn't look more than twenty-five years old. I got to my feet as she approached.

"I am Le Thuy Duong," she said in Chinese. "There is something that displeases you?"

"I am Colonel Milo March. Will you honor me by sitting at my table?"

"It is I who am honored," she murmured as she sat down. "In what way has K'uai Pai Ti Ti given you unhappiness on your first visit?"

"I have been insulted, which is unimportant. But my parents and my grandparents have been offered a dishonor. I am sure that it was not intentional, but it is necessary that it be corrected."

She leaned back and laughed. It was a pleasant sound. "You are an unusual American, Colonel March," she said in English. "You also speak excellent Chinese. But, as you see, I speak English, so let us continue in that language. How have you been insulted?"

"These," I said, holding up the chopsticks. I had noticed that the other American customers also had brown ivory chopsticks, while those served to the Chinese and Vietnamese were of white ivory.

There was a twinkle in her eyes as she looked at me, but she wasn't going to give up that easily. "In what way are you insulted by the chopsticks, Colonel March? You requested them from the waiter."

"You play with me, Madame Le, unless you were completely corrupted by the French." That produced another reaction in her eyes, but I continued, pretending not to notice. "It has been long said that when ivory chopsticks turn brown it is because they were used by women. By giving me these, your waiter was implying that I am not a man. Since I am obviously an American, he probably thought I would be unaware of his implication—and that the people in the kitchen would laugh."

She laughed again and clapped her hands. The waiter appeared immediately with a pair of chopsticks made of the purest ivory. He murmured an apology in his own language and hurried away.

"Did you understand him?" she asked.

"No," I lied.

"He apologized. It was a mistake. He is very sorry. So am I…. You are a strange American, Colonel March."

"I don't think so."

"But you are. I was aware of you as soon as you arrived. I am always aware of new guests. You are an American Army officer and you arrive with a little dog. I have never known such an officer. You speak perfect Chinese—Mandarin as well as Cantonese. You are aware of Chinese customs and you are familiar with Vietnamese cooking. I have already seen your order. When my girls came around, you appreciated their beauty but you did not invite any of them to sit with you. Why?"

"They were very lovely women—but a woman, like a special fruit, needs to reach a certain ripeness. Your girls are most attractive but there is a greenness about them. Give them another five years and it may be a different story. In the meantime, my tastes are somewhat different."

"What are your tastes, Colonel?"

"I would prefer the teacher of the girls—as a luncheon companion." I switched back to Chinese. "Would you honor this humble person and make the meal perfect by adding your presence to the table?"

"You are a most unusual American, Colonel." She clapped her hands and the waiter appeared. "I will have my usual meal," she told him.

The food was soon served, accompanied by a bottle of special wine. The waiter informed me that it was a present from the house. I was surprised to notice that she was having scrambled eggs.

"You see, Colonel," she said, "I have acquired some of your habits, just as you have acquired some of ours."

"I noticed," I said dryly, "and I am honored. I also like scrambled eggs for breakfast, but at the moment I prefer this delicious soup."

"We are pleased that you like it," she said demurely.

This pleasant exchange continued throughout the meal. Everything I had ordered was excellent and I said so. She always found a way to return a compliment.

"It has been one of my most pleasant luncheons," I said. "Perhaps we can do it again someday."

She studied me for a minute. "Why don't you come to

dinner, Colonel? We do much better then."

"Tonight?"

She shrugged. "Why not?"

"Will you join me?"

"Perhaps," she said with a smile. "How long have you been in Saigon, Colonel?"

"One day."

"That is not long. I know that one is not supposed to ask military questions, but are you commanding an American company of advisors?" From the way she asked it, I was certain she already knew better than that.

"No. I am attached to our Embassy. It is a reward for years of service."

"You look too young for that."

"I am not that young," I said solemnly. "It comes from our years of ancestor worship."

She laughed. "I like you, Colonel March. Come to dinner if you feel like it, but don't forget that there is an eleven o'clock curfew in Saigon." She got up from the table and I stood up at the same time.

"I will remember," I told her, and then she was gone.

I had just finished my coffee when the waiter appeared with a small paper bag and said it was for my dog. I thanked him, paid my check, and left.

The Sergeant had the car door open by the time Dante and I arrived. We climbed in, Dante sniffing at the bag of food.

"I was beginning to think you weren't coming out," the Sergeant said.

"We've always come back—so far."

"I'm beginning to believe it. Where do we go now?"

"To wherever General Lawson hangs out. I think I may need that curfew pass."

"I've got to say one thing for you," he said. "You've got guts. How come you've never been busted to a buck private?"

"They haven't thought of it recently. If they think of it now, I'll threaten to resign and write my memoirs."

He chuckled. "I think you would, too. How the hell did you ever make full colonel?"

"Clean living," I said cheerfully.

It was a short drive to the French-style building that was the General's headquarters. The United States flag and the General's flag were both flying over the top of the building. Dan parked and I went inside, leaving Dante with him.

I started with an NCO and worked my way up to a major, who was the General's aide. The General wasn't there. I showed the major my ID and waited until he was satisfied with it.

"I understand that you reported for duty yesterday at the Embassy. Why didn't you report here, Colonel?"

"My orders didn't give me a date when I should. I'd like to request permission to speak to the General."

"He isn't here just now. What can I do for you, sir?"

"I want a pass which will permit me to get back into the city if I happen to be outside after the curfew."

That startled him. "But—that's impossible, Colonel. We give no such passes."

"Major," I said patiently, "I am officially an attaché assigned to the Embassy. Actually, I'm here as a personal representative of General Baxter in Washington. If it seems necessary to carrying out orders, I shall be outside the city after curfew. I'd like to think that I can come back into the city without resorting to physical violence against our own men, but if that is the only way I can, I will do it. I trust that I am making myself perfectly clear, if I may use a small quote from a recent commander-in-chief."*

He looked unhappy. "Exactly what is your assignment here?"

"I have no authority to tell you," I said. "I'm sure that General Lawson knows my mission. If you'd like, you may call General Baxter in Washington. I want the pass and I want it now."

"But the General isn't here now, Colonel March."

"But you are. If you think it's too much authority for you, I will call General Baxter myself and let you explain the matter to him. I'm sure he would understand."

"I'm afraid he would," he said bitterly. "Why can't you come back tomorrow, Colonel?"

"I may need the pass tonight."

"We can't even guarantee that the pass will ensure your safety. You know, the men get a little jumpy when they are constantly under fire."

"Really? No one ever bothered to tell me. In the meantime, I'd like the pass before I get so old I can't make it outside and back."

His face reddened with anger, but he reached into his desk and got a form. "What is your full name?"

---

* President Nixon was often ridiculed for overusing the phrase "Let me make one thing perfectly clear."

"March, Colonel Milo March, the United States Army. You'd better make the pass for Colonel March and dog."

He looked startled. "Dog?"

"Dog," I repeated firmly. "Do you want the dog's name?"

He slapped his forehead. "My God, no! A dog! What is General Lawson going to think?"

"That I'm an animal lover. By the way, did General Lawson happen to leave anything for me?"

"Anything for you?" he repeated hollowly. Then his face brightened slightly. "Oh, yes. He said to give this to you if you came in." He reached into a desk drawer and produced an envelope. It looked fat. I took it from his hand and squeezed it. It felt fat, too.

"Thank you," I said. "I'll be seeing you, Major."

"I hope not," he said. Then he realized how it must sound. "I mean I hope it won't be necessary."

I laughed. "Okay, Major. I read you loud and clear. Don't worry. It all counts on twenty." I put the pass and the envelope in my pocket and went out.

Dante wagged his tail when I got into the car and Dan looked at me. "Did you get the pass?"

"Sure. For Colonel March and dog."

He whistled softly. "You must know where the body's buried."

"The General wasn't there. All I had to deal with was a major who wasn't quite sure on which side his oak leaves were buttered. He almost fainted when I told him to include the dog on the pass."

"I wish I could have seen that. You know, I'm getting very fond of that little fellow. What kind is he?"

"He's a miniature pinscher. They might be the smartest breed of dogs in the world, maybe except for the Hungarian puli. But with the puli's coat, there's no way it could survive in the jungle. Min pins are perfectly adapted to this kind of operation."

"I can believe that about him. Where do you want to go now?"

"I think back to the hotel. Only half of the afternoon is gone. That leaves time for me to take a nap. I may need the extra rest before the night is over. That'll give you time to go home for a few hours; then you can pick me up in time to get me back to the restaurant for dinner."

"Okay."

Again, it was only a short drive. Dante and I got out of the car as soon as it stopped in front of the hotel. "I'll see you later, Dan," I said.

"I'll be here. I'll have the clerk phone you when I arrive."

I went in and stopped at the desk. There were no messages for me. That was fine with me. I told the clerk what time I wanted to be called and we went upstairs. I got undressed, had one drink of Canadian Club, and went to sleep.

The phone awakened me. I thanked the clerk and went into the bathroom and looked into the mirror. I didn't need a shave, but I stripped off and took a shower. I felt better when I came out of it. I dried off and got dressed. I took a small drink from the bottle, then the phone rang again. I answered it and was told that Dan was downstairs.

Dante was waiting for me beside the door. There were times I thought he could read my mind. We went out together and downstairs.

Dan was waiting in the car. I picked up Dante and climbed in the front.

There were only a few cars in the parking space when Dan pulled in, so our timing was about perfect. "Wait here for a while," I told Dan. "If I learn I'm going outside tonight, I'll send a message out to you."

"Good luck," he said.

As I moved away from the car, I became aware of an old Chinese man who was clipping the shrubbery. As I started past him, I suddenly realized he was speaking to me.

"March *hsien?*" he said.

"*Shih,*" I answered. I stopped to light a cigarette, being careful not to look at him.

"I bear a message from your Elder Brother, Tang Lok Hee."

"I trust my Elder Brother is well," I said politely.

"He is well and trusts you are the same and hopes that you will continue in such health."

"My Elder Brother is most kind. What is it that my Elder Brother wishes from me?"

"Only that fortune walks with you. He asked me to bring you a message of most importance."

"I am honored." I knew there was no point in pushing. He would give me a message when he felt like it.

"You are going to see Le Thuy Duong?" he asked.

"I am going to have dinner in her restaurant, and I may see her and I may not. There is no formal arrangement."

"Your Elder Brother says that he has learned that Le Thuy Duong is planning on luring you into the hands of the Viet Cong, where you will be arrested and imprisoned."

NINE

The old gardener moved on to the next clump of shrubs before I could answer him. I shrugged and let it pass. "Come on, Dante," I said, and we headed for the entrance to the restaurant.

As soon as we entered, we were met by a waiter. "This way, Colonel March," he said.

I followed him to a table in a remote corner of the dining room. It was almost hidden from the rest of the room by tall potted plants.

"Madame Le will be with you soon," he said. "Would you like a cocktail or Chinese whiskey?"

"A dry martini, I think."

He bowed and left. He was back very quickly with the dry martini. I noticed it was a double. He placed it in front of me and backed off to disappear through the potted plants. I wondered if the double martini was a comment on my drinking habits or merely generosity. I smiled to myself and went to work on the drink. It was obvious that I was going to get special treatment, and that was the way I wanted it.

I had barely started on the martini when Dante nudged my ankle with his nose. I looked up. There was Le Thuy Duong, framed by the plants. She was wearing thin, clinging pants with a flowing ao dai in delicate pastel colors. She was the vision of classic Oriental grace and beauty. I stood up at once.

"You have honored me beyond my dreams," I said in Chinese. "You are as lovely as the morning sun."

"Thank you," she said in English. "Why do you use Chinese so often, since I speak English?"

"Compliments sound better in Chinese." I held the chair for her, then went around the table and sat down. She clapped her hands and the waiter appeared at once with two double martinis.

"You see," she said as he left, "I not only speak English well, but I have learned to like martinis. It is our great American import. That and men. It was recently reported that we now lead the world in half-breed bastards.* I drink to the bastards." She lifted her glass.

"I'd rather drink to a beautiful woman," I replied. "To Le Thuy Duong."

"You are very kind," she murmured. We drank. "But please call me Thuy."

"Only if you call me Milo."

She smiled. "All right, Milo. It has an Oriental sound. Are you certain you are not partly one of us?"

"I've often been called a bastard," I said, "but never so nicely. And I can neither confirm or reject the thought. I was never that intimate with my ancestors."

---

* There are no exact statistics on the number of Amerasian children abandoned by American G.I. fathers in Vietnam. Estimates from 1971 ranged between 10,000 and 15,000, but Vietnam expert Don Luce claimed the number was between 100,000 and 200,000. Luce's testimony to the Senate may have been the report Thuy refers to here. Wherever in Asia they were, illegitimate children of mixed race were outcasts in their societies. In contrast, intermarriage between Vietnamese and Chinese was common since the French colonial period, when many Chinese settled in Vietnam and even took Vietnamese names. In 1970 the Chinese Vietnamese were around 5 percent of the population, though they were disproportionately influential in commerce. In 1975, probably after this book manuscript was completed, the ethnic Chinese began to flee; many were among the refugees called the Boat People.

She laughed softly. "I am surprised that you haven't asked me about my given names."

"I know that Duong is a masculine name, so I am curious about it."

"My father was a strong-headed man. He expected a son when I was born. He did permit my mother to also name me Thuy, which she preferred, so you might say they compromised. Later, my mother dutifully bore him a son, but I already had the favored name."

We continued to talk, more or less in the same vein, just getting acquainted. She paused to clap her hands and the waiter started bringing food. There were some of my favorite dishes and several which I didn't recognize at all. But all of them were delicious. I noticed that nothing that I'd had at my previous meal in this restaurant was duplicated. It was a big meal and it was nine o'clock by the time we finished.

"That was wonderful," I said, leaning back and lighting a cigarette. "No wonder people say it is the best restaurant in Saigon."

"Most of these dishes are not on the menu," she said. "I made them myself—much to the distress of my chef. Now he thinks that I am not satisfied with his cooking. He will sulk for days."

"You cooked for me? I am overwhelmed."

"It is nothing," she said. She clapped her hands again and the waiter appeared with a small bowl of food. He placed it on the floor next to Dante. "The small one must also eat," she added.

"It's his favorite occupation. Tell me, do you have to stay around to lock the place up?"

"Why do you ask?"

"I thought that if you could leave early, we might go out, perhaps to a nightclub, for the hour or two we have before curfew."

She smiled. "I usually leave well before the curfew since I live outside the city. I think that neither of us would enjoy the nightclubs that are now in Saigon. I might make another suggestion, but there would not be much time for us. Unfortunately, my country is engaged in civil war."

"What sort of suggestion?"

"I would like to invite you to my house. We could have a drink and talk some more, but not for long. An hour at most. Then I could drive you back so you could reach the city before the gates are closed."

"I'd like that," I said. "Could we send word down to my driver that I won't need him tonight and he can go home?"

"Of course." She clapped her hands once more and the waiter appeared at once. I had a feeling that he stayed just behind the plants all the time until she summoned him. She told him what to do in Vietnamese. I noticed that she was watching me to see if I understood, so I kept my face blank as she talked.

"Now we can go," she said in English as soon as he left. "But we must hurry. Give me but a moment."

She was true to her word. She was back within three minutes, wearing a stole that looked like mink. She took my arm and we left the restaurant, with Dante following.

When we reached the parking lot, Dan was already gone. So was the Chinese who had been clipping the shrubbery. Thuy led the way to her car. It was a fairly new Mercedes. I opened the rear door and Dante jumped in. I slid into the seat with her.

"Now it is only a few minutes," she said. We soon left the city, and it was only another three minutes or so until she pulled into a driveway of a house that stood alone beside the road. It was Oriental in design and was quite large, with a three-car garage attached. She parked in front of the garage and we got out.

Dante sniffed around the lawn but his heart wasn't in it. I could tell by the way he acted that we weren't entirely alone.

"Isn't it dangerous," I asked her, "for you to live out here alone?"

"No. It's safer than in the city. I have several employees who look after me. They would not let anyone harm me."

Dante and I followed her into the house. The interior was even more impressive. It was furnished entirely in Oriental style.

"Make yourself comfortable," she said. "I will get us something to drink. There are cigarettes in the jade box on the table."

She vanished. I sat down and looked at Dante, who was staring at me in a way that indicated he didn't think I was too bright. It occurred to me that he might be right.

Thuy returned within a few minutes. She carried a tray on which there was a bucket of ice, a bottle of Chinese whiskey, two glasses, and a bowl of milk. She put the bowl on the floor for Dante.

She poured two drinks and lifted her glass. "May your future be as you wish," she said solemnly.

"It will be," I replied. We both drank.

"You are a strange man, Milo March," she said, putting down her glass. I wished that people would stop telling me I was strange. I didn't think I was. "An especially strange man to be an Army officer. You seem to have no definite assignment and you do as you please. What are you looking for in my country, Milo?"

I took a long drink from my glass and looked at her over the rim. "Can I trust you with a secret, Thuy?"

"Of course," she said softly.

It was like a corny screenplay with a small budget, but I suppressed my smile. "I am really not here representing the Army. I managed to get sent here—but on a private mission."

She looked startled. "A private mission? What can that possibly be?"

"I want to go north, possibly even to Hanoi."

Her reaction was even greater. "You want to go north! But why?"

"It's personal. A very good friend of mine, a civilian, worked at our Embassy here. A company of our men went too far north and were killed just south of Hanoi. They were reported as missing in action. Finally, a small group of soldiers were sent to try and identify the bodies. Among the missing were a few men who were well known to my friend. He was asked to go along for help in the identification. Most of the men in the second group were killed, and two or three we think were taken prisoners. Among them was my friend. It is believed, especially by his family, that he may be in prison. He would have been wearing civilian clothes and may have been arrested and charged with being a spy. But no answers have been received to a number of inquiries. I intend to go to Hanoi, as an unarmed Army officer on a peaceful mission. I will try to get them to see that he has been wrongly charged and should be released. As far as he's concerned, the arrest and imprisonment are contrary to all rules of warfare. My country does not know of my intentions."

"But why are you doing this?"

"I told you. He is my friend. He was in the diplomatic service, not the Army."

She stood up and began to walk about the room. "Of course," she said and the slight tone of sarcasm in her voice was difficult to detect. "Who was this good friend?"

"Martin Rigsby. He was in our Embassy in Saigon."

"Perhaps he was also a spy."

"Impossible. He wasn't the type. One glance at him would convince you of this. To charge him with being a spy is ridiculous. I promised his wife that I would try to get him released."

"How sweet!" she said dryly. She was pacing back and forth in front of me. "How do you expect to accomplish this?"

"I will go as far north as I can through military channels and will then strike out on my own. I will not be armed. When I encounter the North Vietnamese Army, I will surrender and ask to be taken to Hanoi."

"How can you be sure that they won't shoot you on sight?"

"I don't think they will. It isn't every day they can grab an officer without a fight."

She laughed. "Milo, you are amazing." She filled our two glasses again. "But it is too much for a simple woman to understand." She lifted her glass. "We must drink to your journey."

She had stopped walking and was again sitting close to me on the couch. There was only one logical thing to do about it. I kissed her. She stiffened at first, then responded with a passion that surprised me. When she finally pulled away, it was to stand up and take my hand in hers.

"Come, Milo," she said. Her voice was once more soft.

I followed her through the house until we ended up in a large, luxurious bedroom. She let go of my hand and reached for her throat. A minute later, her clothes were on the floor around her feet. She looked at me and smiled.

"Do I please you, Milo?"

"Very much," I said. I held out my arms and she came into them. I kissed her and carried her over to the bed. She smiled up at me as I undressed. Then we were together, our bodies melting into each other.

Much later, I was lying on my back, staring at the ceiling and wondering how it was possible for a woman to be a traitor and at the same time so good in the sack. It's a question that has never been answered and probably never will be.

"Milo," she said from beside me.

"Yes, Thuy?"

"Did I please you?"

I turned my head and looked at her. The dim light in the room made her look like a delicate Chinese watercolor.

"You were the music of a thousand nightingales," I said in Chinese. "And you, Thuy?"

"Could you not tell, Milo? It was you who made the music at all possible." She reached over and put a hand on my chest.

We were quiet for a few minutes. Making love is many things, but mostly it's like dying a little and getting one foot in heaven. So we were quiet as we slowly came back to life on earth. She turned to look at me. "Darling, I didn't mean your visit to turn out this way. ..."

"I hadn't exactly planned it this way either—but I'm afraid I can't complain."

She laughed and stroked my cheek. "Thank you, Milo. I wasn't complaining either. But I have caused you trouble."

"How?"

"It is already past curfew time. The gate to Saigon is closed now. You will have to stay here tonight."

"I can't," I said. "That would cause me more trouble than trying to get back in now. I'll get in. It may take some talking, but that's all."

"You'll probably get away with it, but I won't let you walk back to Saigon. Take the Mercedes. You can leave it at the restaurant anytime tomorrow. I have two more cars, so there won't be any problem." She swung her feet to the floor and stood up. She walked across the room to a closet and took out a dressing gown and slipped into it.

I got dressed and we walked back to the living room. "Since you're already late, why not have a late drink and then you can go?"

"Why not?" I ignored the look Dante was giving me.

She poured two drinks and lifted her glass. "To something that wasn't supposed to happen."

"If it wasn't supposed to happen, it wouldn't have."

"That's not fair, Milo. You're talking like a Buddhist and making me sound like a Christian."

"Are you?"

"A Buddhist or a Christian? I was raised as a Buddhist and have since then been exposed to Christianity. At this moment, I can only say that I find good things in both and belong to neither. Does that matter?"

"No."

"Are you really going to try to go to the North?"

"Yes."

She was silent for a second. "Would you permit me to help you—if I can?"

"I wouldn't ask you, but if you volunteer I'll accept."

"I might be able to help," she said. "Will you give me two days to find out?"

"Okay."

"Then you'd better start. The keys are in the Mercedes. You can bring it to the restaurant tomorrow. I will want to see you anyway."

I finished my drink and kissed her. "Let's go, Dante."

She walked to the door with me, Dante following close at my heels. I stepped outside and walked directly to the car without looking back. I put Dante on the seat next to me and started the car. As I backed out and headed for Saigon, I could see her framed in the doorway.

As I neared the gates a few minutes later, I could see the soldiers facing into the light, their guns held at ready.

"Get out of the car with your hands over your head," a voice said over a loudspeaker, "and approach the gate with your hands over your head. Move quickly or we will attack the car at once." Another voice began to repeat the message in Vietnamese.

I opened the door and stepped out with my hands up. I left the car door open. "Stay," I told Dante. I walked slowly toward the gate, the lights blinding me.

"Halt," a voice said when I was still a few feet from the gate. "Identify yourself."

"Colonel Milo March, United States Army, currently assigned as military attaché at the Unites States Embassy."

"Aren't you aware of the curfew law, Colonel?"

"I was told about it."

"Then why are you outside the city at this hour?"

"I left the city earlier on a mission and was unable to return before the curfew. I do, however, have a pass from the General's office."

"Where is it?"

"In the left pocket of my jacket."

"All right. Take it with two fingers and move slowly. Hold it so I can get a good look at it."

"Just a minute, Sergeant," another voice said. "Colonel March, isn't that car the one that belongs to Madame Le?"

"Yes."

"Why are you driving it?"

"My mission involved talking to Madame Le. When I became aware that I was late, she kindly offered me the use of her car."

"You're a fast worker, Colonel," the voice said dryly. "Just exactly what is your mission?"

"I am not at liberty to tell you. If you desire more information, I suggest that you phone General Lawson here in Saigon or General Baxter in Washington."

"I've heard about you and about your pass. I understand that there is even a small dog mentioned on the pass. Where is he?"

"He couldn't come out of the car with his front legs up, so I left him in it. I'd be disturbed if he were shot." I raised my voice. "Dante!"

He came out of the car and trotted up to stand beside me.

"That looks like the description I have," said the unseen voice. "All right, Colonel. Get in the car and drive through the gate. Be sure to stop as soon as you're inside. And don't make any sudden moves."

I walked back to the car, Dante following, then drove slowly through the gate. A strong flashlight was focused on my face. But it did give me a glimpse of the pair of silver bars on the man's shoulders. "Take it easy, Colonel. You're among friends—maybe."

"Thank you, Captain."

"Smart," he said. "Is that how you got those glorified chickens on your shoulders? But don't try to pull rank on me. It won't work in this situation. You can get away with it tomorrow, but not tonight. Let me see your ID. Don't forget to move slowly."

I did as he suggested. He studied it for a moment, then handed it back. "All right," he said wearily. "Where are you living?"

"Hotel Caravelle."

"Well, you'd better keep your pass handy on the way. Drive slowly and don't make any strange moves. One more thing, Colonel: I don't care how much hanky-panky you play with Madame Le, but just take it a bit easy around here. You may not have heard, but we have a small war going on. You bright boys from Washington are welcome, but don't get in the way of the action. You might get hurt."

"Captain," I said gently, "may I borrow your flashlight for a moment?"

He passed it to me and I turned it so the light was directly on the fruit salad pinned to my left chest.

"Take a look at the action, Captain," I said. "I won't pull rank on you, but I didn't get these by playing what you laughingly call hanky-panky, and that must be right out of Arkansas. Do you read me?"

"Loud and clear, sir," he said unhappily. "You may proceed, Colonel."

"Thank you, Captain." I returned the flashlight, started the motor, and drove off.

I soon discovered there was one advantage to driving Thuy's car. The Saigon police were out in full force, but they would take one look at the car and then quickly look in another direction. Nothing interrupted the drive.

When I reached the hotel, I pulled in and parked in front of the entrance. I noticed that the car next to me looked like the one that Dan drove. Dante and I got out and he confirmed my guess. He looked at the car and started wagging his tail. I walked over to the car and looked in. Dan had his head on the back of the seat and was asleep. I tapped on the window. He awakened and looked out, then rolled the window down.

"Good evening, Dan," I said. "I hope I didn't wake you up."

"Not at all. How did you make out?"

"If you want to talk, come on upstairs. You may be right about the hotel not being bugged, but what about the grounds? Come on."

He got out of the car and we went inside. I stopped at the desk and asked the night clerk to send up a bucket of ice and a bottle of Canadian Club. Then we got in the elevator and went up.

"What happened?" he asked.

"Later. After the waiter brings up some ice and booze. In the meantime, what were you doing sitting in the car out front? Why weren't you home asleep?"

"I was nervous, and it was my wife who suggested that I wait over here for you. I guess I was getting on her nerves. I wanted to know what happened."

There was a knock on the door. I went over and opened it. The waiter came in and set the tray down. I signed the check and he left. I poured two drinks and handed one to Dan. He took a sip and looked at me. "Well?"

"Everything went fine. I had an excellent dinner with Madame Le and then she invited me to her home for a drink, warning me I wouldn't have much time. It was worth it. She made several veiled hints to discover what my assignment was really about. So I told her."

"All of it?"

"In a way. I told her the truth with a few lies to spice it up a little. There's a funny thing about most people, Dan. If you tell them the plain truth, they usually won't believe you; then someone along the line may think it's partly true, but will also think it's too dangerous to accept as being true. In this case, I helped them to believe what they think about Americans. They imagine Americans are overly sentimental, so they find it easy to believe. Madame Le has promised that she can help me get to Hanoi and to meet the right people so I can rescue my best friend. Touching, it isn't?"

"From everything I've heard," he said, "I think she is dangerous. I don't think you should believe anything she says or anything she promises."

"You're wrong, Dan. In the first place, the enemy will do pretty much as I do, if they're smart. And don't forget that Madame Le is damned smart. They will also tell a mixture of truth and lies. I like the truth part of her offer. It's much better than anything I could have devised. In the meantime, all roads lead to Hanoi, but this is the only one I have access to—and that is where I have to go soon."

"Why do you have to be there?"

"Because my orders are to get to Hanoi in any way that I can. Madame Le offers the only available road, and I am sure she will see to it that I get there safely. That's half of my mission. The other half is that I have to rescue my friend and get out. For that, I will have to depend on the realization that I am colonel in charge of an army of one. Me. But if I can't get there, I won't be able to get out or to get anyone else out. It's that simple."

"It don't sound so simple to me. And maybe you shouldn't have told me."

"Why not? You're the only one who knows that much about what I'm going to do. It's safe with you. I'm sure you don't talk in your sleep."

"My wife wouldn't believe it if I did. She'd think I was making it up. It just makes me nervous knowing about it."

"You'll live through it, Dan. Why don't you go home and get some sleep? I won't need you until after lunch. Come to the restaurant and send word to me that you are there. I'll be right out."

"Okay. I guess I am pretty sleepy at that. See you later, Milo."

"Right."

I watched him go through the door. Then I got undressed, shaved, and took a shower. After calling the desk and telling them I wanted to be awakened, I poured another drink and stretched out on the bed with it. When it was finished, I fell asleep.

I was awakened by my call. I glanced at my watch. I had just about the right amount of time. I got up and dressed. I took out the envelope full of money I had gotten at the General's office the day before. I had part of a roll of adhesive tape in my suitcase and fastened part of the money to the inside top of the dresser. The rest of it went into my pocket.

I went down to the Mercedes and drove to the restaurant. It was a peaceful drive. No one followed me. No one stared at me.

I parked the car in the rear of the restaurant and went around the building to the front. Again, Dante and I were met by the same waiter who'd met us the night before. He must have been watching for me.

"This way, Colonel March," he said. He led the way to the table that Thuy and I had occupied the last time.

"Just a minute," I said before he could scurry away. "My driver may be in for lunch. If he is, please give him a table and put his lunch on my check."

"Very well, Colonel March."

"I'd like a dry martini while I'm waiting for Madame Le."

He bowed and left. He was making me nervous the way he appeared and disappeared through the potted plants.

He came back with the martini. "Madame Le will be with you in a minute." And he was gone again.

She was as good as her word. I had barely taken a sip of the drink when she appeared. "Hello," she said, slipping into the seat across the table. "I was worried about you this morning, until someone told me they saw you arrive and park in the rear. I'm glad there was no trouble."

"I had a friendly little chat with the soldiers at the gate, but it worked out all right. Aren't you going to have a drink?"

"Not now. We're going to be very busy today. Come back for dinner and I may have some good news for you. Have you made any further plans?"

"Not exactly plans. I did spend some time this morning looking at maps. I think I've found a good spot for taking off for the North."

"Where?"

"Bien Hoa. It is near enough to Saigon to make it easy to reach. At the same time it is near an area persistently held by the Viet Cong."

She nodded. "Are you busy this afternoon, Milo?"

"Yes. I have to go to Headquarters and fill out some stupid papers covering my assignment here. And I have to do some shopping for clothes."

"Shopping? We won't be going to a fancy dress ball, you know."

"That, my dear, is why I'm going to shop. I don't imagine we are going to drive the Mercedes all the way to Hanoi. I presume we'll be walking. I need things for that."

"You're right, of course. We'd both look pretty silly marching along the trail in what we wear at the moment. Take the Mercedes and run your chores. Then come back here for dinner. I may have our news by then."

"When do you think we might go?"

"It might be tomorrow morning. Are you in a hurry, Milo?"

"I'm in a hurry. How far do we have to go beyond Bien Hoa before we meet your escort group?"

"A few miles. Why?"

"I might be able to pull rank at Bien Hoa and get a jeep for us."

"That would be wonderful, Milo. Don't forget. Back here for dinner." She stood up. So did I. "I'll see you later, darling," she said as she came around the table. She stretched up and kissed me lightly on the lips and left.

I had my lunch, then asked for the check. The waiter told me that it was on the house. He also reported that my driver hadn't been in yet. I went outside.

Dan was sitting in the car, waiting. I opened the door and let Dante in. He seemed glad to see Dan.

"Did you have some lunch?" I asked.

"Sure. At home. Where are we going?"

"You drive to the PX and I'll follow you in the Mercedes. Let Dante go with you. He doesn't like shopping unless it's for food." I went to get the Mercedes, then followed him.

Dan had been right about one thing. It was a good PX. I bought two heavy fatigue uniforms, a couple of shirts, and a pair of heavy marching boots and several pairs of socks. I picked up a small roll of tape. I also bought a duffel bag that would be easy to carry and a box of shells for my smaller gun. I went back outside.

"Take these things to the hotel," I told Dan, "and ask the clerk to have them put in my room. Then you can go home, or drive Dante around, for a couple of hours. Then go to the General's headquarters and wait. On the way you might stop somewhere and buy a hamburger for Dante. You may have a long wait. But stay there until I come out."

"What are you going to do?"

"The General doesn't know it yet, but he's going to help me slip out of the city. I'll be back in two or three hours." I turned and went back to the Mercedes.

When I reached the Army quarters, I parked the Mercedes in a conspicuous place and went in. After a short delay I was told to go to the Major's office. The Major didn't seem too happy to see me when I entered.

"Well, Colonel," he said, "I understand that you used your pass last night."

"That was the reason I requested it," I said cheerfully.

"What do you want now?"

"I would like to speak to the General."

He managed a combination expression of unhappiness and relief—which meant that the General was there, so he wouldn't have to make a decision. He picked up his phone and pressed a button. "Colonel March is here, requesting to see you, sir." He listened for a minute. "Yes, sir." He replaced the phone and looked at me.

"General Lawson will see you now," he said. "Through that door." He indicated a closed door to the left of where I stood.

"Thank you, Major." I crossed the door, opened it, and stepped inside. I closed the door behind me and looked at the General. He was a trim, well-built man with gray hair and the usual worried look of a field officer. There were two stars on his shoulders.

"Colonel March, sir," I said, saluting him, "requesting some assistance."

"Sit down, Colonel March." He didn't sound happy, but he waited until I was seated. "By this time, I know quite a bit about you. Yesterday, you came in here and bullied my aide into giving you a pass. Last night, you used that pass to enter Saigon after curfew and you were driving a car belonging to Madame Le. Since then, I have had a conversation with General Baxter in Washington. He suggested that I give you any assistance possible."

"Yes, sir," I said politely.

"Damn it, Colonel," he suddenly exclaimed, "why do you G-2 characters always have to butt in? And why the hell does General Baxter let you bring a mutt with you? We even have to supply the damned dog with a pass!"

"In the first place, sir, he is not a mutt. He's a purebred

miniature pinscher, a certified military working dog, and he was chosen to come with me because he's smarter than any man they could find to send with me."

"I don't doubt that last statement. Now, what is it you want us to do?"

"I want to go to Bien Hoa today, and I would like to avoid being observed by any stray members of Viet Cong. I would also like to be assured complete cooperation from the officers there."

"You don't expect much, do you? I don't suppose you can tell me what this is all about?"

"I'm afraid not, sir."

"Are you also aware that by being seen with Madame Le and by driving her car all over South Vietnam you are guilty of committing treason and could be tried for that?"

"I'm quite aware, sir. About Bien Hoa?"

He sighed. "All right, Colonel. When do you want to leave?"

"As soon as possible."

"You'll have to wait a short time. Go back to the receptionist and he will tell you where to go and when. We'll have you change into the uniform of a sergeant, then taken to a helicopter and delivered to Bien Hoa. How long do you expect to be there?"

"One hour, I think. Two at the most."

"That will be all right."

"Thank you, General."

"Don't thank me. To be perfectly frank, I'll hate every minute of it, but I have no choice. Now, get out, Colonel March, and let me attend to my regular duties."

I saluted and left. I stopped in the outer office and smiled at the Major. "You see, there was nothing to it. But if I were you, I'd let him brood for a few minutes before you present him with another problem."

I didn't wait for him to respond. I left the office and went downstairs. I explained to the receptionist why I was there and sat down to wait.

It wasn't long. His phone rang and he answered it. When he was through, he looked at me. "Go to the rear of this floor, Colonel, and you will see a door marked *Private*. Open the door and go in. You're expected."

Thanking him, I strolled down the corridor until I saw the door he had mentioned. I opened it and walked in. There wasn't anyone there, but there was a sergeant's uniform neatly folded on top of a table. I changed clothes quickly and strapped my gun on beneath the jacket. I folded my uniform and placed it on the table, fixing it so that the eagles didn't show. I barely made it before there was a knock on the door. It opened and a lieutenant looked in.

"You're the guy who's going to Bien Hoa?" he asked.

"That seems to be the idea."

"Then let's go, Sarge. I'm Lieutenant Greene."

I followed him out of the room and through a rear exit where there was a car. Another sergeant was sitting behind the wheel. The Lieutenant and I got in the back seat and we drove off.

When we reached the airfield, we went directly to a helicopter on the field, its motor already warming up. I followed the Lieutenant inside, dodging around an M-14 rifle fixed to fire out the doorway.

"Welcome to *Baby,*" the Lieutenant said with a smile. "If she likes you, she'll treat you fine."

"I hope so," I said. "Every time I climb into one of these, I feel like I'm back with the Wright Brothers."

He laughed. "Here we go." There was a sudden roar and it lifted off the ground, dipping sharply to the right and soaring over the trees.

Saigon soon fell behind us and we were over fields and small forests. I could see a few animals grazing in the fields, surrounded by scars from where shells had fallen. It seemed peaceful enough—then, suddenly, there was a sound that reminded me of the Fourth of July.

"Old Charlie is out today," the Lieutenant said. "We've already taken a round." He pointed to a starred section in the windshield.

"It's pretty near to Saigon."

"Sure, and it keeps getting closer every day. I think they're trying to get even for last night."

"What happened last night?"

"We defoliated a village very near here. A Rome plow. It does a neat job."

I digested that for a minute, then figured out that it meant a village had been completely destroyed. It had been accomplished by a huge bulldozer that could destroy houses, people, animals, and even trees. It did, as the Lieutenant said, a "neat" job.

"I thought we were no longer at war in Vietnam. Didn't our dear president say something about peace with honor?"

"We're not at war with anyone, Sergeant. We're only

defending ourselves. Where have you been? Kitchen police back in the States?"

"Learning how to dodge bullets, but I never passed the course."

He laughed. "Well, I just hope you can stop being peaceful long enough to handle that gun next to you. I'm driving."

"Which end of it do I point?" I asked innocently. I reached for the gun with one hand and for the edge of the open door with the other. At that moment a bullet hit the window right next to me and made a beautiful star-pattern.

It didn't thrill me, but then I'd never been that good at art appreciation. I only knew what I liked—and I didn't like this.

TEN

I took a closer look at the ground below. I could see figures scurrying from bush to bush. Each time one of them stopped, there would be a shot. In the meantime, I swiveled the gun so it was pointed in the general direction of the figures. When I saw one of them stop, I swung the gun slightly and pulled the trigger. The figure slumped to the ground.

In the meantime, I was aware that the helicopter was shifting every few feet, but I had braced myself against the side of the cabin and ignored it. I concentrated on the job at hand. Then I was aware that the shots were coming from farther away and I didn't see any more scurrying figures. At the same time, the Lieutenant spoke.

"At ease, Sergeant. We've outrun them. That was a nice bit of shooting. I counted ten myself and I was pretty busy at the time."

"Who counts?" I said lightly. I swung the gun back against the wall and closed the door. I took out a cigarette and lit it. "It was the way you maneuvered the helicopter that made it possible."

He laughed. "Sergeant, I predict you'll go far in the Army. Well, if *Baby* holds up, we'll be there in a couple of minutes."

"That reminds me. Why do you call it *Baby?*"

"I hate to disappoint you, Sergeant. I would like to say that it was in honor of some glorious babe I met in Saigon, but I haven't even seen one. It's because it's a baby chopper. We have big choppers that carry troops, and they are known as slicks. Then we have choppers that carry forty-eight rockets in addition to machine guns, and we call them hawgs. That's all there is to it.... We're coming in now, Sergeant."

He turned on his radio. "George Able calling Green Fox." He flicked the switch.

"Come in, George Able," a voice said over the loudspeaker.

"Baby and I are coming in with a passenger."

"Okay, George Able. Over and out."

We started losing altitude and I could see the field. We were slanting in for a landing, so I had a good look at the planes that were on the field. There were a number of big cargo planes, the type that the Air Force brags that it lands on a dime and flies on a rubber band. Another part of the field looked like F-105 fighter-bombers. Then we were down and the Lieutenant shut off the motor. I opened the door and we climbed out.

"Thank you, Lieutenant," I said. "How do I get back?"

"I'll wait for you, Sergeant. After that little display of shooting, I wouldn't think of going back without you. In fact, if you'd like to shift outfits, I'll be happy to have you on every flight. I'll be waiting in the officers' club when you're through. I'll leave word for you to be let in."

"Thank you, Lieutenant."

While we were walking, I'd been aware that there was an MP sergeant trotting toward us. He arrived just then. "Sergeant March?" he asked.

"Yes," I said.

"Come with me. Colonel Blake is waiting to see you."

I followed him across the field where we got into a jeep and drove to a nearby building. The MP led me into the building and turned me over to a staff sergeant, who in turn took me to the office of a Colonel Blake.

I stood at attention and saluted. The Colonel returned my salute and waited until my guide had left.

"Relax, Colonel," he said to me then with a smile. "The General briefed me on you. Glad to help in any way I can. Sit down."

I took the chair beside his desk and lit a cigarette. "I gather that the General told you that I was a colonel?"

He nodded. "And told me it was an important secret. Now, what can I do for you?"

"How near are we to the Viet Cong?"

"Depends. Some days you can stand here and spit and you'll hit a few no matter which way you spit or which way the wind is blowing. And there are more of them almost every day. Look over here." He stood up and pulled down a wall map, then pointed out to me various Viet Cong strongholds.

He talked for about thirty minutes, and by that time I had a pretty good picture of the surrounding territory.

"Thank you, Colonel," I said when he'd finished. "I'd like to ask one more thing."

"Yes?"

"Do you have an expendable jeep?"

"Not very many of them, but I might be able to scare up one that can be patched up so that it will run maybe forty miles, fifty at the outside, before it dies. When it does die, that will be the finale for it. How soon do you need it?"

"Tomorrow morning."

He thought for a minute. "I can do it. I've got one mechanic here who is a genius. I'll take him off the other jobs and make him responsible for it. You'll have your jeep in time."

"Thank you, Colonel."

"You're welcome. Now, if you're finished, may I ask you a few questions? They will be off the record and I will forget the answers as soon as you walk out of here."

"Why not?"

"I get the feeling that you have some thought of trying to infiltrate the Viet Cong. Is that true? If you don't feel like you can answer that, I'll change the subject."

"I don't think it was a secret even before I got here. There have been three attempts to kill me, starting about two minutes after I landed. So my general reasons for being here are a hell of a secret. I think, however, that I have confused the issue. At least a small part of the local Viet Cong has started to think of me as a simple-minded American who can be used. I like the role. But 'infiltrate' is the wrong word. I expect to be escorted and assisted in everything I want until I'm in Hanoi. Then there will be a sharp change. And that will be when I have problems. One half of the journey is already arranged. The other half is strictly my own affair."

He nodded. "Do you have any relatives in the Service, Colonel?"

"Not that I know about."

"I've been in South Vietnam several years," he said. "I

came here as a captain. I remember that a couple of years ago that there was an Intelligence officer who spent most of his time up in the hills. Stories about him drifted down from the hills. He didn't have a dog with him, but his name was March and he had a very unorthodox way of working. He was the favorite topic in the officers' clubs. Half of the officers hated him for breaking rules. The other half were in the cheering section."

"That's what I call the coffee parties," I said. "I prefer, however, to call it a kaffeeklatsch. A bunch of grown men sitting around gossiping like a clutch of old ladies with nothing else to do."

"That's a pretty good description. All right. I'm not even sure I remember your name now." He stood up and held out his hand. "If I don't see you when you get back, good luck, Colonel."

I stood up and shook his hand. "Thank you, Colonel."

"The sergeant who brought you here will return you to the chopper. He's just outside."

I turned and left his office. The MP sergeant was sitting outside. "The Lieutenant ain't returned to the chopper yet. You want to go to the NCO club?"

"Not just now," I said. "Can you tell me where the officers' club is?"

His eyebrows went up. "How long you been in the Army, Sarge? Didn't they ever tell you the officers' club is off limits to enlisted men?"

"I've heard rumors, but the Lieutenant told me to meet him there. I was told never to disobey an officer."

He grinned. "I guess you got something there. Their club is the third building down that way. Want me to show you?"

"I'll stumble along." I walked in the direction he had indicated. I opened the door and found a corporal just inside.

"Sorry, Sergeant," he said, "this is for officers only."

"I know. There's a Lieutenant Greene inside. He told me to come here."

"Sergeant March? He's expecting you. Go on in."

I went into the bar. There were only three officers there. One of them was Lieutenant Greene, sitting at the end of the bar by himself. There was another enlisted man behind the bar. He looked at me and waited.

"Do you have whiskey?" I asked. A foolish question.

"We have it. How do you want it?"

"With a water chaser."

"The water isn't so good."

"Then drown it in ice cubes."

He nodded and brought me my drink. He collected the money from the Lieutenant.

"Well," he said when I'd finished my drink, "maybe we better start back."

I nodded and we went out. An enlisted man drove us out to the chopper in a jeep. We climbed in and he started the motor.

"Better check our departure," he said, switching on the radio.

I looked around. "Where's the tower?"

He laughed. "Well, it isn't exactly a tower. It's merely a tall building—which is two floors here…. George Able to Green Fox. Can I get out of this joint?"

"Green Fox to George Able. Take her away."

The motor roared and we lifted from the ground. As soon as we were above the buildings, he straightened out on a course across the fields. It was an uneventful trip and we were soon in Saigon. The jeep and driver were waiting for us. When we reached headquarters, we entered the building from the rear entrance. I thanked the Lieutenant and went to the room where I had changed clothes.

I quickly removed the uniform I was wearing and carefully draped it over the back of the chair. Then I got into my own uniform. It felt better. I opened the door and stepped into the corridor.

Lieutenant Greene was coming back down the corridor. He saw me and stopped short and saluted. I returned the salute.

"Well," he said, "I didn't know that promotions were coming that fast. For riding in a helicopter over and beyond the call of duty, I suppose? I must look into it."

"That's a good idea," I said gravely. "And the next time I see you, Lieutenant Greene, remind me that I owe you a drink in the local officers' club. Thanks again." I strode past him and continued through the building and out the front door.

The Embassy car was still parked and Dan was in it. Then I saw Dante's face at the window. I walked over to the car and gave Dante the sign to get down. He obeyed and I opened the door.

"How'd it go?" Dan asked.

"Fine." I leaned against the open door. "How would you like to have the rest of the day off?"

"What's the booby trap?"

"There isn't one. You definitely have the rest of the day off. If things go right, you can have several more days off as far as I'm concerned."

"You're going outside again!"

"Tonight. And, if I'm lucky, I will leave for Hanoi tomorrow morning. Keep your lip buttoned about that."

"I don't think you should," he said stubbornly.

"But the United States Army thinks that I should. I also think that I should. That is the end of the conference. I will know tonight if I'm leaving in the morning. I'll call you at home. But if you don't hear from me, you'll know that I have left. Come on, Dante." I scooped him up from the seat and held him.

"You're taking him, too?"

"Right. He's been living off the fat of the land since we arrived, and it's time he started working for a living. Keep your chin up, Dan."

"Okay," he said glumly. "I'll see you when you get back. Happy landings, Milo."

"Thanks, Dan. We'll be seeing you." I turned around and walked to the Mercedes. I got in, put Dante on the seat next to me, and started the car. I snapped a salute to Dan as I went by.

Everything I had bought at the PX was in my room when I reached it. I poured myself a drink and sipped it while I considered what I had to do. Then I changed clothes, putting on one of the heavier uniforms I'd bought earlier. I removed the fruit salad from my duty uniform jacket and used the tape to fasten it to the back of a drawer. No one would see it without taking the drawer completely out. I did pin the eagles on. Then I got down to essentials. There were two guns and a knife. I decided to leave the Python. Using adhesive tape, I fastened it to the lid of the toilet tank. After consideration, I voted to leave the knife behind, too. I taped it to the inside top of the shower curtain.

The small, flat gun went inside one combat boot. Taped. I took some more of the money in my pocket and taped it inside a boot near the toe. I also taped my lock picks inside the other boot. When I reached Hanoi I'd transfer all three items to another hiding place. Then I put on my jacket and I was ready.

Downstairs, I stopped at the desk and told them that I would be gone for a few days but wanted them to hold my room. The clerk said he would and asked no questions.

I drove straight to the restaurant and parked the Mercedes. Dante and I went inside. We were met by the same waiter, who led the way to the same table. This time, my martini was already on the table for me. I thanked him and he vanished through the potted plants. It was getting to be too much of a routine.

Then Thuy came in and the waiter reappeared with a martini for her. He left.

"You were fast, darling," she said. "I have good news for you. We start for Hanoi in the morning."

"And I have good news for you, Thuy. When we reach Bien Hoa, I have arranged for us to have a jeep. We can take it as far North as we wish to on the road. Then we abandon it."

"My people could use an extra jeep," she said. "How did you explain the need for a jeep?"

"That was simple. I explained to the general in Saigon and the colonel in Bien Hoa that I could not tell them what my mission was but only that I wanted to make an inspection of the area within a few miles of Saigon. They accepted that."

"Why?"

"Because I know a general in the United States who made it possible for me to come here and try to rescue my friend. They don't dare oppose the Washington general, so they put up with the situation."

She laughed softly. "That is good, Milo. But let us not talk about that now. We shall enjoy ourselves."

We did. We each had another drink and then a wonderful dinner completely different from the one the night before. When we finished dinner we left, taking food with us for Dante, and drove in the Mercedes to her house. This time she put the car in the garage, then we went into the house. I carried the duffel bag with me.

"What's in that?" she wanted to know.

"The results of my shopping today. All clothes except for some cigarettes and adhesive tape."

"You know where the bedroom is, darling. Put your things up there and I will have drinks for us when you come down."

I told Dante to stay where he was and went upstairs. I dropped the duffel bag on the floor in one of the closets. Then I went back downstairs.

There were two glasses of Chinese whiskey on the table, and Thuy was sitting on the couch. Dante was standing in the middle of the room giving me a scornful look.

"I tried to make friends with your little dog, but he wouldn't respond at all. Why do you take him with you? The jungle is no place for a small dog."

"I take him there," I said, "for the same reason I take him anyplace. If I left him alone, he would stop eating and would die. I will take care of him while we're in the jungle. If the United States Army can put up with him, then so can the Viet Cong."

"All right," she said, laughing. "I merely thought it was being unkind to him. If you say it is necessary, I believe you. … You know, you never introduced me to your little dog."

"Sorry. Dante." He looked up. "I want you to meet a friend of mine. Her name is Thuy. Say hello to our friend."

He looked at her and wagged his tail, but I could see his heart wasn't in it. "How delightful," Thuy said. "I don't blame you for wanting him with you."

"Thuy, can I really leave tomorrow morning—with help?"

"Unless something happens between now and the morning, we can leave early tomorrow morning. We will call a taxi from Saigon and take it as far as Bien Hoa, where you will get the jeep. Within twenty miles we will be deep inside the Viet Cong lines."

"We?"

"Yes. I will go with you."

"I won't hear of it," I said. "It's much too dangerous for you, and you have too much to lose here. I'll accept any other sort of help you can give me—but not if it's going to damage you in any way."

She laughed. "My dear Milo, I am the only one you know who can give you what you want. You would not get ten miles, my darling, without being killed. If I am along, I think I can guarantee you will stay alive—and you will at least have the opportunity to plead for your friend."

"But—"

*"Chut!"** she said in French.

*"Certains amis sont pires que des ennemis,"*** I answered.

"I am not your enemy, Milo," she said, switching back to English. "We will start early in the morning. So now let's forget about it and enjoy tonight."

Dante looked at me with disgust.

I still made a show of not wanting her to make the trip, but I gave in slowly but gracefully. We had a few more drinks and talked about many things far removed from the Vietnam War. Finally, she again took my hand and led the way upstairs. Dante stayed where he was.

We made love and it was even better than the night before. Then she curled around me and went to sleep. I was awake for a while, thinking what a strange world it was. Here we were, two people involved in and dedicated to different ideologies. Each of us had approached a more intimate relationship with ulterior motives. She sensed that I might be an important capture for the Viet Cong. I saw her as an easy way to reach Martin Rigsby. At the same time, there was a warmth between us, and we already found ourselves in conversations which were as close as making love. It created a problem for both of us. With no solution in mind, I fell into sleep, wishing I were back in Washington with Marya.

---

* Hush!
** Some friends are worse than enemies.

I was awakened in the middle of the night by a sound. I opened my eyes and lifted my head slightly. There was enough light coming through the window from the moon so that I could make out a dim figure bending over at the closet. Finally, I could see what he was doing. He had lifted one of my combat shoes and was holding it upside down and shaking it. I guess he thought that was a better method than reaching inside. It was for me. When the shaking produced nothing, the figure straightened up and slipped from the room. I went back to sleep.

It was about five when I awakened again. Thuy was still asleep. She looked beautiful and innocent. It was as hard to believe that she was the enemy as it was to believe she was over twenty-five. I reached over and touched her lightly.

"Milo," she said sleepily, "why didn't you stay wherever you were? Why did you have to come into my life?"

"It was written in the sands of time."

"Don't give me that Oriental claptrap," she said sharply. Then, more softly, "Just kiss me. It's too early for philosophy."

I kissed her and then we made love again. We reached the apex together and held it for a long, long minute. When I felt her relax, I rolled over and reached for my cigarettes.

"Cigarette?" I asked.

"No, thanks, darling. I feel wonderful."

I finished my cigarette while her head rested on my shoulder. I put it out in the ashtray and slapped her gently on the bottom. She raised her head and stared indignantly at me.

"What was that for?"

"We're making a trip this morning, remember? Now it's shower time, and ladies go first. Then, while I'm showering, you can make certain that I get a breakfast that will last me through the day—or longer if necessary."

She sat up in bed and glared at me. "You learned too much about the ancient Chinese way of life. Things have changed." She swung off the bed and marched into the bathroom.

After a while the sound of water stopped and a few minutes later she came out, her body golden and rosy. She looked down at me. "I have decided that I like you better without your uniform."

"And I like you better without yours."

The laughter fled from her face. "It would be nice, Milo, if the world could stop right here—but you wouldn't like it, because you'd be hungry." She took a robe from the closet and slipped into it. "Take your shower, darling, while I make you a huge breakfast. And a small one for Dante." With that she swept out of the room.

When she was gone, the first thing I did was cross the room and look at my shoes. Everything was still in place. I went to take my shower. When I came out, I got the small gun and the bullets from the boot and used the adhesive tape to fasten them to my back, just above the hips. They were flat enough to not make any suspicious bulge. The shorts and heavy pants would take care of that. I decided not to shave. I might look more like I belonged in the jungle if I didn't.

When I went downstairs, Dante was already eating from a bowl on the floor. There was a glass of Chinese whiskey on the coffee table with ice cubes floating around in it. I sat down in front of it. I took a swallow and was ready to admit that morning had arrived.

Thuy came in, carrying a tray, and put it down in front of me. It was scrambled eggs and fried pork, with two pieces of toast. And there were two cups of tea.

"I made you an American breakfast," she said. "You may have to eat Vietnamese food until we reach Hanoi."

"Toast," I said. "I don't believe it. Where's your breakfast?"

"I have already had it. I drank some juice and had a large piece of melon and a cup of tea."

"That sounds more like an American breakfast than what I have," I said. "Are you sure that some of your ancestors didn't stray across the line?"

She laughed. "No, I'm not sure. But I am sure that I'd better get ready. I phoned for the taxi when I first came downstairs." She went into the kitchen and came out carrying two pint bottles.

"What the hell's that?"

"Whiskey. You may need a drink or two while we're in the jungle. May I put them in your duffel bag?"

"Sure. Put anything of yours into it that you want to. I think there's plenty of room. Yell and I'll come up and get it."

She was staring at me. "What happened to all of your ribbons?"

"I left them in the hotel."

"But they're a part of you," she protested.

"Not an essential part. I'm wearing the insignia of my rank and I'm wearing a proper uniform. If I also wear the ribbons, it'll only look like I'm bragging about my military experience. I'm going to Hanoi on a peaceful mission and I'm wearing my uniform only so it won't look like I'm trying to sneak in.

The ribbons are out just as much as a gun strapped around my middle would be."

"That's very smart," she said at length. "I won't be long, Milo." She went upstairs. I waited and thought about what was ahead of me. I was sure that the first few hours with the members of the Viet Cong we were meeting would tell the story. If I passed muster with them, I might make it.

Thuy called from upstairs and I went up. I picked up the duffel bag and followed her down. She was wearing a pair of heavy, dark green slacks with the bottoms tucked into the ankle-high boots, and a green blouse of the same material. She was tying a green scarf over her head.

"The taxi should be here any minute now," she said. "Why don't you take Dante outside and walk him while I lock up."

I nodded and went out, with Dante right at my heels. I stood on the lawn while he investigated. Several times he seemed more interested in something else. I suspected there were some people around somewhere but staying out of sight. Thuy joined me just as the taxi arrived.

"When we reach Bien Hoa, have the cab stop just this side of the entrance. We'll both get out and you can walk in and get the jeep. When you come out, turn to the right. Drive slowly, because you won't see me until you're almost on top of me."

"Okay."

We got in the cab and I told the driver where to go. "When you reach Bien Hoa, stop just this side of the entrance and we'll walk inside. Then you can go back to Saigon."

He nodded to show he understood, and the car started forward. Thuy and I were quiet on the ride. It was only twelve miles from where we were, and there was no traffic on the road, so we were there in twenty minutes.

The driver stopped where I'd told him we wanted out. I paid him in American dollars and included a good tip. I knew he'd get a profit by selling them to the black market in Saigon, so he probably wouldn't tell his interesting story until much later.

"Take care, honey," I said as I picked up the bag. She nodded and blew a kiss to me. I turned and went through the gate.

There were two MPs standing just inside the gate. I showed them my ID and told them I wanted to see Colonel Blake. They conferred for a moment and then decided that one of them would escort me to the Colonel's office.

The Colonel reassured the MP and dismissed him. "You look like you're dressed for the bush," he said to me when we were alone.

"In a way I am. I intend to visit a number of native villages but will limit it to those not occupied by soldiers from the North."

"That's a hell of a mission they've sent you on. There are times when I think that Washington believes this is a tea party. I have no authority to give you orders, Colonel March, but my advice is to forget it."

"Sorry, but I'm afraid I can't do that. I doubt very much if you would pick up and go back to Washington with the report that you had been advised not to carry out your orders."

"You're right, Colonel. I apologize." He glanced down at Dante, a puzzled look on his face. "Is that your dog or did he merely follow you in here?"

"He's my dog."

"You're going to take him with you?"

"Yes. He goes wherever I go. Don't be fooled by his size. I'd rather have him with me than any man I know."

He shook his head. "You must know what you're doing or you wouldn't have lasted this long. The jeep is just outside. Don't worry if you can't return it. Here's a pass that permits you to take it out." He stood up and handed me the pass, then held out his hand. "Happy landings, Colonel."

We shook hands. "Thank you," I said. "I'll see you on the way back."

"I hope so," he said warmly.

I saluted him and walked out. There was a sergeant there who showed me the jeep. The key was in it. I started it and drove out, stopping at the gate to let the guards look at the pass. Once outside, I turned to the north and drove slowly. I was well out of sight of the guards when Thuy popped out of the bushes. I stopped and she got in beside me.

"I told you I'd be here," she said, snuggling up beside me.

I put the jeep into gear and drove ahead. "I know what you are," I said. "You're a bush bunny."

She laughed as the jeep picked up speed.

It was mostly a narrow country road, and once in a while I had to steer around a hole that had been made by a shell. We didn't see a car or a person. After ten miles, Thuy told me to take a road that branched off to the left. It was a winding road, and we were soon winding through a scrubby jungle. Once we saw a few wild cattle.

We'd driven fifteen miles from Bien Hoa when we rounded

a sharp curve, and suddenly men began to magically pour out on the road. They all wore baggy, ragged uniforms that looked like black pajamas and carried rifles. The rifles were pointed at us as the men placed themselves solidly across the road.

"You'd better stop, darling," she said.

ELEVEN

There was something to be said for her suggestion, although it was hardly necessary. I was not about to charge twenty men who were pointing rifles at me. I braked the jeep and came to a stop a few feet away from the man who was apparently the leader. His pajamas were not quite so faded and ragged.

"Get out," he said in Vietnamese.

Staying in character, I looked puzzled to show that I didn't understand.

"He wants us to get out of the car," Thuy said in Chinese. "Don't worry. We will not be harmed."

"Okay," I said. I reached back and picked up my duffel bag, then stepped down on the road. Thuy jumped down before I could help her.

The officer gave a quick order and one of his men climbed into the jeep. He drove it a few yards up the road, then turned off and vanished into the jungle.

"This way," the officer said. "Hurry."

"He wants us to follow him," Thuy said. "In single file."

I nodded and the officer set out through the shrubbery, with us following him and several soldiers coming along behind us. As we left the road, I noticed that we were on a narrow path that had been invisible from the road. Dante stayed at my heels, sniffing quickly at plants when there was time for it.

We must have marched ten miles without stopping. By then, we were deep into the jungle and in front of a large mass of shrubbery. The officer had stopped and gestured to some of his men. They ran forward and parted the shrubs, revealing a large cave. We marched inside. There were several gasoline lamps burning, and I could see there were many members of the Viet Cong there, but couldn't tell how many.

"Over there," the officer said, gesturing toward an empty section of the cave.

"This way, darling," Thuy said, putting a gentle pressure on my arm.

I let her guide me across the cave. The officer and a few of his men came with us. Thuy turned to face the officer.

"This," she said in rapid Vietnamese, "is the man I told you about. As I told you, he does not speak our language, but he does speak Chinese and French. Do not treat him in your usual way. He is much too valuable." She turned to me, smiling. She hesitated and then spoke Chinese. "Colonel March, I would like you to meet Captain Le Ton Kuang. He is my younger brother."

"Hello," I said to him. Then I did a double take. "Your brother?"

"Yes. That is part of the reason I said I could help you make the trip."

"Enough," her brother said. He gestured to one of his men. "Search him," he ordered.

"One minute," Thuy said sternly. "You may take his weapons away from him—if he has any. But that is all. Remember that." She turned back to me and switched to Chinese. "They want to take any weapons you may have, Milo. Let them, if you have any. I know you don't, but let them find out for themselves."

"Okay," I said.

The soldier stepped forward and felt my pockets and patted me under both arms. He turned and looked at my duffel bag.

"There is no reason to go through that. I packed it this morning and I know everything in it. There is nothing in it that can be considered a weapon."

The soldier turned and looked at my feet. "He is wearing a fine pair of boots," he said. "I think they would fit me."

"No," Thuy said sharply.

The soldier looked at Le Ton Kuang, who merely shrugged his shoulders. The soldier turned his gaze to Dante. "What about that one? He would make a good meal."*

Le Ton Kuang shrugged again. "The only trouble with the Association of the People," he said to the soldier, "is that they sometimes give too much authority to mere women. In the good times of our people, the women only produced babies and served meals."

"Yes, dear younger brother," she said, "and sometimes mere women do as much as or more than the brave soldiers in the jungle who hit and run. And much better than the brave soldier who helps invade a defenseless village and rapes a young girl after killing her mother and father."

He grunted something under his breath and the soldier fell back. "We leave in fifteen minutes," the Captain said. He turned and walked away.

---

* Dog meat is big business in both China and Vietnam (as well as some other countries). On Vietnamese menus it is called Cho.

"We'd better rest," Thuy said, sitting down on the ground with her back to the wall. I joined her.

"I don't understand," I said to her. "You were obviously giving that soldier orders and he obeyed. Does that mean that you are part of the Viet Cong?"

"These are my people," she said gently. "Ton is my brother, but these are my people. As long as I can remember, especially under the French, our land and even our lives have not belonged to us. We have fought back in the only ways we knew or could." She put her hand on my arm. "I told you before we left my house that I am sorry the way things have turned out. I wish it were possible for us to go to the island, or up in the hills, but we can't. Please try to understand that, Milo."

"I'll try," I said. I took out two cigarettes and lit them both. I passed one to her. "What are you going to do with me, Thuy?"

"Give you what you said you wanted."

"And then?"

"That depends on you," she said simply. "I think there is something special about you, Milo. There has to be for you to risk your life to see a friend and try to get the government to release him. You will see him. Then, perhaps, you will find that I am not so bad. Perhaps you will even agree to stay here and work—with me. There are many things to fight—maybe even my own brother."

I picked what I thought was the wisest position. "I don't know, Thuy. I didn't come here to fight."

"I know, darling. We don't want to fight either. We want to live and grow things and raise babies. We are very similar to the people in your country at the time of your Revolution. All of my people do not agree with this, but most of them do. And I think that you agree, too, or you wouldn't have traveled so far to help a friend. Isn't that true?"

"I suppose so," I said. I had a feeling that Dante was looking at me accusingly, but I must have been wrong. He couldn't possibly understand that much!

Le Ton Kuang returned. "We are leaving now," he said to his sister. "Tell your man to remove the insignia of his rank from his uniform. It may cause trouble. And tell him that we have a long march ahead of us—unless he's too soft to make it."

"He'll make it," she said. "And speaking of rank, younger brother, you might remember that I hold a higher rank than you do. Everything that happens on this march will be especially noted in Hanoi."

"In Hanoi, yes," he said softly, "but not in the jungle. Hurry up." He turned and walked away.

"What did he say?" I asked innocently.

"We must go now. And he requests that you remove the insignia of rank from your uniform. It might cause trouble with some of the soldiers, and we have a long march ahead of us."

I took the eagles from my jacket and put them in my pocket. I put out my cigarette and stood up. "Let's go."

We walked over to her brother. He nodded curtly, raised his hand to the soldiers, and started walking. Several soldiers fell in behind him, and I scooped up Dante and put him inside my jacket. Thuy and I fell in behind them, and the remainder of the soldiers followed us. We headed toward the rear of the cave. There was another entrance there, and we soon emerged into the jungle with only a narrow path to follow. We walked in single file.

We marched through the jungle for nine hours with only two brief stops. There was only time for taking care of bodily needs and a fast cigarette. We saw nothing on the march except thousands of insects and a few wild animals. Finally, when it was already dark, we left the path and entered a small area sheltered by huge rocks on three sides. As soon as we were established there, several soldiers left and disappeared into the darkness.

Thuy and I sat down a few feet away from the rest of them. It was so dark we could barely see them. I heard Thuy fumbling with my duffel bag and then she placed a bottle in my hand. It was one of the pints she had brought with us. I took a long drink from it and felt a little better. I handed it back to her.

I was tired, but I wasn't going to admit it. The Viet Cong soldiers had been watching me all the time on the march, expecting me to weaken any moment. I lit two cigarettes and passed one to Thuy.

"How are you feeling?" she asked.

"Fine," I said, lying only a little. "It's not as easy as the cocktail circuit, but we can't have everything."

In the meantime, several soldiers were building a fire. Shortly thereafter, the missing soldiers returned. They were carrying a large wild pig. It was wounded, but not yet dead. They hung it up by its hind legs, cut its throat, and started butchering it.

The pig was on a wooden spit over the fire when one of the

soldiers came over to us, carrying two cups. He offered one to Thuy, who accepted it, so I took the one he offered me.

"What is this?" I asked her.

"A native drink," she said. "I suggest that you drink it even if you don't like it. If you drink it fast, you won't notice the taste so much. She took a big drink and I noticed that her face paled, but she still managed a smile.

Well, I had been warned. I noticed that the Viet Cong soldiers had stopped everything and were watching me. I tilted the cup and drank until it was empty. It wasn't until I lowered the cup that I got the taste. It wasn't good. It was a heavy, warm liquid with a sickening flavor—but somewhere in it, there was also alcohol, which helped keep it down. I put my cup on the ground and smiled.

There was a buzz of conversation among the soldiers. I couldn't catch all of it, but I gathered they approved of my conduct. They lost interest in us and turned their attention to the pig.

"Hand me the bottle," I told Thuy.

She put it next to me. I checked but no one was looking, so I took a hell of a big drink and gave the bottle back to her. My stomach felt better, but the taste was still in my mouth.

"What the hell was that?" I asked.

"The blood of the freshly killed pig mixed with wine," she said with a hint of laughter in her voice. "It is a favorite drink of many of my people who haven't yet been introduced to martinis."

"I always knew that we must have made some social progress since the Chinese invented spaghetti, but I wasn't sure what it was. I guess that what we just had must be a more recent invention. I have a name for it. We have a Bloody Mary, so why not call your drink a Bloody Pig?"

She laughed softly. "It is pretty awful, isn't it? But you did well, Milo. If you had stopped after the first sip or made a face, they would have thought there was something wrong with you."

Sometime later the food was ready, big chunks of roast pork and some nuts they brought from the forest. We were given two battered mess plates. There was no cutlery except for our fingers. Once I had tasted the pork, however, I didn't care. It was delicious. Dante agreed when I gave him some.

After eating, we all rested, stretched out on the ground. We used my duffel bag as a pillow. Thuy moved closer to me and Dante curled up on my other side. It must have been a picture of domestic tranquility: man, woman, and dog relaxing before an open fire. I should have had a photograph of it to send back to General Baxter.

We must have rested an hour or so before Le Ton Kuang was moving among us to say that we were marching again. We got up and brushed the dirt from our clothes. I put Dante back inside my jacket and we started while a couple of soldiers stopped to put the fire out.

We were soon back in the jungle. It was so dark that it was almost impossible to see anything. There was enough starlight so I could just make out the form of Thuy ahead of me. Occasionally I could hear the cough of a big cat in the distance. I thought it was a tiger. Each time it happened, Dante gave a low growl from the inside of my jacket.

It was impossible to tell how much time was passing. There was enough light for me to see my watch. I knew I was getting tired again, but was determined not to show it. My guess was that we had marched steadily for four or five hours when Le Ton Kuang stopped.

"Stay here," he whispered in Vietnamese.

"He says we must wait for him here," Thuy told me, her lips brushing across my lips as she whispered.

We waited there in complete darkness, the only sound the drone of insects. It seemed to me that somewhere ahead there was an area that had been cleared, but there wasn't enough light to be certain.

It was probably another half an hour before Le Ton Kuang returned. "Come," he said.

We followed him through the jungle for about ten minutes. Then suddenly we were in a large open field. There were no visible lights, but I could see there were several buildings, two light planes, and a crude runway on the field.

We marched straight to one of the buildings. Then Le Ton Kuang stopped and gave an order to his men to wait.

"Bring your man and come," he told Thuy.

I waited while she translated this and then the three of us went up to the door. He knocked and it was opened. We entered a small room lit by gasoline lamps. There were four men in the room, all of them wearing black pajamas. There were no insignia of rank on their clothing, but I guessed they were high-ranking officers. Both Thuy and her brother saluted them.

They spoke in Vietnamese after Thuy explained in that

language that I didn't understand it. I continued to pretend that I didn't know what they were saying while Thuy explained that I was the man she had told Hanoi about. I gathered from their responses that they considered me a fairly important catch. That could mean only one thing to me. There must have been a leak and they knew I was from Intelligence. That would also explain the grenade that had greeted me when I got off the plane. I also guessed that they were going to fly Thuy and me to Hanoi.

She confirmed it at once. "I was explaining why you are here," she said. "One of these men is a pilot and will fly us to Hanoi at once. In the meantime, they all wish to welcome you to the Association of the People."

I hadn't heard any mention of that. "Us?" I asked.

She nodded. "You and me."

"And me," said her brother in his own language, but he obviously understood some English.

Thuy was obviously surprised. "You? But your job is here."

"Yes. But I have been ordered to go with you to make sure that your lover does not try any tricks before he reaches Hanoi. If he does, you can tell him, I will kill him. Once you are safely in Hanoi, I shall return to my command."

"Is Hanoi where my friend is?"

"Yes," she answered. "You can probably see him tomorrow."

Her brother muttered something vulgar and Thuy gave him an angry look.

"My younger brother," she said, turning to me, "does not approve of our relationship, I fear. But then he has always been jealous. He does not think that a mere woman should have been involved in our war before he was old enough to take part in it or that she should hold a higher rank than he does. But one day he will grow up."

"I'm sure he will," I said without conviction in my voice.

His face darkened with anger but he kept quiet. Thuy turned to one of the four men. "Shall we go, Captain Tran?"

The man stood up and nodded. Everybody said good-bye politely and we left the office. Outside, Le Ton Kwang snapped some orders at his men and we went on to the airplane.

It was an old prop-driven Russian model. It had probably once been a small bomber but had been converted to a cargo plane. I could see that it was armed, the guns being controlled by the pilot. Back of him there was nothing but bare floor. It was obvious that was where we had to sit. Thuy and I took one side, leaning against the wall of the plane. I took Dante from my jacket and he curled up between my legs.

Le Ton Kwang sat across from us, glaring. He still held his gun as if he expected me to make a dash for it at any minute. The plane roared to life and began to trundle down the runway. A few minutes later, it was airborne. I had to admit the pilot was good, because I knew there were no lights around the field.

"Relax, younger brother," Thuy said. She was really bearing down on the younger brother bit. "You will soon be back with your comrades in the jungle where you can sit and fight the bugs and pretend you're a hero. What will you do when we win the fight for independence? Go sit in the jungle all by yourself?"

"Shut up, woman," he said harshly. "This gun is not only for him. It might also be for you. Too many years of decadent living have softened you—even to taking an enemy as your lover."

She laughed. "Jealous. You've always been. You were a little boy when I had my first lover and you wanted to kill him. With a slingshot."

"Love and politics do not mix," he said through gritted teeth. "Especially love with the enemy. I spit on him. You should do the same."

"You are still a child," she said. "Yes, I like this man. If things were different, I might spend the rest of my life with him. But the fact that he is here on a peaceful mission proves that I do my duty—even better than some who hide out in the jungle and pretend to fight. You are killers, not fighters. Tears may flow from my heart, but that is personal. Tears do not come because of this man. I will never do things which hurt my country and my people. I do not expect him to do so in regard to his country. It is partly that which brings us close to each other. If you do not understand, ask them in Hanoi."

"I know what they will say," he answered sullenly. "Perhaps you also convinced them in bed."

"Pig," she snapped.

I put my hand on her arm. "I know that none of this is my business, but could you tell me why he was getting so excited?"

She explained it to me quickly and left out nothing.

"May I ask him two questions? In Chinese?"

"Yes. He speaks Chinese, even though he denies it. He

claims to love his country but professes to no love for his ancestry."

"Captain Le," I said, "you said that politics and love do not mix. Tell me how that fits in with what happened when a man killed an old man and his wife and became so excited at the blood running from their bodies that he raped their young daughter. Were the father and mother and the girl the wine from which you know how to mix a drink that will protect you from thinking too much?"

"How—?" he started, only to break off quickly. "You do know our language!"

"Only enough to catch a few words. When one is picking up a strange language, he first learns the words that come from the gutter. But that doesn't answer my question."

He was sitting in a tense position, his hand gripping the gun so tightly, his knuckles were almost white.

"I know you would like to kill me," I said calmly. "Your life draws its food from killing and raping. You are not a hero. You are a coward. You won't kill me. You might fire one bullet that would hit me somewhere, but I would reach your throat before you could press the trigger a second time."

He seemed to come apart all at once. He still held the gun, but the point of it was wavering in the air. His eyes were still full of hatred, but now it was joined by fear.

"Put the gun away," I said gently. "I'm sure that your sister, who is kinder and more intelligent than you, will not report this incident in Hanoi. And I think you will also learn that every time you kill a man, you also die a little." I turned to Thuy. "I'm sorry, Thuy. I could not listen to any more."

"It's all right, Milo. It is something that had to be said some-time. Let us forget about it for the rest of the journey."

We did no talking for the remainder of the flight. Thuy began to doze with her head on my shoulder. Her brother stayed awake, but it was obviously an effort for him.

It wasn't a long flight even though the plane was slow. It finally came down to a bumpy landing and rolled to a stop. The door was opened and we got out. Thuy left the plane first, then I got out, with Dante once more tucked inside my jacket. Her brother followed, doggedly guarding me to the very end. I glanced at my watch. It was a little past four in the morning.

We were met on the field by two men dressed in civilian clothes. They both greeted Thuy, then one of them looked at her brother. "Thank you for your assistance, Captain Le," he said. "You may now return to your command. You will be there before daylight."

Le Ton Kuang saluted. He frowned as he looked at Thuy and me, then turned on his heel and climbed back into the plane. The four of us walked across the field to the small terminal.

Thuy waited until we were inside the terminal, then intro-duced me to the two men. They were Tran Xuan Ngo and Ngoc Dinh Binh. I gathered that both were important. The latter was short and fat, wearing horn-rimmed glasses. He beamed at me as he was being introduced.

"This is the man I told you about," Thuy said quickly. It was strange, but suddenly her own language seemed awkward in her mouth. I thought it was because she had learned that I knew more of her language than I had admitted. "He has come here bearing no weapons and he says his sole interest is in seeing the man known as Martin Rigsby."

It was the short, fat man who spoke. "Welcome to Hanoi. We are honored to have you and regret that your journey was so difficult. You must be very tired."

"No," I said, lying. "I am honored to be accepted. I am only sorry that the time of my arrival has disturbed your rest."

"It is nothing," he murmured. "First we must see that you and our dear friend get some rest. We will talk afterwards. Come, we will take you to a hotel." He suddenly caught sight of the alert eyes peering out from my jacket. "A dog! What kind is it?"

I sighed. "A miniature pinscher. A very old European breed."

"Ah," he said in delight. "You see! We are already comrades. Come."

We followed the two men out to the car, also a Mercedes. We drove a few blocks through the city, which was quiet and deserted except for the occasional glimpse of patrolling soldiers, and finally arrived at a large building that could have come straight out of turn-of-the-century Paris. They parked the car in front of it and we got out.

"This," said the fat man, "was the Metropole Hotel when our French friends were here. It is no longer called by that name. It is now the Reunification Hotel—but you will find it just as comfortable, perhaps more so.* We will make certain that you are properly cared for." I was surprised. I had expected to be put in prison until they talked to me.

---

* The hotel was renovated in 1987 and renamed the Metropole. Today it is called the Sofitel Legend Metropole Hanoi.

We went inside. A sleepy-eyed clerk became suddenly alert as he recognized the two men.

"This is the couple I told you to expect," the fat man said. He had switched to Vietnamese. "You have everything ready for them?"

"Oh, yes," the clerk replied.

The fat man turned back to me and resumed in Chinese, "Is there anything you would like, Colonel? Perhaps some food?"

"We had a very good meal a few hours ago in the jungle," I said. "But I am tired. I wonder if there might be some whiskey available."

"American whiskey?"

"I would prefer Chinese whiskey if possible."

He smiled. "Of course." He gave the order to the clerk and turned back to me. "I trust you will have a good rest. We will see you about noon or shortly thereafter."

"Thank you," I said.

The clerk came back with the squat bottle of whiskey and a wooden bucket of ice cubes.

"You see," said the fat man, "we have everything. Good night, Colonel March, Major Le."

We both said good night and the two men left. The clerk led the way upstairs and opened the door for us. "Should I tip him?" I asked Thuy.

"I think not, under the circumstances, Milo. Normally, I am sure he would be pleased, but since we were escorted here by two important members of the Democratic Republic of Vietnam, it might frighten him."

"Good night," we said to the clerk as we entered the room.

It, too, was a surprise. Once it must have been an elegant suite. It was still better than an average hotel room in any country. I tossed my duffel bag to the floor and released Dante from my jacket. He wandered around the room, sniffing, and then settled on the floor to stare at me.

"Sack time, Dante," I said. He wagged his tail.

"I'm tired," Thuy said, bouncing on the bed. "How about you, darling?"

"I think so. I'm either tired or just numb. I'm not quite sure which."

She laughed as she slipped the shoes from her feet. "Shall I race you to the showers?"

"Go ahead," I said. "Ladies first. Besides, I just want to sit for a minute and enjoy a drink before I make the transition from jungle to shower."

"I'll be right out." She was almost to the bathroom door when she stopped and looked back. "Milo?"

"Yes?"

"You're not sorry that you came?"

"It's what I wanted. Why should I be sorry?"

"I just wondered," she said. She went into the bathroom and closed the door.

I took off my jacket and shirt and removed my combat boots. I unfastened my belt, loosened the adhesive tape on the small of my back, and removed the small gun and the spare ammunition. I was amazed that those Viet Cong soldiers had not found the weapon back in the jungle, but it was a huge relief to know that I was still armed. One man with a pistol in the middle of a hostile country was hardly in a position of strength, but the gun gave me some relief from a sense of complete helplessness.

I put the gun and ammunition under the bed, taping them to the springs. I had decided that was probably the safest place. If Thuy was curious enough to reach inside my boots, all she would find was money. My picklocks were in the suede case in my jacket, but if anyone opened the top flap, all that could be seen was a comb and a fingernail file. I removed the rest of my clothes and poured myself a drink.

Thuy came out of the bathroom, a towel wrapped around her. She looked like a combination of roses and old ivory.

"It's all yours, darling," she said. "Do I look all right?"

"Lovely," I said. "I'm going to see if a warm shower will take some of the stiffness out of my legs. Will you fix me a drink while I'm gone?"

"I'll make drinks for both of us. Hurry."

I went into the bathroom and started the shower. When it was the right temperature, I stepped into it. I took a long shower, feeling much of the soreness leaving my muscles. Finally I got out and dried myself and walked into the room.

Thuy had already discarded the towel and was stretched out on the bed. A quick glance told me that none of my things had moved from the position in which I had left them.

"A man," I said, "should always be greeted by such a vision when he comes to bed."

"Thank you, sir. You look rather special yourself. Your drink awaits you."

I went over and sat on the edge of the bed. I picked up a cigarette and lit it, then reached for my glass.

"Milo?" she said.

"Uh-huh?"

"What are those red streaks on your back?"

I hadn't thought about the fact that the adhesive tape would redden my skin. I reached back to the spot. "You mean these?"

"Yes."

"Someone threw a hand grenade at me the first day I arrived in Saigon. I grabbed it up and threw it away, and my back was slightly strained. They put some tape on it. It was taken off yesterday before I came to meet you at the restaurant. I did that myself."

"Who threw the grenade at you?"

"He didn't stay around long enough to answer any questions. Want a cigarette, Thuy?"

"Please."

I lit one and passed it to her. "Comfortable, Thuy?"

"Of course. Milo, why did you lie to me?"

"What did I lie about?"

"The fact that you do know our language."

"I didn't lie. You asked me if I spoke it and I said that I spoke Chinese and French. I also speak several other languages. I know enough Vietnamese to understand a little of it. But not much."

"Why didn't you tell me just that?"

"Call it self-protection, if you like. I trust you, Thuy, but I don't trust anyone else."

"All right. What did you think of the two men who came to meet us?"

"They were friendly enough. That one little character certainly is fat, isn't he?"

She giggled. "Ngoc Dinh Binh? He is called—but never to his face—Beo, or Fat Boy. But he is a very brilliant man. He just likes to eat too much."

"Martin Rigsby is here in Hanoi?" I asked.

"Yes."

"I will be able to see him?"

"Yes."

"When?"

"Tomorrow or the next day."

"Where is he? In prison?"

She hesitated only a minute. "He's in prison, Milo, but he is well cared for in every way. You will soon see this for yourself."

I turned to look at her. "And what about me, Thuy? Will I also be sent to prison?"

"I hope not. It will depend on you. You will have the opportunity to speak to important officials about him. It is very possible that they will send both of you back to Saigon at once."

"Okay," I said lightly, without believing it. I finished my drink and put my cigarette out. I reached for her and she came into my arms, her body trembling with desire.

Daylight was coming through the windows when we finally went to sleep.

TWELVE

It was noon when I awakened. Thuy was still asleep, curled up with her back to me, looking almost like a child. I slipped quietly out of bed and took clean clothes and my razor from the duffel bag. I took the gun and ammunition from beneath the bed and went into the bathroom. First I taped the gun and ammunition to my back again, got dressed, and then shaved.

She was just awakening when I returned to the room. She stretched like a cat and opened her eyes. She smiled. "Good morning, darling."

"Good morning," I said cheerfully. I bent down and kissed her. "It is already high noon and time we were up."

"All right." She swung her legs from the bed and stood up. "I will be out in minutes. Don't go away without me." She had the door opened when she turned to look at me. "You know what I think you should do?"

"Not offhand. What?"

"Put the eagles back on your shoulders."

"Why? You're the one who told me to take them off."

"I think it's all right now. You are an American Army officer even if you are on a peaceful visit. You're entitled to your rank, and under the circumstances they cannot charge you for that."

"Okay, but get a move on or they may charge you with being tardy."

She made a face and disappeared into the bathroom. The door closed gently. I looked closely to make sure it was completely closed. I sat down on the chair and took the picks from the suede case.

I bent over to Dante, who was beside my feet. He had a very special collar. It was decorated with a line of brass studs running almost completely around it. If the right stud was pushed gently, it gave access to a secret pocket in the collar. I manipulated it and shoved the picks inside the collar. I closed it and pushed the stud back to a lock position.

Thuy came out of the bathroom just as I finished pinning the last eagle on my shoulder. She stretched up and kissed me. "You look so much more dignified with those on, Colonel March. I'll be dressed before you realize it."

"You don't have to rush," I told her. "I will take Dante down for his morning walk and meet you downstairs. Where are we going to eat?"

"In the hotel restaurant. If I'm there first, I'll order for both of us. Martini?"

"By all means. I haven't had any juice yet today. I'll race you to the restaurant."

She laughed. "Then you better get started."

"Come on, Dante," I said. "We're not wanted here. Let's go." He followed at my heels as we left the room. No one paid any attention to us as we walked through the lobby. We went out on the grounds, and Dante took off on his own business. He didn't care who owned the shrubbery, as long as it was there.

Dante finally decided he'd had enough of the place, so we went inside. I stopped at the entrance to the restaurant and looked in. I spotted Thuy sitting at a table. There were already two martinis on the table. There was also a Russian officer standing in front of her. As I watched, I saw him say something and then walk away. From the expression on his face, I guessed that he'd made a pass and it had been incomplete.

I took a quick glance around the room. It was pretty well filled up, although many customers were still at the bar. The majority of them were Vietnamese, a few in civilian clothes and the rest in uniforms. It was quite a change, seeing North Vietnamese regulars in actual military garb instead of the black pajamas that the Viet Cong and North Vietnamese soldiers wore in the jungle.

Aside from the Vietnamese soldiers and civilians, the remainder looked as if they were Russian. A few of these were in uniform and the rest in civilian suits. I guessed the latter were probably technicians. Thuy was the only woman in the restaurant. I walked across the room to her table.

"I notice," I said, "that you are also popular with other foreigners and not only Americans."

She smiled at me. "He wanted me to have lunch with him. I told him I already had a luncheon date. Think what it will do to him when he sees that my date is an American officer."

"Serves him right," I said. I lifted my martini. "To the speedy defeat of all other candidates for your company."

"I'll drink to that," she said. She laughed as we touched glasses and then we drank the toast. She laughed again, but the laughter suddenly ended and she looked sad. "We are all out of time, Milo. Why couldn't we have met at another time and somewhere else? We could have been happy just lying on the beach."

"One is never happy just lying on the beach. One usually feels that he must do something to earn the pleasure."

"Do you feel that way, Milo?"

"No. You know, Thuy, you were right about something."

"What is that?"

"About martinis. They are somewhat better than pig blood and wine."

She laughed, but suddenly stopped again. She was looking past me. "My admirer is coming over here. Don't start anything."

"I never start things. I only finish them." I turned in my chair so I could see him. He was walking straight for us. There was an arrogance in his stride. I looked at his rank. He was a general. That explained some of his arrogance. But his uniform also boasted an emblem that revealed the branch of military service he was in, and that explained the rest.

He came straight to the table and bowed to Thuy. He turned and made a slight bow to me, politely excusing himself in Russian. *"Izvinite. Govorite li vwi porusski?"*

I shook my head. "Try French or English."

"Ah, you speak English. So do I. I was going to ask if you would do a favor for me. Haven't we met somewhere before?"

"I've been somewhere before, but I don't remember meeting you there. What's your favor?"

"I have been admiring your luncheon companion. Perhaps you will introduce me to her."

"Perhaps I won't," I said. "You've made a small mistake. I don't run a dating service."

His expression hardened. "I am sure that you and I have met. I would recognize your face anywhere. Perhaps in America?"

"I don't think you would be welcome there. Why don't you go to the telephone and call the KGB in Moscow? Maybe they can revive your faltering memory."

The expression on his face made me realize I had made a mistake and I knew the answer to his question.

"That is it," he said triumphantly. "You have given me the key to it. I have not met you, but I have seen photographs of you. In a minute I will remember it all."

"Don't strain yourself," I said. "It can be dangerous." I meant that it could be dangerous for me.

"I have it," he exclaimed. "You were in Russia several years ago. You were calling yourself Peter Miloff. The Soviet Union employed you to teach us how to make vending machines. But your name is not Miloff. We have photographs of you. We also have a complete dossier on you, including your fingerprints. Your real name is March. Milo March, is it not?"

"My name is Milo March, but I assure you that it is a very common name. There are hundreds of people with the same name. By the way, what is your name?"

"I am General Igor Gershuni of the Komitet Gosudarstvennoy Bezopasnosti."

"I've heard of you," I said. "You have a reputation, even in Russia, that matches that of Rasputin in his day. If you ask me, I would guess that you have one of your famous little bloodbaths in store for the people in this country. You will probably try to implicate the Chinese so that Russia can wind up as the sole supporter of North Vietnam and will leave hundreds of slaughtered North Vietnamese in the laps of the Chinese. Like the time there was a small group of Italians who were considered too progressive by the Soviet Union. You were assigned to straighten them out. You did, too. You made part of the group believe that you were there to help them. Then, one night, there was a meeting of sixteen men. The top fifteen men, solid comrades of yours, and you. You, personally, killed all fifteen. I will do my best to see that you are stopped before you repeat that story here. Yes, I know you, General. And so will the people of North Vietnam by the time I'm through with you."

I turned to Thuy. "Let's go, my dear. We have an important engagement, and I think they might be interested in the way this mockery of Communism works."

Her face almost haggard, she took my arm and we walked out into the lobby. As we appeared, the clerk saw us and waved to attract our attention. "A phone call for Major Le," he said. "You may take it here."

She went to the desk and I waited where I was. Things, I suspected, were going to start getting tight. Thuy finished her phone conversation and came to join me. Her face was more relaxed.

"That was Ngoc Dinh Binh," she said. "He had intended to be here but has been detained on business. He suggested that I show you Hanoi. He ordered a car to be left out front for our use." It was one to which she had a key. We went out and got into the car. Dante sat in between us.

She took a deep breath and looked at me. "Milo?"

"What?"

"How much of that, back there in the restaurant, was lies and how much the truth?"

"A little of each." I lit two cigarettes and passed one to her. "I am Milo March. I have been in Russia. Twice. I have been questioned by Russian officials. They do have pictures of me and my fingerprints. I have not been a Peter Miloff. I am not an expert on vending machines.* I'm not even a neophyte. I have never been charged with a specific crime by Russian officials. My name does not appear in the files of Interpol. On the other hand, everything I said about the General is true. Substantiation of these charges exist in the files of many nations."

"We don't have them in our files."

"If you ask around, I think you may learn that you do. When it comes to a matter of world power, the Russians are apolitical. They bore from within, no matter who or what is involved. They have, for instance, had many agents collecting information and setting one group against another in China for years. Look in the embassies of any country and you will find ten times as many attachés and aides in the Russian embassy as there are in any of the others. This is true of your own country."

"But you are an American agent?" she said.

"I am not at present. Thuy, I served in the United States Army for many years. Then I retired and became an officer in

---

* In *Wild Midnight Falls*, Milo goes to Russia on an espionage mission, posing as a vending machine specialist named Peter Miloff.

the Army Reserves. I have been recalled to active duty several times to deal with matters of security. I was sent to Saigon once to investigate Americans. It involved such petty things as the theft of American products which were supposed to be for the people, not the few. I also investigated American participation in such charming industries as wholesale thefts, drugs, prostitution, and murder."

"I remember," she said, "that an American agent was said to have been in Saigon on such a mission."

"That was me. On my present mission, I was recalled to active service and appointed military attaché of our Embassy at my own request. After considerable talking, they finally agreed to permit me to come here on a mission of my own. You know all about that. Trying to negotiate the release of Martin Rigsby is entirely my own idea and will be carried out as I have outlined to you. I will not even accept his release under conditions which can harm me or my country or harm you or your people."

She thought for a minute. "I believe you," she said, "but I doubt if others will. If that is so, I will be unable to help you. They will make certain of that."

"A long time ago," I said, "I invented an ancient saying: Bedfellows make strange politics. You and I, my dear Thuy, are a perfect illustration of the truth of my coinage. We are bedfellows—and very delightful ones—and as a group we certainly represent strange politics."

I heard a noise from her and looked at her quizzically. She was laughing with her hand over her mouth. "How do you arrive at that conclusion?"

"Easy. We have talked very little about politics. When we have, we usually end up silently agreeing with each other on the specific points which have come up."

"Why do you say that?"

"I'll start with me. Making a generalization, I would have to say that I like people. Some individuals I like and some I detest. There isn't much that can be done about that. I would like everyone to get a fair shake in life. Then I might like them all. I think men and women should have equal rights. I think all races should have equal rights. So should all nationalities. No one should take those rights from them. One can forfeit his rights, but that should be the only way he can lose them. I believe that you think much the same way."

She was silent for a minute. "I guess I do. But others have to agree with you if you are to have a platform or a policy."

"They do, but they are no more obliged to agree with you than you are with them. Sometimes I think we should return to the open forums of the Greeks.* You also agree with me on many specifics—such as the one argument you had with your brother considering his actions in a peasant village—which I also referred to later. You and I can both look at Ngoc Dinh Binh and see a fat man. Like many others, we may have an inner picture of a fat person being cuddlesome and nonhostile. We could think of many examples. The Buddha, for one."**

---

* The Agora of the ancient Greece was an open space in the center of the city where, among other activities, citizens (usually just men) gathered to discuss politics and other topics in a free, egalitarian manner. The Agora of Athens is viewed as the birthplace of Western democracy.
** The familiar statues of a fat, laughing Buddha represent a monk of Chinese legend named Pu-tai (or Budai), not the Buddha who was the founder of Buddhism. Pu-tai is revered as an enlightened buddha in Zen Buddhism.

She started the motor, then looked at me. "I will think about it. Would you like to see Martin Rigsby today?"

I was surprised. "Do you mean it?"

"Yes. Ngoc Dinh Binh also said that he has arranged it at the prison and that I could take you there if you wanted to go. Do you?"

"Very much."

"Then you shall see him." She put the car in gear and we drove off. "It will have to be a brief visit today, but you will have time to tell him about his family and to inform him of your reason for being here."

We drove for a few blocks and she parked in front of a forbidding stone building that looked like an old French fortress. We got out of the car and, with Dante following, went to the entrance. Thuy showed her identification and told him our reason for being there. He opened the gate.

We met another guard inside who told us how to reach the cell. It was on the second level, which was reached by worn stone steps. I was amazed that they would let us wander through the prison unescorted, especially with a dog, but I guess they knew they could stop us if we tried to smuggle anybody out—emphatically including Martin Rigsby.

There was little natural light here, but the electric lights were very bright. At one end of the cellblock there was a soldier on a raised platform with a machine gun. He must have had word about us, for he merely saluted Thuy and grinned.

We walked slowly along the cellblock. I was watching intently so I could identify Rigsby in advance. Then I spotted his face in a cell slightly ahead of us. There was no mistaking his features.

"You will soon see your friend," Thuy said softly, putting her hand on my arm. "Of course, you will recognize him."

So they still had to set traps. I smiled to myself and said nothing. I waited carefully until we reached his cell.

"Martin," I exclaimed. At the same moment, I gave Dante a hand signal. He immediately dashed down the block, barking madly. Thuy and the guard were both startled, and for a few seconds their attention was on him. It was enough.

"I'm Milo March, an old friend of yours," I said in an undertone. "Just follow my lead." He nodded and I turned away from the cell. "Dante!" I yelled. "Come back here."

He stopped, then came back with his tail between his legs. The guard laughed and lowered his gun. Thuy turned back to watch me. I ignored her and looked at Rigsby. "Martin," I said, "it's good to see you. How are you?"

"I'm well, Milo," he said, playing up to it. "I'm surprised to see you here. Are you a prisoner, too?"

For an American who had been held in a North Vietnamese prison, he looked in pretty good shape. There were horror stories about the way the North Vietnamese treated American fliers who'd been shot down, and other POWs. I imagined that they had never heard of the Geneva Conventions, or maybe they thought they didn't apply to them. My guess was that they'd decided that Rigsby was too valuable to send home as damaged goods.

I told him, "No. I'm here to talk to the officials about getting you back home. Helen is worried about you, and so are Jason and Maria." Those were the names of his wife and two children.

"Are they all right?"

"They're fine, but they do miss you. Have they treated you all right here?"

"Sure. Gee, it's good to see you, Milo."

"The same, old buddy. I am to have a meeting with some of the government officials and will try to get you released and take you home to your family. Just relax and you'll be there before you know it."

"You were always a great one for ignoring regulations and thinking of people."

"Why shouldn't I?" I said indignantly. "You saved my hide once in Hong Kong." I knew he had once been stationed there.

"It was nothing." He probably said that because he didn't know what I was talking about.

"It was the time I got in trouble with that British general over his Chinese girlfriend. The fortunes of war." We both laughed, and it sounded fairly authentic.

"Milo," Thuy said softly. "It's time we have to meet General Ngoc Dinh Binh."

"I'll be right with you. Relax, Martin. You'll soon be out."

"Thanks, Milo."

"It's nothing. See you soon."

"Sure," he said. He was trying to put his heart into it, but it didn't quite come off. I decided we'd better leave before he tried to improve the image.

We walked back through the cellblock and down the stairs. Thuy said good-bye to the officer at the gate and thanked him.

We went out to the car and got in. She looked at Dante. "Why did he act that way?"

"He doesn't like guns to be pointed in his direction. It doesn't make any difference who does the pointing. I think he's trying to tell the person with the gun that it is usually the first person to draw a gun who gets shot first."

"You just made that up," she said, starting the car. "What was that about the Chinese girl?"

"What Chinese girl?"

"The one you got in trouble with in Hong Kong. What was her name?"

"Shen Mai. But why ask? It was a long time ago, and besides, the wench is dead."*

"What caused her death?"

"A firing squad. I think she was accused of consorting with the enemy."

I pretended not to hear her small gasp. I lit a cigarette and watched the scenery. When I felt the car braking, I looked ahead to see where we were stopping. She parked in front of a two-story building. With Dante tagging behind, we entered a large office on the second floor. The walls were covered with maps, instead of charts, and the desks were covered with papers.

"Ah," said Ngoc Dinh Binh, standing up, "the lovely major and Colonel March. Did you have a good visit with your friend, Colonel?"

---

* Milo is playing on a famous line from English literature that Thuy could hardly be expected to recognize. It is from a play by the 16th-century poet Christopher Marlowe. One character begins, "Thou hast committed—" and the other completes the sentence: "Fornication: but that was in another country; and besides, the wench is dead." What makes this quote especially ironic is that Marlowe had a reputation as an espionage agent.

"It was nice to see him again. He seems to be in good health, but he does miss his family."

He sighed heavily. "That is an unfortunate part of quarrels between countries. It is a sad fact of life that not all casualties are suffered on the battlefield. I understand from our people in the South that when you arrived in Saigon, you were wearing many colored ribbons, indicating much experience on the battlefield. I have not seen them in evidence since you arrived in Hanoi."

"Since I was coming on a mission of peace, I felt it would be in bad taste to display the awards of battle. It would seem to be a boyish flaunting of the opposite of my mission here."

"Of course. I remember that you even removed the emblems of your rank until after you arrived in Hanoi. Very considerate of you. The Association of the People believes in peace, Colonel March. So we welcome you, even if you did not bear an olive branch in your hand." He smiled at me, but there was a hint of cruelty in his face I had not seen before. I realized that the General Ngoc I was looking at was quite different from the cuddly teddy bear of a man I had met the night before.

"I also did not bear the lightning bolts of the gods of war."

"That is true," he admitted. "We have had a pleasant meeting, Colonel March. It is unfortunate that there are many unpleasant sides to so many of our pleasures. Tell me, have you ever heard of Yuan Mei?"

"Yes. The eighteenth-century poet and artist. He also wrote a famous cookbook."

"Ah! Then you may have read this line from his verse: 'In the casual life of meetings and partings—' "

" '—there is much sadness to endure,' " I finished.

"You are a very unusual man, Colonel." He sighed. "I only wish there was time to know you better. You are also a fortunate man. You traveled all the way from America, then walked all the way from Saigon to Hanoi. Today you have had a nice visit with your friend Rigsby. And I understand that you met another old friend last night."

"I don't recall meeting a friend last night."

"He says he has known you for many years and he is most anxious to see you again." He smiled, then raised his voice. "Please come in, General."

A door on the other side of the room opened and a man came in. It was General Igor Gershuni.

THIRTEEN

"Ah, Colonel March," the General said, "I was hoping you might be here. I have some interesting news for you. I put in a telephone call to Moscow last night, as you suggested. They were very happy to learn that you were here and that I would be seeing you today."

"I can imagine," I said dryly. "Had you missed the usual shop talk over a glass of tea with your comrades at KGB?"

"Nothing so trivial. I told them that I had encountered you and they were delighted to hear it. They expressed the hope that they would have the opportunity of meeting you again. I convinced them that I would do my best to get you to accept their invitation."

"I didn't know you cared, General."

"I also have some other news for you, Colonel March. When you left the restaurant last night, you very kindly left your glass on the table. I walked over and took possession of it. With the assistance of General Ngoc's men, I lifted the prints and classified them. This information, as you can understand, brought joy to my comrades."

Well, that blew it. In a way, I was almost glad it had happened. I had never expected anything to come from the talks in Hanoi. My only choice after that was to get Rigsby out of prison and somehow get him safely back to Saigon. The first would have been easy, but the second presented problems I hadn't been able to solve. Now all I could do was visit.

"You know, Colonel, you have been one of my responsibilities for years. It almost prevented my promotion to the present rank. Starting years ago, I have slowly built a file on you. I have several photographs of you and many samples of your fingerprints. I have a complete record of your last trip to the Soviet Union. I know when you left Moscow and went to the beach. You took Irina Simonova with you. She was a trusted journalist at *Pravda* until you corrupted her. I know about your meeting with Grigory Masinov, whom you killed on the beach at Leningrad. Then you escaped with Irina, crossing the Baltic Sea to Helsinki. You may remember that Masinov was an officer in the KGB. Oh, I have a very complete file on you, Colonel. It will be complete when I add you to it."

"What do you intend to do about that part of it?"

"We are not looking for revenge," he said loftily. "We are more interested in what you will tell us. You and your friend."

"My friend?"

"Yes. The one you came to so gallantly rescue. When both of you talk, it will make fascinating reading for the whole world."

"Okay, General. Let's go."

"In good time. There is a plane due from Moscow tonight. You will be on it when it leaves in the morning."

"Colonel March," General Ngoc said, "we have agreed that our comrades from the Soviet Union should have the first opportunity to question you."

"How chummy," I said. "Do I understand that I'm free to go until the morning?"

"Not quite. You seemed disappointed in the shortness of time with your friend whom you came to see. I think you indicated that you would like to see him again. We are granting your wish. Please open the door, General Gershuni."

The Russian crossed to the door in the front of the office and opened it. Three North Vietnamese soldiers were standing there. They came in and stood at attention. They were heavily armed. "Take this man," said Ngoc Dinh Binh, "and put him in the same cell where we are holding an American named Rigsby. Both men will be picked up early in the morning, so it will not be necessary to give them breakfast. Tell the captain in the prison they are to be left alone." He looked at me. "You see, you will get a long visit with your friend."

I glanced at Thuy. She was staring at me, a sad expression on her face. Her lips moved as though she were going to speak, but no sound came forth.

One of the soldiers nudged me with his automatic rifle and told me, in Vietnamese, to get moving.

"He doesn't understand our language," Ngoc Dinh Binh told the soldier. He glanced at a paper on his desk. "Only Chinese, French, and English."

"What about the animal?" the soldier asked.

"It hardly looks savage enough to give any trouble," General Ngoc said. "Let him go with it. The man may get hungry by morning."

The soldier prodded me again with the rifle. *"Allez,"* he said.

I walked out of the office and down the stairs with the soldiers behind me. They had a large jeep which looked like a Russian model. I was put in the front seat with the driver. Dante crouched between my feet. I patted him on the face. The other two soldiers sat in the rear, their guns pointing at my head.

"Take a last look," the driver said to me in French.

"Lorsqu'on presse trop un poisson il vous échappe," I answered. "When you squeeze a fish too much, it escapes you."

"Not when I squeeze," he said boastfully.

We soon reached the prison and they escorted me inside. The captain of the guard searched me, but it consisted mostly of patting my pockets and just above my belt. He didn't pat the small of my back. He did, however, find the money in my pocket and took most of it. I decided that the money he found was a small enough price to distract him from the small gun and ammunition taped to the small of my back.

The captain signed the paper the soldiers presented, then called to prison guards to escort me to my cell. We went upstairs and stopped in front of Rigsby's cell. They opened the door and shoved me inside. Dante darted in before they could shut the door, and the guards laughed.

Rigsby was lying on one of the two cots, but he sat up as they opened the door. He squinted at me and waited until they had left.

"Aren't you Milo March?" he asked. "The American who came to see me yesterday?"

"The same," I said cheerfully. "Colonel Milo March. It's nice to meet you in privacy—old friend."

I put out my hand and he shook it. "I'm afraid I didn't quite understand what was going on, but I tried to play along."

I sat down on the other cot and lit a cigarette. I offered him one, but he shook his head. "You did fine," I said. "I'm not here with you because of anything you said or did."

"Do you really know my wife and children?"

"No," I admitted, "but I was told that they are fine—except for being worried about you. Do the guards speak English?"

"I don't think so. Anyway, the nearest guard now is the one on the platform with the gun. He will remain there until he is relieved by his replacement."

"What about the prisoners on either side of us?"

"They speak only Vietnamese."

"I received two orders when I left Washington," I said. "They were to get you out of here and back to Saigon. Then you will go immediately home."

"Good God, how do they expect a man to do that?"

"They love me," I said. "At least I've gotten the first half of the orders almost finished."

He laughed, but it wasn't a happy sound. "I noticed. What do we do now? Rot here together?"

"I don't think so," I said slowly. "To tell you the truth, their idea is that we will be taken out of here early tomorrow morning and flown to Moscow, where we will be questioned. I believe that was the word they used."

He was silent for a minute. "Well, so much for the rest of your orders," he said bitterly.

"Relax, Rigsby. You have to realize that it was impossible to do any intelligent planning about getting you out of here and back to Saigon since there was no information to serve as guidelines. It is possible that their new plans will make it easier for us. I can only tell you that I've been in this business a long time and I'm still alive. I plan to stay that way."

"Sorry, Colonel. I take it that you are not regular army."

"I am, but I nearly always work on special assignments. I'm wearing this uniform because I'm presently the military attaché at our Embassy in Saigon. Wearing the uniform to come here was much smarter than trying to make it in civilian clothes."

He groaned. "Attaché at the Embassy? Some cover!"

"It gave me the essential freedom of movement."

"Why are you in this cell with me?"

"Two reasons. They're making the grand gesture of offering the Russians the opportunity of questioning me first. And the Russians want me very badly. On the other hand, Hanoi will be very happy if I just disappear, since everyone tries to act as if they are living up to the cease-fire agreement that was signed in Paris. No one is living up to it. Did you ever shoot craps, Rigsby?"

He was startled. "What does that have to do with it?"

"Everything. I rolled snake eyes last night. Tomorrow there will be a new set of dice."

"In Russia? That's where we'll be going tomorrow, isn't that what you said?"

"We'll be starting for Moscow tomorrow. I expect us to end up in Saigon."

"How? You have a plan?"

"No. I never make plans in advance, and I wouldn't tell you what it was if I did."

"This is a strange place to bring a dog," he said. "What kind is he?"

I sighed. "Min pin. If you're curious, he's with me because he's worth it. Besides, he's the only friend I have. Do you like dogs?"

"Yes."

"Dante," I said, "go over and say hello to the man. He's a friend."

Dante padded across the cell, wagging his tail, and let Rigsby pat his head. Then he came back and curled up on the floor.

"Did he understand what you said?"

"He understands everything I say in every language I know. He sometimes understands things that I don't say. That's one of the reasons he's with me."

We stopped talking when a guard came around with food for the prisoners. Rigsby was handed his plate and then the door clanged shut.

"He didn't leave any food for you," Rigsby said when the guard was out of hearing range. It was a brilliant observation.

"That was the idea."

"We'll divide this," he said.

"No. I've been on a better diet recently than you have. Eat it all. You need it. I expect that neither of us will be served any breakfast in the morning."

"I insist."

"Forget it," I said. "That's an order. We'll have lunch in Saigon tomorrow." I wished that I felt as confident as I sounded.

He ate. I knew he was feeling guilty, but it would be good for his soul. It might make him feel guilty enough to not make any move on his own the next day.

Later, another guard came to collect his plate. I had an idea. "Can these guards be bribed?" I asked Rigsby as I heard the guard's footsteps coming closer to us.

"Not to get us out of here, I'm sure."

"I mean a safer bribe than that," I said impatiently. "For extra favors?"

"I've never tried it, but I believe so."

"Do you speak Vietnamese?" He nodded. "I'm not supposed to understand the language. When he takes your plate, ask him what it will take to get him to bring me a bottle of whiskey. If there is any bargaining, translate for me so he won't guess that I do understand it."

"Do you think we should?"

"Definitely. If it makes you feel better, it's an order."

The guard arrived and asked for the plate. Rigsby gave it to him and asked him about the whiskey.

"Fool," the guard said. "You have no money."

"No, but my friend does."

"Perhaps I should come in and take it away from him," the guard said.

Rigsby translated for me. "Tell him," I said, "that such action would catch the attention of the other guards, who would want a share. And tell him that if he brings the whiskey, I will pay him in American dollars, which he can easily exchange in the black market."

I watched the guard's face as Rigsby translated. There was

suddenly a crafty expression on his face. He scratched his head while he thought about it. "I can give him a pint of Chinese whiskey for two hundred and fifty piastres." He had already jacked up the price to about three dollars.

"Tell him I'll take it," I told Rigsby. I reached in my pocket and pulled out the money the downstairs guard had left me.

The guard chattered again. Rigsby turned to me. "He says you can have the pint of whiskey for two hundred and fifty piastres or three dollars, whichever you prefer—in advance."

I separated five singles and put the rest of the money in my pocket. "Tell him that I will give him one dollar in advance and four dollars when he delivers, after I have determined that the bottle does contain whiskey." Rigsby dutifully translated correctly.

The guard grumbled but he finally agreed, and I handed Rigsby one dollar to give him. The guard took it and went on down the line, collecting plates. Finally, there was no more sound except the mumbling of prisoners.

I knew it was risky trying to bribe the guard, but the kind of duty he was stuck with seems to breed corruption anywhere in the world.

A few minutes later, the guard reappeared at our cell. He stood up close to the bars and produced the bottle. I went over and reached for it. He pulled it back and told Rigsby that I would get it as soon as he had the rest of the money.

"Just tell him," I said the minute Rigsby finished the translation, "he can take his bottle back and keep the one dollar I gave him. Or he can let me test the contents and determine whether it is whiskey and then he can depart five dollars richer than he was before. I remember one time, years ago, I was in a prison and I bought a bottle of whiskey, paying the guard in advance. I smelled the contents and the bottle contained urine. I had already paid for it and the jailor had vanished."

Rigsby translated it, but omitted the last three sentences. The guard handed the bottle through the bars. I uncapped it and smelled. It was whiskey. I handed him the four dollars and went back to my cot. He hurried out of sight.

"Would you like a drink?" I asked Rigsby.

"No, thanks. I don't drink." He sounded disapproving.

"Too bad," I said. I took a big drink and stretched out on the cot, lighting a cigarette. I didn't feel like making conversation, and we were quiet. I had another drink and another cigarette during the time that passed. I wouldn't want to spend a long time living like this, but I'd anticipated worse.

"You seem to feel pretty sure of yourself," Rigsby said at last.

"I have to be. If I'm in a jam, I'm the only person who is going to get me out of it. Washington won't sacrifice another agent by sending him to save me. I'm expendable. Does that bother you?"

"No," he said, but I could tell he wasn't being truthful.

"They'll probably come for us early in the morning. We'd better get some sleep." I snubbed out my cigarette, put the bottle under the flat pillow, and picked up Dante so he could lie on the cot next to me. I was asleep almost immediately.

They came for us shortly after daylight. I'd already finished the bottle and had a cigarette, but Rigsby looked as if he had been awake all night. Two guards opened the cell door and motioned us out. I picked up Dante and we left the cell.

"Colonel," Rigsby said as we walked down the block.

"Not now," I said. "Don't say anything to anyone until I tell you it's all right."

We went down the steps and were checked out by the captain of the guards. The same three soldiers were waiting for us, but this time they were driving a small sedan. I was put in the front seat again with Dante while Rigsby was pushed into the back with the other two soldiers. We drove straight to the Hanoi airfield.

At least we were expected. General Gershuni, General Ngoc, Tran Xuan Ngo, and two Vietnamese noncoms were there, and there were three Russians busy about the plane. I guessed that two were pilots and the third was a guard.

"Good morning, Colonel March," General Gershuni said gaily. "I trust that you had a pleasant night."

"Not quite as pleasant as Reunification,* and the room service was terrible."

The General laughed. "But we are providing you with first-class transportation. I am sorry I will not be on the plane with you, but I will soon see you in Moscow."

"You always save the worst for last, don't you?" I said.

The Russian made way for General Ngoc. "I am sorry for this turn of events," he said in Chinese. He sounded sincere. "I had no choice about the matter. Major Le has requested that she be permitted to speak with you before you leave.

---

* Reunification of North and South was achieved gradually. It began with the fall of the Saigon government in April 1975 and was completed in July 1976.

Privately. She has been given three minutes." He bowed and to my surprise nodded to the other men, and they withdrew far enough so that I knew that if we kept our voices moderately low they wouldn't be able to hear anything we said.

Thuy came to stand close to me. She looked as if she, too, had had a bad night. "Milo," she said, "I have brought a package of cigarettes, and the rest of your things are inside the plane." I noticed she was looking off to the side of us.

"Rigsby," I said, "will you please move a little farther away, but don't be foolish and make a run for it. Major Le and I have things to discuss privately."

He obeyed me, but the expression on his face told me that he didn't understand and didn't approve. To hell with him, I thought. I turned back to Thuy.

"What about you?" I asked. "Will they let you return to Saigon?"

She nodded. "You might say that I am temporarily on probation. I'll be all right once I am home. I am so sorry that this happened, Milo. So is General Ngoc, but he had no choice but to grant the Russian's request." She laughed nervously. "Why is it I always fall back on old Chinese expressions? 'Bind women's feet and you bind the women.' "

"When will you be in Saigon?"

"I leave Hanoi in the morning, and it will take about the same time that it did for us to reach Hanoi. It will be empty without you, and it will be sad to think of you in Moscow."

"I make you one promise, Thuy. I will meet you or phone you in Saigon very soon. Now I think your three minutes are up."

"But how—," she began.

"They're looking impatient. Take care of yourself, Thuy."

"You, too, Milo." She sounded as if she were on the verge of tears. She turned suddenly and walked away. I watched her go. She was a brave woman in many ways.

"Who was that woman?" Rigsby asked.

"A friend of mine," I said shortly. "The Russian is returning. From now on, Rigsby, please remember to be completely silent. If anyone asks you a question, refuse to answer by shaking your head. I'm sure you don't like being given orders, but your life depends on it, as well as mine."

I saw his gaze go beyond me and knew that somebody was walking up behind me. I turned and it was General Gershuni.

"It's time to go," he said. "I'll see you in Moscow in a few days, but you will be cared for gently until I arrive." He nodded to the Russian soldier and walked away.

The soldier swung his gun to indicate that we should go up the few steps into the plane. We did so. He followed us and closed the door behind him.

It had once been a medium-size twin-engined fighter-bomber but had been converted to a sort of passenger plane. I could see that the old wing-mounted machine guns were still in place, and wondered if they were loaded and ready to fire. There were single seats on either side, and next to each seat there was a single handcuff, one end welded onto the interior of the plane. It was obvious what sort of passengers they expected to carry.

The guard waved me into a seat on my left and snapped the cuff on my left wrist. He put Rigsby across from me and cuffed his right wrist. He then dropped into the seat behind Rigsby. He raised his voice and told the pilots we were ready for the takeoff. I quickly picked up Dante and put him in the seat next to me.

As the plane took off, I went to work on Dante's collar. It took no more than two minutes for me to get out the picks. I only took three that I thought would be the right size for the cuffs. I put one of them into my left hand and waited.

As the plane left the ground and went into its climb for altitude, I went to work on my cuff. It took no more than a minute until I felt the lock open. I reached over and removed the cuff quietly. I put the pick in my pocket. I turned my attention to the window.

The plane swung to the right and headed north. It had reached its altitude and leveled off. I could hear a voice from the cockpit that sounded as if one of the pilots was on the radio reporting to the ground. The plane felt like it was on automatic pilot. This was my chance—and it might be my only one. I leaned across the aisle and stared through the window next to Rigsby.

"What kind of plane is that?" I asked in Russian.

The guard pressed his face against the window. "I don't—," he started to say.

I stepped quickly into the aisle and as the guard started to turn, I hit him a slashing blow across the back of his neck. He slumped down in his seat.

"What—," Rigsby began.

"Shut up," I told him. I took the pick from my pocket and unlocked Rigsby's cuff. "Keep quiet and watch the soldier.

If he starts to move, take his rifle and bend it over his skull."
I went quietly up front until I was standing behind the two
pilots. The copilot must have heard me.

"What is it, Nicolai?" he asked, starting to turn his head.
I hit him with another blow across the back of his neck. He
fell against the instrument panel. Without waiting, I whirled
and threw a hard right at the pilot. It caught him on the jaw
just below his ear, snapping his head back. It hit the window
with a solid sound and he was out.

I reached behind me and pulled my shirt out of my pants.
I reached down, got a good hold on the adhesive tape, and
ripped it out, bringing the gun with it. I tore the rest of the
tape from the gun and stepped back out of the cockpit. I was
just in time.

The Russian soldier was recovering and groping for his
rifle. I couldn't have reached him in time, so I did the only
thing that made sense. Rigsby was just sitting in his seat,
watching the soldier with fascinated horror. I leveled the
automatic and pulled the trigger.

The Russian grabbed his chest and coughed as he began to
slide to the floor. I never had much confidence in small auto-
matics, so I pulled the trigger again and saw the bullet strike
his tunic where it was already turning red.

Rigsby was staring at the body on the floor. "You killed
him," he said.

"I believe I did," I said calmly. I put the gun in my pocket.
"Stop admiring my work and come up here. You have work
to do and not much time to do it in. Come on."

He came toward me, but he didn't look like he'd make it.

His face was pale and drawn. "Okay," I said. "I'll do this one by myself. Get back and stop by the first seat on either side."

He retreated. I put my hands under the copilot's arms and dragged him out of the cockpit. Then I pulled and pushed him into the seat. I pushed him against the window and got the handcuff locked on his wrist.

"I'll bring the other one back," I said. "You make sure that this one doesn't have a gun on him. And do it quickly. He may wake up any minute and do some damage to you even if he is handcuffed. Check his pockets, under his arms, and under his belt."

I went back to the cockpit and dragged out the pilot. I pulled him all the way to where the soldier was lying and put him in the seat right across from the body. That might give him second thoughts if he had the urge to be brave. I searched him quickly and found nothing. I went back to the front of the plane.

"I couldn't find any guns," Rigsby said as I reached him. "Do I have to keep at it?"

"No. If you haven't found any, he's probably left them in the cockpit. I'm going there now."

"The plane!" he said with a new panic. "Who's flying the plane?"

"It's flying itself. They had it on automatic pilot. I am going to switch it back to manual control. That's better if there's any sort of emergency."

"Do you know how to fly it?"

"No," I said, "but I can always learn, can't I?" I went on to the cockpit and sat down in the seat that had been the pilot's. I studied the instruments in front of it. Identification of instruments and instructions on what they would do were in Russian, so I had no trouble reading them. I figured out how to disengage the automatic pilot and the location of almost everything I would need.

It was true that I didn't know how to fly a plane, especially this one. I had flown a plane once, not very far, but I brought it down from a high altitude and landed it. I was talked down by a pilot in the tower. That was the only solution for the present problem. If I could get within radio distance of Saigon or one of the military fields, I might contact them on the radio and get talked down again. It was a long shot, but even that was a hell of a lot different from being well on my way to Moscow.

In the meantime, I leaned back and remembered the map of South Vietnam. When it was fixed in my mind, I sat up and stared at the instrument panel as if I expected it to give me an answer. It was then that I heard a voice. Then I realized it must be from the radio receiver that was in the pilot's helmet. It was on the floor beside me. I picked it up and put it on my head.

The voice was clear and in Russian. I waited until it stopped at the end of a sentence. I pushed the button marked *Transmit*.

"Calling Hanoi," I said in Russian. "Ready and over."

"You're off course," the voice said angrily. It sounded like General Gershuni speaking. "What's wrong?"

"Engine trouble," I said in Russian. "I'll try to circle around and head for Hanoi." I kept my fingers crossed that he wouldn't recognize my voice speaking in Russian.

"You'd better turn quickly," the voice said. "You are already too far south."

"At once," I said and turned off the radio before all of the second word could be heard. I turned back to the instruments. The plane had already strayed slightly to the east. I got it back on due south and turned the radio back to *Receive*. I turned my attention to the gadget and finally found the button that fired the guns that were on the wings. I fired a short burst to make sure they worked. Then I concentrated on heading for Saigon as fast as I could.

It was about ten minutes before the radio started squawking again. This time the voice was speaking Vietnamese. It identified itself as belonging to a major in the army of the Democratic Republic of the North and ordered us to return to Hanoi or be shot down.

I kept watching the skies, and it wasn't long before I spotted them. Two fighter planes were barreling toward me at about three o'clock. My guess was that they would merely make a warning pass and wouldn't fire until they were certain that there was something wrong with the regular pilots. I made a couple of small tests with the bomber and got a good idea of what I could get out of it. So I sat and waited.

"Hold on, Rigsby," I shouted.

The first plane came in to sweep just over the nose of the bomber. I timed his approach the best I could, then pulled sharply back on the yoke, a gadget a lot like a steering wheel with an arc cut out of it. The nose of the bomber tilted up just enough for me to see the fighter plane edging into view in the gunsights, and I tripped the guns. I pulled back again on the yoke and increased the power of the engines. I saw the bullets hitting the fighter plane. It went into a dive and smoke began to pour from it. It fell out of sight as the bomber went over it.

Bringing the big plane back to the level course, I looked out the window. Far below, the first fighter was still falling in fire and smoke. The I spotted the second one.

He was well above me and was swinging in a circle meant to carry him over the tail of the bomber. "Rigsby," I called, "get down and stay there, but hold on to something. It's going to get rougher."

I couldn't outrun the fighter, and I certainly couldn't maneuver faster than he could. My only hope was to amble along like a sitting duck and try to outguess him. I looked out the window and could no longer see him. It meant that he was over me and behind me and must have started his dive.

As if to reassure me, I heard his guns firing and the bullets hitting the bomber. I braced myself and waited. I knew that when I saw the shadow of his plane over me, it would be time to go into action.

The sound of the bullets striking the bomber became louder and closer. Something hit me in the left shoulder and jammed me against the instrument panel. As I straightened up, I saw the shadow starting to cross the canopy. I yanked the yoke back as far as I could and triggered the guns.

The bomber stood on its tail and the fighter plane came into view, holes appearing in its belly as though made by a gigantic sewing machine. Flame burst from it as the pilot tried to swing it to the right. It was already out of control as I shoved the yoke forward to level off the bomber. I noticed that the instrument panel was partly smashed, but enough had escaped damage for my purposes. "Rigsby," I shouted, "come in here. It won't be so tough for the time being."

Rigsby showed up, looking frightened. I didn't blame him. I wished that I were back in a nice, air-conditioned bar in the States myself. "Fun and games," I said. "Are you all right?"

"Y-yes. I guess so."

"What about the others?"

"The bullets did some damage, but the two pilots weren't hit."

"Okay. Do me a favor. Somewhere back there, you'll find a duffel bag that belongs to me. Bring me a bottle of whiskey, a shirt or a pair of shorts, and some adhesive tape."

He nodded and left. I'd been thinking while I was talking to him. I remembered the installations I'd seen on the map, and it seemed to me that there were a number of them between Hanoi and Saigon. I turned the plane to the left and headed for the China Sea—I hoped. It would probably be a safer route.

When I reached the water, I turned and followed the coast-line. We flew over a number of sampans, some of which opened fire with rifles, but none of the shots even came close. I watched the instruments, and when the bomber reached a point which I thought should be directly east of Bien Hoa, I pointed the plane in that direction and put it back on automatic pilot.

Rigsby returned with the items I'd requested. My shoulder was beginning to hurt. I asked Rigsby to help me get my jacket off. He did so without fainting, which made me feel better about having him around.

My shirt was already red with blood. I took the pair of shorts and asked him to pour some whiskey on them. He did so, but he looked puzzled. I folded the shorts into a pad and put them inside my jacket, right on my shoulder where the bullet had gone. The alcohol burned smartly, but it was the only antiseptic I had. Then I asked Rigsby to tear off a couple of strips of adhesive tape and fasten the pad to me. He managed that, too.

When he was finished, I took a big drink from the bottle of whiskey. It revived me to a degree. I put the helmet back on my head. I could hear the hum of power on the radio.

Flicking the switch to *Send,* I adjusted the mouthpiece on the helmet. "This is Milo March calling Green Fox," I said. "Colonel Milo March calling Green Fox. Over." I pushed it back to receive and waited.

There was no answer.

FOURTEEN

Every few minutes, I tried calling again, then waited for an answer. Over and over again, until I couldn't tell whether I was feeling weak and dizzy from the attempt to reach Bien Hoa or from the wound in my shoulder. But I continue methodically. Once I got an answer in English, but the voice had an accent, which made me think it was a Viet Cong station. I immediately changed my course slightly and continued to send out the call.

I lost track of time and had almost given up hope when I got an answer.

"Green Fox to Colonel Milo March," the voice said. "Identify yourself further."

"This is Colonel Milo March," I said again. "Military attaché to the Embassy in Saigon. I believe I am near you, flying an old Russian fighter-bomber now converted to a transport. Can you put Colonel Blake on the horn?"

"Just a minute. Hold, Colonel March."

It must have been no more than two or three minutes before I heard another voice. "This is Colonel Blake. What was your rank the first time I met you?"

"Sergeant," I said. "At least, that's what the stripes said. I arrived in a chopper that was called *Baby*."

"All right, Colonel. I've already ordered a fix on you. What is your present altitude?"

"Fifteen hundred feet. I'm flying a Russian plane, so tell your boys not to shoot me down."

"Take it up to seven thousand and circle. Four of our planes will come up and escort you in. Can you land the plane?"

"I don't even know how to keep it in the air, so how the hell would I know how to land it?"

"When you're over the field, one of my men will get on and talk you down. What are the markings on the plane?"

"Russian."

I could hear him suck in his breath. "Well, you certainly go first class, Colonel. Are you alone?"

"Not quite. There is an American Embassy employee and the three men who were originally with the plane. One of them is dead and the other two are handcuffed to the sides of the plane. There is, also, a very fine dog."

"Like I said," he said wearily. "First class. You should see our four planes any minute now. And hold."

"Thanks," I said. "You might bring a bottle of whiskey with you. I think I need something. Out."

When I reached seven thousand feet, I put the plane into a circle and waited. I felt like I was going to sleep. "Rigsby," I called. Maybe he would keep me awake.

"Is anything wrong?" he asked nervously, coming into the cockpit.

"Everything is just fine," I said dryly. "We'll be on the ground within a few minutes. Tell me something, Rigsby. Are you really an intelligence agent?"

"Me?" He sounded flattered. "Goodness, no! The only contact I ever had with them was when I was transferred from

Egypt to the Saigon Embassy. I was asked to report anything that seemed to be unusual in the documents which came through the Embassy. It was a harmless chore, so I did it."

"Why were you with the group that went into North Vietnam?"

"I was the only person who could identify two of the men who were lost on that mission. Did I do something wrong?"

"I'm sure you didn't," I said. The radio came to life before I had to say anything else.

"This is Green Fox One," a voice said. "Identify yourself."

"Colonel Milo March."

"All right, Colonel March. Follow us."

I looked through the windshield and saw the four planes swoop around in front of me and dart away.

"Hey, fellows," I said into the microphone. "This ain't that kind of jet and, I might add, I'm not a flyboy."

"Relax, Colonel," the voice answered. "We won't run away from you."

It wasn't long before I thought I recognized Bien Hoa below us, but I couldn't be sure. Just then the escort planes began to dip away.

"See you on the ground, Colonel," the voice said on the radio. A second later, another voice broke in. "Colonel March, do you read me?"

"Loud and clear," I said.

"You are now over the landing field. Is your landing gear up or down?"

I squinted at the instrument panel and found the word for wheels. They were up. I reported this over the radio and was told to lower them. I pushed the button and was glad to see the instrument show that the wheels obeyed.

"Wheels down," I said.

"Good. Fly beyond the field for six miles. Then turn back to the field, lowering your altitude as you approach. You will be able to see the runway. Aim for the nearest point, on a slant. I will continue to give you instructions as you come in."

I did as he told me, and he started talking again. It was a calm voice that made me feel better. I just listened to it and didn't bother to look. When he told me to lift a wing, I did it. When he told me to cut down on the throttle, I did it.

I vaguely felt the wheels touch the ground, then applied the brakes as the voice told me to. The plane rolled to a stop. The first person to enter the plane was Colonel Blake.

"Welcome, Colonel," he said. He put something into my hands. It was a bottle. "You look as if you need this. Take a good drink. There's a medic right behind me, and he may stop you if you don't beat him to it." He was still standing where he blocked the entrance.

He leaned over and shut off the motors as I took the drink. I felt a little better, but not much. The Colonel took the bottle from my hands. "Who's this?" I looked up and saw Rigsby, looking as if he wanted out.

"That's Rigsby. From our Embassy."

Colonel Blake stepped farther into the plane, making room. Rigsby stepped forward to the exit, then stopped and looked at me. "I want to thank you, Colonel March, for rescuing me from Hanoi. And I apologize for not having more faith in you. I—I haven't ever met anyone like you."

"It was nothing," I said dryly. "Go on back to the States and see your wife and children."

He stepped out of the plane, and almost immediately a medical captain stepped in. Without saying a word, he was looking at my shoulder and then probing it, more or less gently. The next thing I knew, he was sticking a needle into my arm. He pulled it out and left.

I manage to focus on Colonel Blake. "One thing," I said. "The dog goes with me."

"Don't worry, Colonel," Blake said. "I'll take care of everything. Just relax."

I didn't need to be told that. I was already relaxing. I started to say something else, but fell asleep in the middle of the sentence.

When I finally recovered consciousness, I was obviously in a hospital room. Everything was white and antiseptic. There was a smell of alcohol—but the wrong kind. There was a man holding my wrist. He was wearing a medical gown, but I could see his shirt collar. He was a major in the Army Medical Corps.

"Good morning, Colonel," he said cheerfully.

"Is it?"

He was startled. "Is it what?"

"Is it morning?"

"Well, not exactly. It's early in the afternoon."

"Where am I?"

"The military hospital in Saigon."

"How long have I been here?" I asked.

"This is the third day, Colonel. You took a fifty-caliber bullet in your left shoulder. It did some damage, but we're sure you'll recover before too many days. You also lost a lot of blood. We've been giving you transfusions and feeding you intravenously. How do you feel?"

"Fine," I said. "How soon can I get out of here?"

"In a few days. There's a special ambulance plane coming to take you back to Washington. You can be released about the time it arrives."

"Precision," I said. "That's what I like about the army. Where's Dante?"

"Dante?" he repeated uncertainly.

"My dog."

"Oh. One of the nurses has been taking of him. I believe he's fine."

"I'm not interested in what you believe. Send him in."

"We'll see," he said stiffly. "I'll send the nurse in on my way out. I'll see you sometime tomorrow." He picked up his bag and marched stiffly out of the room.

A moment later the door opened and a pretty blond nurse came in. I noticed that she was a lieutenant. "Well, you've come back to us," she said cheerfully. Too damned cheerfully. "How are you feeling today?"

I decided that she also needed to be taken down a notch or two. "I feel fine," I said. "I want a quart of whiskey, a rare steak, and a girl." I looked at her. "Cancel the last request. I'm still a sick man. I think you should stay with me."

Her face turned slightly pink. 'You know better than that, Colonel. You can't have the whiskey. I think you can have the steak. Period. In the meantime, you have several visitors waiting to see you if you feel up to it."

"Who?"

"There's a Sergeant Daniel Farrow. There's a Mr. Wilson from the Embassy. There's a Lieutenant Greene from the General's office. And there's Colonel Blake from Bien Hoa."

"We'd better go by rank," I said gravely. "Send my dog in first and then Sergeant Farrow. Then Mr. Wilson, Lieutenant Greene, and Colonel Blake, in that order." Based on army protocol, I should start with the highest-ranking officer, but I figured I was some kind of war hero and could get away with a little lapse of manners. "And hold the steak," I added.

"All right, Colonel. I will have to give you some medicine later."

"Okay. Can I make a call to Washington later?"

"I haven't received any orders about it, so I suppose it's all right. The phone is on the small table next to your bed."

"Fine. Now scoot."

She gave me a smile and left. A moment later, the door opened and Dante came in. The nurse looked in. "I'll give you three minutes. He's a lovely little dog."

"Three minutes, hell. He's going to stay here as long as I do—except for occasional strolls outside. I'll arrange for that. You can bring in the next visitor in three minutes, but Dante stays."

"I'll see you in three minutes." She went out and closed the door. Dante came over to the bed and looked up at me. I reached down and put my hand under his chest and lifted him up to the bed. He came over and sniffed at my shoulder, then licked my nose. He wagged his tail and went to curl up at the foot of the bed.

The door opened and Dan Farrow came in, almost on tiptoe.

"Relax, Dan," I said. "I'm not quite ready for a military funeral. Are you still my driver?"

He grinned at me. "Sure, Milo. How are you feeling?"

"Great. How's the wife?"

"Fine—except she can't understand why I've been so nervous."

"She will in time. I want you to do two things for me. Get me a map that shows all of Vietnam in as much detail as possible. Tell the nurse that I've sent you for this and you'll be right back. I also want some whiskey, but don't tell her about it. Do you have enough money for that? I'll give it back to you when you return."

"No sweat." He leaned over and patted Dante on the head. "Welcome back, Dante." He turned and left. I started to turn and make the phone call, but suddenly realized it was a bad time for it. I lit a cigarette and leaned back to wait.

He was back sooner than I expected. He handed me the map, then took two pints of bourbon from his pockets. He placed them on the table beside me. I pulled over the water glass and poured it half full. Another pocket yielded a small bag.

"Ice cubes, too," he said with a grin. He dropped two of them into the glass. "Anything else can I do for you?"

"One more thing. I had on a pair of combat boots when I came in here. They must be around somewhere. See if you can find them."

He started looking around and finally stood up, waving them. "You are not going to put them on now, are you?" he asked.

"No. Just bring me the one for my right foot."

He brought it over. I reached down and found the folded money I'd put there. I worked the tape loose and pulled the money out.

"Money?" he exclaimed. "Where the hell did that come from?"

"Washington. Expense money. I didn't want the Viet Cong getting their fingers on it, so I stashed it in the boot. I figured if it gave me a blister, it was worth it. How much do I owe you?"

He hesitated but finally named the figure. I peeled off the amount and handed it to him. "Thanks, Dan."

"But—," he started.

"Don't give me that stuff. You've been in the Army long enough to know that a colonel makes more money than a sergeant. Besides, this is expense money, and the way I feel, General Baxter wants to buy me a drink." I reached for the drink beside me and held it up. "To General Baxter. There's probably another glass in the bathroom, if you'd like to join me."

He shook his head. "My wife wouldn't like it if I smell like booze."

"I guess you're right," I said. I leaned to my right and put the bottles of whiskey in the drawer with the money. "Will you take the two glasses into the bathroom and rinse them out, Dan?"

"Sure," he said. He picked them up and went into the bathroom. I could hear the water running, then he came back and replaced the glasses. "Anything else?"

"Yes. Take the rest of the day off. Come back at about ten

tonight. It's important, but I won't keep you long. On your way out, tell the nurse I want to see her before she sends any more visitors."

"Got it. I'll see you later." He left.

She came right in. "Well," she said, "having a visitor must have been good for you. Do you want something?"

"I want you to do something. Tell Mr. Wilson that I won't be able to see him today, but he can rest better. I am informing him officially that I am resigning as his military attaché and he may date the resignation prior to the day I left Saigon, if he likes. Then you can send in the lieutenant."

She bustled out. I lit a cigarette and waited, but not for long. The door opened and Lieutenant Greene came in. "Good afternoon, Colonel March. General Lawson asked me to stop by and see if there's anything you want."

"Plenty," I said, "but they won't let me have them. How are things in the outside world?"

"They have been pretty hectic, but they're straightening out. General Lawson has been on the phone to General Baxter in Washington and things are working out fine. You dumped a pretty package in our laps when you landed in Bien Hoa."

"It was nothing, Lieutenant," I said lightly. "Tell General Lawson to consider it an advance Christmas present."

"It almost is, but in the beginning it looked more like a funeral wreath. It is difficult to explain a Russian plane, two handcuffed Russian pilots, and a dead Russian sergeant in our possession."

"Into each life some problems must fall," I said. Then curiosity got the best of me. "How did you solve it?"

"I wish I had," he said wistfully. "The two generals had several talks with the leading authorities of South Vietnam, and they have generously accepted the whole package as a present to them. We could not lodge a complaint against the Soviet Union nor explain why it was delivered to us in Bien Hoa. South Vietnam can make such a complaint and justify the action that followed. I understand that already there is considerable worldwide press coverage and sympathy for the South."

"It was made to order," I admitted. "I had intended to suggest something of the sort, but they wouldn't let me talk. In fact, they won't let me do anything. What else?"

"There hasn't been much talk of anything else. General Lawson asked me to convey his congratulations to you and to tell you that Washington is sending an ambulance plane to pick you up."

I nodded. "That should brighten up his life as much as being relieved of a plane and prisoners he didn't want. Give him my congratulations. If he reacts as I think he will, you may end up running the whole headquarters while he takes sick leave for a few days. Thanks, Lieutenant."

"I was glad to do it. If I don't see you before you leave, happy landing." He left.

The next visitor was Colonel Blake. He was carrying a box tied with bright ribbons. He stopped at the foot of the bed and looked at me. "They tell me you might survive," he said. "But can we say the same for the Army? I brought you a survival kit to use while you're waiting for your Purple Heart."

"Then open it. Having the use of only one arm, I don't think I can manage to open it and still catch myself when I swoon."

He tore the ribbons and wrapping from the box and produced quart of good bourbon.

"Ambrosia for the wounded warrior," I said. "I'm touched. There's a clean glass on my right. The one that has been used is mine. There may even be a couple of ice cubes left in that little bag. Pour us two drinks and then slip the bottle into the drawer, away from prying eyes." I watched him as he poured. He picked up his own glass.

"I want to propose a toast," he said, "to the only man, so far as I know, who has succeeded in hijacking a Russian military plane."

"Sounds fair enough. I'll drink to that." We both did. "What are you doing down here? I thought you were running a war."

"They let me drop in once in a while just to see how the other half lives. Anything I can do for you?"

"There might be. Can you manage to send a telegram to Hanoi for me?"

"You don't want much, do you? But I just might be able to do that. I know a sergeant in the Army of the Republic of Vietnam who is a telegraph operator. He has a girl in the North and he's pulling for the war to be over. And I think there's a least one cable operating between Saigon and Hanoi. What's your message?"

"I want it sent to General Igor Gershuni in care of the People's Revolutionary Party in Hanoi. The message: Sorry you missed the trip. Milo March."

"Who is Igor?"

"The one who talked a General Ngoc of Hanoi into turning me over to the Russians for questioning. He's also the one who put me on the plane for Moscow."

"I'll do it. I've always said that there are too many generals in the world."

"Agreed. Incidentally, I heard about the way that General Lawson and General Baxter put their heads together and came up with the idea of turning over the whole Russian package to the South Vietnamese. I had exactly the same idea while I was driving that Russian bus into your lap, but today is the first time I've been permitted to talk."

"The Army takes care of its own," he said. "General Lawson got the idea from me—in a roundabout fashion. He asked me what I thought we should do about that problem. I told him I didn't know and suggested that he ask you what you thought. Obviously, he didn't. I'm sure that he didn't think of it himself. There was only one way I could have gotten it from you, and that would be by ESP. I don't think the Defense Department has gotten around to recognizing things which are not included in the Articles of War or the officer's manual."*

"To hell with that," I said. "I just hope it costs General Gershuni a couple of grades in rank. And it may."

He took time to take another drink, then looked at me uncertainly. "May I ask you a question?—and I don't have the right to know the answer."

---

* In 1978, several years after this book manuscript was written, the U.S. Army began a secret program (the Stargate Project) to investigate the potential of ESP and remote viewing for military use. The research was terminated in 1995, having produced no practical results.

"Why not? Go ahead."

"What about that Rigsby? He baffles me."

"I expect he does everybody. But you still haven't told me what your question is."

"Is he an intelligence agent?"

"No," I said. "He's always worked in an embassy, and I suspect he has never been any more than a glorified office boy. He was, however, approached when he came to the Saigon embassy and asked to obtain copies of any unusual or strange messages going through the offices. Nobody knew anything about this except the agent who recruited him, including Hanoi. They didn't even think he was important except for propaganda. I doubt very much that I would have been sent to rescue him if we had known that was the situation."

"He's a strange one."

"I'll tell you about him," I said. "Stranger than you think. He's an innocent. He's unaware of most of the things that go on in the world. He's a nice little innocent man who wouldn't knowingly hurt a fly. But let's look at him. In the past week, solely because of him, three men have been killed, two men wounded, one lady has lost her position in the world and may even lose her life, three governments have been disturbed, two Russian officers were kidnapped—and nothing has happened to him. He also has no awareness that he played any part in these events. The things which have happened, however, resulted in his release from prison and saved him from possible torture or disgrace. When it's all over, he says thank you as if speaking to someone who told him the correct time. Think about it sometime in the middle of the night."

"No, thanks," he said hastily. "I've got better things to think about. Are you sure there's nothing else you want me to do?"

"Nothing else. Just the telegram to Igor."

"Okay. If I have the chance, I'll drop in and see you again. If I don't make it, give my regards to the Pentagon."

"I'll let Dante do that," I said as he left the room.

I leaned back against the pillow. I felt a little tired. I was about to ring for the nurse when she came in carrying a small tray. There were a couple of tiny dishes on it with two capsules in each one.

"That doesn't look like a rare steak," I said.

"Antibiotics. Do you want the steak now?"

"I think I'll wait. Give me the pills and I might take a nap."

"That sounds a little more sensible." She looked at the stand with the two empty glasses. I think she sniffed the air a little. There was a smile on her face when she looked at me again. "When you die, it'll probably be from drinking too much milk." She picked up the two glasses and went into the bathroom. When she came back, she was carrying a glass of water and the empty second glass, which was clean. She set the empty one on the stand.

"You're in the wrong branch of the service," she said. "You should have gone into the Navy. Now, take the capsules."

I downed them one after another until they were all gone. "Now," she said, "in the event that you're the worrying kind, the things you've had in your stomach in the past hour won't hurt you. They may help you sleep a little longer, and that may be better for you than the medicine. Go to sleep. I'll tell the night nurse to let you sleep as long as you can and to serve you your steak when you wake up."

"Thank you, Lieutenant," I said gravely. I looked at my watch and decided to make a phone call. But before I could pick up the receiver, she was back, carrying a medium-sized bowl.

"If there's anything I hate," she said, "it's the sight of a man drinking straight whiskey without even ice cubes in it. Here's some ice for you." She set the bowl down with a thump. "Good night, Colonel."

"Good night," I said. I didn't want to waste the ice, so I put two cubes in the glass and covered them with the bourbon. I took a swallow and then picked up the receiver.

I gave the operator the number of the K'uai Pai Ti Ti restaurant. It rang a few times and then a man answered.

"I would like to speak to Madame Le," I said in Chinese.

"Just a minute. Whom shall I say is calling?"

"Tell her Dante wishes to speak to her."

I waited for about three minutes. I was just about to hang up when I heard her voice. It was barely above a whisper. "Milo," she said, "is it really you?"

"It's really me. How are you, Thuy?"

"Confused. And sort of beaten up. Inside, not outside. I can't say any more right now. Where are you?"

"In Saigon. Can you come to see me tomorrow morning?"

"When?"

"Hold on. I'll find out." I pushed the bell on the stand.

The nurse opened the door almost immediately. "Not asleep yet?"

"I always talk in my sleep. How early can I have a visitor in the morning?"

"Eight o'clock. You mean you'll be ready to receive one that early?"

"Yes. Good night again."

When the door closed, I spoke into the phone. "Thuy?"

"Yes."

"This is very important for you. Listen closely. I'm in our military hospital here. I must talk to you. Can you get here at eight o'clock?"

"Yes. You'll be there?"

"Unless someone carries me off. Good night, Thuy."

"I have to go now. I'll let you hear the minute I know anything." There was a click and she hung up.

I put my phone back and leaned against the pillow. I smoked a cigarette and finished the rest of my drink. I was asleep almost the minute my head was down.

It was a few minutes past ten when I awakened. I felt better than I had all day. I pushed the button next to me.

The door opened and a night nurse looked in. She also was a lieutenant. "Ready for your steak, Colonel?" she asked. I nodded. "In ten minutes." She stepped back and closed the door.

She was as good as her word. It was just under ten minutes later when she came back in with a tray. The only things on it were a bowl and a plate with the most beautiful steak I had ever seen. I realized that I was hungry. The nurse put the bowl down on the stand. "Lieutenant Summers said I should bring you some ice and to not tell anyone about it. I guess you don't want any coffee or milk."

"Smart," I said. "I'm expecting a Sergeant Farrow to be here to see me. Please send him right in."

She glanced at her watch and frowned, but she shrugged and left. I put some ice in a glass and poured bourbon. I was still working on it when the door opened and Dan came in.

"Sorry I'm a little late," he said. "There was some military traffic through town, and I had to wait for a time at several intersections."

"No damage. Make yourself a drink, then pull up a chair and listen. I want you to hear it so you can plan things."

He nodded and crossed to the stand. He poured himself a small drink, dragged the chair over, and sat down. "Shoot."

I swallowed another drink and lit a cigarette. I picked up the phone. "This is Colonel Milo March," I said when the operator answered. "I am at the moment a patient in this hospital. I want to make a person-to-person phone call to General Baxter in the Pentagon in Washington, District of Columbia, in the States." I listened to what she had to say. "There are two ways you can handle it, honey. You can just charge it to the Army and I can tell General Baxter to okay it, and if he's too cheap to do that, then I'll pay for it myself. In cash. American dollars. Or I can get the doctor who took a lot of lead from my shoulder to turn the lead over to you. I don't know what the price of lead is today, so don't bother asking me. Put the call through. I'm a wounded man and don't want to wait all night for it. ... Okay. Thanks." I held the receiver to my ear and waited.

"Hey," Dan said, "are you going to talk to the General that way?"

"I might. Look, Dan, I hurt, and when I hurt, I don't give a damn how the other person feels. He's a big boy. In fact, I know what he'd do. He would take a quarter out of one pocket and put it in another. That would mean that he'd made a bet with himself about what I would say and he won the bet." I held up a hand indicating silence.

I had heard muffled voices on the phone before, but suddenly a voice came in clear. It sounded familiar.

"Is General Baxter there?" I asked.

"Milo!" she said. "This is Marya. How are you feeling?"

"Great," I said. "But if you were planning on scheduling a few matches of left-handed ping-pong, you'd better cancel them."

"General Baxter is waiting to talk to you," she said hurriedly. "I have permission to meet you at the airport when you arrive. Good-bye."

"Congratulations, Milo," the General said. "You did a great job."

"Just get me out of here. I'm tired of getting all of these Purple Hearts. You can't raise a dime on them at a hock shop. You deserve the congratulations, sir. You thought of a way of keeping the alien population down and avoided being stuck with what might be called a piece of hot property. That was smart thinking."

"I agree that it was. But I was told by General Lawson that it was you who came up with the idea, so you'll be getting more than a Purple Heart.

"Don't get some guy to pin it on me who will want to kiss me on both cheeks. Now, don't hang up on me. I want you to do something for me."

"What?"

"There's a sergeant here. His name is Dan Farrow. He was assigned to be my driver. He's a good man and I owe him a few. He's put in enough time in this joint. He's a career soldier and he should be permitted some coasting on the remaining years of his twenty. I want you to have him transferred to the States. The guy needs some breathing spell."

"Damn it, Milo, you can't just move men around like they were checkers."

"No, but you can. Just get him out of here or I won't be on that plane. Don't argue; it's costing the taxpayers money."

"All right," he growled. "I'll see what I can do." He hung up quickly. I guess he was afraid I'd ask for something else.

"Hey, you can't do that," Dan said as I replaced the receiver.

"I just did. He said he'd see what he can do. That's his way of saying yes. And that means you'll be transferred soon. You may even be there almost as soon as I am."

"But I can't let you—"

I interrupted him. "You can't do anything else. I've already arranged it, and if I know General Baxter, I doubt if even the Commander-in-Chief can stop it now. Weren't you ever told not to argue with superior officers?"

He grinned. "Obviously *you* weren't told. How do you get away with talking like that to a general?"

"Clean living. I can add to the bit of advice you have now had. Never pass up a pass, a leave of absence, a furlough, a promotion, an award, or a transfer that you really want. You're going as soon as the machinery can work. I don't want to hear any more about it."

"Okay. The wife will be pleased. We haven't seen the kids in some time. Of course, we get letters, but it ain't the same thing. Thanks, Milo."

"It was nothing."

There was a light knock on the door and the nurse looked in. "It's time for your medicine, Colonel March."

"Bring it in, Lieutenant."

Leaving the door open, she went back for her tray.

"Want me to beat it?" Dan said. He sounded eager to go.

"Not yet. She won't take long, and I have another order to give you."

He nodded as the nurse returned. This time there was a glass of water on it. She put it down and put her hand on my wrist. I knew she was taking my pulse, but I decided not to warn her that she might raise my heartbeat.

"Perfectly normal," she said with a smile. "Now, wash down the pills—with water."

I obeyed. I realized I was starting to get sleepy again. "You should sleep through the night," she said, "and I'm certain you will feel much better in the morning."

"When is the plane coming for me?"

"Day after tomorrow."

"What time does the day nurse come on in the morning?"

"Seven-thirty. Why?"

"I want you to give her some information from me. Tell her that there will be a Chinese lady here at eight o'clock to visit me. She is not to ask the lady what her name is and is to send her in at once. If it's necessary, you can tell the nurse that is an order."

"Yes, sir," she said with a smile. "Please don't stay too long, Sergeant. If Colonel March does what I expect him to, he might go to sleep in the middle of your most important sentence." With that, she was gone. I poured another drink, thinking it might keep me from sleeping too long.

"Madame Le is coming to visit me at eight in the morning," I said. "She'll be here for at least an hour, maybe longer. You come between nine and ten. I have some errands for you. Nothing difficult."

"I'll have all day," he said, standing up. He hesitated. "I just hope you'll be careful with that Madame Le. I got a feeling that she is very dangerous."

"So are ice cubes," I said, "if you try to walk on them. ... Good night, Dan."

He said good night—which was the last thing I heard.

FIFTEEN

When I finally crawled out of sleep, it was seven o'clock. I reached over to the stand and was not surprised my drink was no longer cold. There were still some small pieces of ice, so I poured them into the drink and took a sip. It tasted better than any drink I'd had in several days. With that, I realized I did feel much better. I knew better than to find out how well I could move my left shoulder, but the rest of me felt as if I were back in business. I reached over and pressed the button for the nurse.

"Good morning, Colonel," she said from the doorway. "How are you feeling this morning?"

"A lot better," I admitted. I noticed she was looking at my glass on the stand. "I was just thinking that the two of us together would make one hell of a good doctor."

She laughed. "I have just enough time, before I'm relieved, to get you some breakfast. What would you like?"

"Just scrambled eggs and toast. Maybe a glass of milk."

"Now I've heard everything. Coming right up, sir."

While she was gone, I finished my drink and lit a cigarette. Even that tasted better.

She was back so soon, I knew she must have peeked in earlier and had ordered it from the kitchen as soon as she saw I was stirring. She had the tray on a bed table which she placed across my lap. In addition to the food and the glass of milk, there were two bowls. I couldn't see what was in them.

"I'll get another pillow from the closet and we can prop you up. You'll be more comfortable." She got the pillow and put the two of them behind me.

"You know," I said, "I may just miss that plane when it comes. I've never had such service before. What're the two bowls for?"

"One is for this." She took two cubes out and dropped them in the glass I had been using, then poured bourbon and put it next to the milk. "The other has some meat scraps for your dog."

"Dante is grateful and so am I. Just put it on the floor."

She did and I could hear Dante going to work on it. "We try to please our visitors to fun-loving Saigon," she said.

"This is a good start. What else do you offer?"

"That's about it. We understand that there are a number of establishments here which offer a variety of services for the pleasure of our fine fighting men—but some of them haven't been exactly pleased and have ended up here for post-coitus treatment. I hope you enjoy your breakfast, Colonel." She was gone before I could think of an answer.

When I'd finished, I rang for her. She came in and took away the dishes, the table, and the tray. I freshened my drink and lit a cigarette. I'd discovered that as long as I didn't try to move my shoulder, I felt normal.

Just before eight, the day nurse put her head in. "Good morning, Colonel March. I hear you had a good night. How do you feel now?"

"Excellent—as long as I don't move too much."

"Is that why you are being visited so early in the morning by a Chinese lady?"

"I've begun to think that you have an unhealthy attitude about life—probably from carrying too many bedpans. But believe it or not, the lady's visit has solely to do with my mission in Vietnam."

"Really? What is your mission about? The investigation of sexual variety among the native population? Are you going to write a book? How about one called *Chinese Whiskey as an Aphrodisiac in the East?*"

"If I ever write one, it will be called *Frigid Nurses in a Torrid Clime.* Mailed to purchasers in an unmarked envelope."

"Touché," she said with a laugh. "Okay, Colonel, I will send in your Chinese princess without asking her any questions." There was a twinkle in her eyes as she departed.

It was impossible to guess what changes might have taken place in Thuy. It would depend on how she'd been treated in Hanoi after I'd left and what had happened after they learned the fate of the Russian plane.

The door opened and in she came. I almost didn't recognize her. She wore a body-hugging cheongsam, unlike anything I had seen her wear, and her hair was styled differently. The alluring cast of her eyes was more pronounced than the last time I saw her. The rest of her makeup was also different. She was, if it were possible, even more beautiful.

"Thuy," I said, "now you really dim the beauty of the lotus flower. Why don't you help yourself to a drink? The glass beside the bottle is a clean one, and there are ice cubes in the bowl."

She walked around the bed and fixed a drink. Then she dropped two more cubes into my glass and filled it. She handed it to me. Bending over the bed, she gave me a kiss, then raised her glass.

"A toast," she said, "to Milo March and a few wonderful days." We both drank and she sat down in the chair. I realized that she was staring at me fixedly.

"Milo," she asked, "are you wounded?"

"That's what they claim."

"What happened?"

"I was shot through the left shoulder. It's awkward and painful, but it's nothing serious if I get the right care. I'm already feeling much better."

"Tell me about it."

So I told her most of the story, leaving out a few unimportant things.

"You knew how to fly the plane?"

"No," I admitted. "I was all right as long as I was up in the air because all I had to do was read the instrument panel and pay a lot of attention to the compass. When it came to landing, they talked me down. I was told what to do and how to do it. A good thing, too. By that time, I could barely see the instrument panel. But it worked out fine."

"Except for a bullet through your shoulder. I'm sorry, Milo. It was really my fault. I don't expect you to believe me, but I really thought I was helping you to accomplish something which I also believed would help my people with favorable publicity. I was wrong. I believed it only because I wanted to. It was foolish and childish of me. … You are an agent, aren't you, Milo."

"Yes. And what happened wasn't your fault, Thuy. And it wouldn't have happened if it hadn't been for General Igor Gershuni."

"Then you did know him? What he said about you was true? You were guilty of the things he mentioned?"

"Yes. But it's not quite that simple. I helped a lot of Russian people who badly needed help. I worked with a lot of Russians who were part of a people's underground, perhaps something like your Viet Cong. And everything I said about Gershuni was true. He's a part of a group who bears little similarity to Marx or Lenin or to their ideals."

"Is or was?"

"I think he is a member. But, any day, the word may change to the past tense. Were you followed here, Thuy?"

"No."

"How did you manage that? I should imagine that they will be watching you closely now."

"They already are. Do you know why?"

"Because of me."

"Only partly, Milo. But chiefly because of my brother. He has just been taken to the bosom of Hanoi. Partly as a soldier but also as what they think is a coming activist and philosopher of the Left. Among other things, he is in charge of checking my every action."

"How did you manage to throw them off?"

She smiled. "Did I ever tell you about my grandfather?"

"I don't think so."

"My grandfather is still alive. His name is Le Chin Kuang. For several years he has lived in Saigon, in a small apartment in a section primarily Chinese. They are Chinese who still cling to the values of the old Chinese. They respect him and they are all ready to protect him at any time. They do not know that my grandfather and I are related. My brother does not even know that our grandfather is still alive. That is how I managed."

"I don't understand."

"For years, when things were too much for me, I have slipped away and spent the night with my grandfather. He helps straighten things out when I'm confused. And other times, we just talked…. He knows about you."

"How?"

"He is most observant. He catches every little change in me. And so it was last night. He asked questions of me and he came up with the answer. He likes you and he feels sorry for us because we come from two separate worlds."

"East and West?"

"No. He means our training and our political experiences, not our culture."

"There is some truth in that," I said, "but it is not the whole truth. Are you talking, or even thinking, about marriage?"

"No. The word has no meaning. I confess that I have had a few thoughts about us spending the rest of our lives in companionship. I have never felt that way about any man before. It may even be a childish fantasy. I do not dwell on it for long."

"I understand," I said gently. "Do you have time to do a personal favor for me?"

"I think so. What is it?"

"I want to buy a jade pendant for someone. I'm not rich, so it shouldn't be the best. But it should be something that would make a woman feel beautiful when she wears it and feel that it's from a friend."

"An old or a new girlfriend?" she asked with a smile.

"Neither. She's the patient woman who is married to a man who has done favors for me, and I would simply like to have her feel that everything in her life hasn't been in vain."

She nodded. "I can get it and have it back here within an hour."

"That will be perfect. How much will it cost? I'll give you the money in advance in American dollars."

She shook her head. "Wait until I return." She stood up and moved toward the door.

"Thuy," I said. She turned and looked at me. "Don't take any chances," I finished.

"I won't, Milo. You have already noticed that I look different. They have never seen me dressed like this or look like this. They have never seen me in the conveyance I will use. A pedicab. When I've vanished before, they have always thought I was with a lover. Today, it will be true." She opened the door and was gone.

I reached for the phone and called Dan Farrow's number. A woman answered. "Is Dan still there?" I asked. "This is Milo March and I would like to talk to him for a minute."

"I'll get him, but first I would like to say one thing, Colonel

March. Dan told me what you're doing for us. I want you to know how grateful I am."

"There's no need for that. Dan is getting only what he deserves."

"I—here he is now."

"Milo," he said. "How are you feeling this morning?"

"Better. I had plenty of sleep and I think it did more for me than the medicine did. Madame Le has left, although she will be back in about an hour. Come over as soon as you can."

He said he'd be over immediately and hung up. I made another call to the hotel and asked them the amount of my bill. To my surprise, they told me General Lawson had already sent someone over to pay it and that my things were still in the room I'd used. I thanked them and told them my driver would be over to pick them up.

I was beginning to get tense. There was a lot to do and not very much time to do it in. I filled the glass with ice and bourbon and tried to relax as I sipped the drink and waited.

Dan arrived sooner than I expected. He shook his head when I motioned to the bourbon. "You're really feeling better?" he asked.

"Why shouldn't I? Everybody around here hovers like an avenging angel. Two generals, one colonel, a medic who's a major, a sergeant, two lieutenants who are nurses, Madame Le, and others who will probably drop around before the day is over. They are afraid I won't eat enough, I'll drink too much, I'll fool around with girls too much, I'll have a relapse or some other damn thing. If it keeps up, I may just walk out of this joint and thumb a ride on the first plane I see going my way. And I have a lot to do before I can leave."

"What do you want me to do?"

"I thought you'd never ask. First, take Dante out for a walk and don't leave the grounds. Hurry back because I need action."

"Yes, sir," he said with a grin. "Come on, Dante."

The two of them strolled out. The nurse strolled in. "Colonel," she said, "are you trying to turn this room into a Mecca for everyone who is strolling around Saigon with nothing to do?"

"It's not a bad idea, but I have a better one. I do intend to turn it into a waystation for people who will run through here, looking for something to do."

She smiled. "Are you trying to suggest that we should move a desk and secretary in here, install a switchboard, and maybe a receptionist?"

"It's a good idea," I said solemnly, "but it would only interfere with what I have to do. In the meantime, the Sergeant and Dante will be back any minute and the Chinese lady will be back in less than an hour. Then the Sergeant will be back again with all of my personal things from the hotel, and you can never tell when there might be a visitation from military gentlemen who have nothing else to do. And later there will be an old Chinese gentleman coming to see me."

"To inquire about your intentions concerning his daughter?"

"I doubt that. Granddaughter, maybe. He may want to inquire about such things as my health, the health of my dog, and perhaps whether any of my ancestors were feeble-minded."

"I can't imagine why," she said with sarcasm. "I forgot to add that any minute I expect a bar and a bartender to be installed. It's too much work for you to do yourself."

"Your concern, Lieutenant, touches me very deeply. Now, will you trot along and carry a bedpan somewhere?"

She laughed as she closed the door behind her. I decided that I needed another drink and poured it. With that, Dan and Dante arrived. The traffic, I had to admit, was getting a little heavy.

"What now, Milo?" Dan asked.

"I've got two errands for you to run. You know where the floating restaurants are?" He nodded. "Go there and ask for the boat of Tang Lok Hee. When it's pointed out to you, take one of the smaller boats out to it. When you get aboard, ask for Tang Lok Hee and tell them that you come from his Younger Brother. Tell him that his Younger Brother will be honored if he will visit me as soon as he can. He may not know that I'm in a hospital, but I think he will. And he speaks English, so don't worry."

"Okay. What's the second one?"

"Go to the hotel. The bill has been paid and I told them you'd be there to pick up my things. They'll let you into the room to pack my things. In addition to the regular things, you will find a gun taped to the underside of the toilet bowl and a knife to the top of the shower curtain. Open the two top drawers of the dresser and feel on what is the bottom of the dresser top. You'll find several things there, including money, fastened with tape. Bring all of them. Throw everything into the suitcase and bring it here. If you see anyone following, try to ditch them before coming straight here."

"That's all?"

"It is for now." I thought of the time schedule. "Make it as fast as you can." I didn't wait to watch him leave. I poured myself a fresh drink and tried to think ahead.

The time passed quickly and I was surprised when the door opened and Dan came in with my suitcase. "Got everything," he said. "The old Chinese said he would be here in less than two hours. What's next on the schedule?"

"Nobody followed you?" I asked.

"No."

"Okay. Take a break for about three hours, then come back. Take some money out of the drawer and bring me a bottle of Canadian Club if you can. I may have something more for you to do then. Don't forget to keep an eye out for anyone tailing you."

I leaned back and closed my eyes when he was gone. I was beginning to get tired, and there was still a lot to do. I went over it again, making sure that I wasn't forgetting any part of it.

Thuy came into the room quietly. I opened my eyes. "You don't have to be so silent," I said. "It'll make me think the place has mice."

She held up a brightly wrapped package. "Here it is," she said.

"Do I get to look at it?"

"Why not?" She started taking the string off.

I didn't answer, but just watched her taking off the paper and string. Finally, she lifted a jewelry box that looked as if it were made from teak. She handed it to me and I opened the lid. What I saw, to put it mildly, was beautiful. So beautiful that it made me suspicious. I rubbed my fingertips gently over the surface of the stone. I looked at her.

"Ke yu?" I asked.

"Damn you to hell," she said violently. "Why didn't you stay in the United States and concern yourself with agate marbles? Why did you have to come east and learn our language, our customs, and everything else? Couldn't you keep your hands off sacred things?"

"How much did this cost?"

"One hundred dollars," she said defiantly. "But there's a story about why that is what it cost."

"There's a story behind everything in China," I said. "Just don't make a three-hundred-page book out of it."

"The man who sold it to me is a friend of my grandfather's and I have known him since childhood. He also has very strong feelings about the China of centuries ago. I told him about you and why you wanted to buy the best piece of jade you could afford. He insisted on selling it for one hundred dollars. He said if you do not believe my story, he will come to see you and convince you."

"Nobody ever won an argument with a Chinese and I don't have the time try again. Sit down. I want to ask you some questions."

"What?" she asked, sitting down.

I put some ice in a glass and poured whiskey over it. I held it out to her, but she shook her head. I took a drink of it and lit a cigarette.

"Thuy," I said, "what are your plans?"

Her face was tense as she looked at me. "I'm not sure that I have any. I thought and talked about it all night until almost this morning."

"What does your grandfather think?"

"That I should leave Vietnam. He thinks I should do so at once. What do you think, Milo?"

"I also think you should leave—but I am not the one who must make the decision. You are the only one who can make it."

"Do you know what leaving Vietnam means to me?" she asked passionately. "It means that I will be considered a deserter—a defector."

"That," I said gently, "is what others will say it means. I don't believe that it is what you believe deep within yourself. I think that it could also mean that you need time to step outside a social maelstrom and think for yourself. I believe you need to be somewhere that will receive you and love you for yourself—not to be judged by a word or a slogan painted on your forehead or on your back. You have to learn to say more things for yourself instead of being the echo of the mouthings of others, no matter how brilliant they are or were. Have you thought of leaving Vietnam?"

She nodded. "It will not be easy to do so. I am known by sight in Saigon and not only by the Viet Cong. It would be impossible for me to get within fifty feet of a passenger plane or a ship about to sail without being detected. To be caught in such an act would mean staying here, dead or alive. At the moment, I see no difference between the two. And there are other problems."

"What?"

"Money," she said simply. "It's not that I don't have money, but getting it out of Saigon is impossible. I have spent fifteen years running the best restaurant that has ever been in this city. Of course, a lot of money went to the Viet Cong. The restaurant building and my house in the country and my cars can all be taken by the Viet Cong. But it is not possible to cash a large check, especially when it's not a habit you have displayed before, without the whole city knowing it in minutes. In that respect, North and South are the same."

"Where would you like to go?"

"Macao or Hong Kong. I have a small bank account in each city. Less than two hundred dollars. But there is no way to get money from here to the banks there. Don't forget that the Viet Cong now hates me as much as the South Vietnamese, and they'll be watching more closely than usual. Either city would be fine for me. I could make money with a restaurant in either, but especially Macao. The tourist business there has grown immensely."

"Thuy, what would you say if I told you that I can get you and your money safely out of here and have it delivered to any place you name."

"You would do that?" she asked in surprise.

"Yes."

"But how?"

"You are the easiest. I can guarantee that part of it. I cannot tell you the exact moment just now, but I should know before the day is over. It might mean leaving tonight, but certainly within two or three days. Getting the money out may be a little tougher. Do you have a friend whom you can trust and who can legally get out of South Vietnam? One you can trust with your money for a few days?"

"I do have one friend like that, but I would hate to put her in that much danger." She thought for a minute, then looked at me. "I do have another friend whom I would trust with anything—and have. His name is Milo March."

It was my turn to be astonished. "That can't be true, Thuy. Everyone would tell you that I am the Enemy."

"Not everyone. My grandfather wouldn't and I wouldn't. I have already trusted you as far as one can go. I trusted you with my body, my love, and my soul. If you had scorned those, there would have been nothing left to protect. You have asked all the questions, Milo. I want to ask one."

"Go ahead."

"That first evening when we went to my house in the country. You had indicated that you wanted to go north and I had given you the impression that I might help you. It was shortly after that when we made love. I do not want you to think there was any connection between those two events. I was eager for us to make love and I believed that you were, too. And I did not have regrets later."

"I know, Thuy," I said gently. "When you took my hand and led me upstairs, it did occur to me that there might be more than one reason for the gesture. It was the latter reason which won after a very brief struggle. But we must get back to details about the future. If it's possible, could you leave Saigon tonight?"

"Yes."

"I will know this evening. Can you be back by then?"

She nodded. "I had already made up my mind not to go back to the restaurant. I found a place for my grandfather. He has several friends in the new community, and they will move him and his possessions into the new apartment tonight shortly after dark. They will look after him."

"Get back here as soon as you can and I will give you instructions for meeting Tang Lok Hee. What are you going to do without your money?"

"I will bring it with me," she said.

"How much is there?"

"More than fifty thousand dollars. In American money."

I whistled softly. "How did you manage that? They must be watching your bank as well as following you except for the times you manage to give them the slip."

"You remember that I told you about the man from whom I bought the jade for your friend?"

I nodded.

"He has the money for me. I gave him my check for the amount, dated three days from now. He will deposit it in his account at that time. It is doubtful if they will even think of checking on him. The Viet Cong will be here in a few days. I will be gone. He will be gone. And it will still take time for them to discover that neither of us left much money behind."

"Very inscrutable," I admitted. "But that's still quite a bundle of money. Especially in cash."

"It's perfect, Milo. Nobody will even think of you as the bearer of money. Their thinking is very primitive. Especially that of my brother, and I'm sure he will manage to be put in charge of trying to find me. And you. About me, they will think, 'Her body, maybe; her money, no. Her body to save her money, definitely yes.' "

"Are you calling the restaurant again before you leave?"

"Yes. And I'll give them the same story. I'm still resting up from the march to Hanoi and back. I'll see you later, Milo." She came over and kissed me, then left without looking back. The nurse came in as soon as she was gone.

"Are you on a hunger strike?" she asked. "It's past the usual time, but don't you want your lunch?"

"I don't think I'll have time for it, but I'll make up for it at dinnertime. Another rare steak, but a big one."

"All right," she said. "More visitors?"

I nodded. "The Sergeant should be here now. Then there will be the Chinese gentleman I mentioned. That's about it."

"No more Madame Butterfly?"

"You've got your nationalities mixed up, but she won't be here until later. After you're off duty. By the way, what do you do when you're off?"

"Write down all the witty things that have been said by the patients. I'll bring your medicine in before you decide to skip that, too."

Once I was alone, I went over everything in my mind to see if I was missing anything. I thought it sounded as if it might work.

The nurse was back with my capsules. I swallowed them just as Dan arrived.

"Bring me a newspaper," I said as she went through the door.

"Yes, Your Highness," she muttered while I could still hear her.

Dan had brought my suitcase and placed it on the floor. "I saw the old Chinese man," he said. "That's some boat he has."

"And a good restaurant, too."

"He wanted to know how I knew you and I told him. Then he invited my wife and me to have dinner there tonight. I said I'd let him know."

"Take your wife and go, Dan. You've probably been to some of the floating restaurants, but his is the best. And I won't need any errands run tonight. Did Tang Lok Hee say he would come to see me?"

"Yes." He looked at his watch. "He ought to be here any minute now. I'd better get going."

"Okay." I picked up the package Thuy had brought. "Here's a present for your wife. Tell her it should have an engraving with it but I didn't have enough time. It would have been: 'For service above and beyond the call of duty.' "

"What is it?" he asked.

"You'll know when she tells you—or shows you. Good night, Dan."

"Good night, Milo," he said. He hesitated. "If you don't mind, I thought my wife and I might come out tomorrow and see you off."

"I don't mind at all, Dan. I'll see you then."

Two more visits, I thought, and I might be able to relax. Or something could go wrong and I might never relax again. I took another drink and rang for the nurse. She came in with the paper and shook her head at the sight of the glass in my hand.

"The old man should be here soon. He is of the old school of traditional Chinese. Before we can discuss what we must, there will be a few minutes which he must spend in wishing good health to our ancestors and in offering toasts to each other and to the ancestors. Would you please bring two fresh glasses and some ice cubes?"

"Yes, sir," she said. "Anything else, sir?"

"Just a fleeting glimpse of you before you retire to whatever you call that section beyond the door."

She made a face at me and departed. She was back almost at once with the glasses and ice. She put them down and went back to the door. "I think he is coming up the hall now," she said. "Have a happy ancestor worship, or whatever." She stepped out.

A moment later he came in. He closed the door behind him and bowed slightly to me. "I am greatly honored," he said, "by the invitation to visit my Younger Brother on his bed of pain. It is hoped that he will soon recover."

"It is I who am honored," I said, "that my Elder Brother can spare the time to visit with one who is so unimportant. I trust you are well."

"The mere sight of my Younger Brother restores me to the scenes of my youth. It is as if the morning sun had consented to guide me through the darkness of life."

I jumped into the conversation before he could think of the next sentence. "Perhaps my Elder Brother will join me in a toast in the honor of the gods who have once more restored me to his presence."

He bowed his head in consent. I poured two drinks and handed one glass to him. "And I wish to also drink to the success of the trip my Elder Brother plans on taking soon."

A startled expression darted across his face and was gone. We both drank, then he glanced at me in a way that indicated that the ceremony was finished. "Where did my Younger Brother get the thought that I might be planning to depart on a journey in the near future?" This was said in English, another indication that the ceremony was over.

"I remembered that the last time we spoke, you mentioned that you might move back to Macao or Hong Kong soon. I believe the times have gotten worse since we talked."

"The times are not good."

"How much worse?"

"It is difficult to say for certain, but when the water becomes clear, the stones will be seen. I am told that a plane will leave Saigon tomorrow night or the night after. It will carry Thieu's family away from the country. Another plane will leave the day after that, carrying the president and his gold. One of my informants tells me that the plane is already loaded. And the soldiers from the North will be in Saigon within forty-eight hours. When do you go, Younger Brother?"

"Tomorrow. And you, Elder Brother?"

He glanced quickly at the door, then back at me. When he spoke, he had switched back to Chinese. "Tonight at midnight."

"After the dinner hour?"

"Immediately after the dinner hour. It is better to leave quickly and feel foolish than to stay and regret it. Why do you ask?"

"Would you be willing to take someone with you?" I asked.

"Who?"

"Madame Le. She intends to go to Macao. The quicker the better."

"I heard that she is no longer in favor. She goes to stir up more trouble there?"

"She says not and I believe her. She says that she wishes to go there to think. I believe that, too. You will be paid for her passage."

"If what you believe is true, there will be no charge. And her grandfather?"

"He does not wish to go, but he approves of her going. He is old and he lives in a sector where he considers everyone his friend and does not wish it to be otherwise. Madame Le found him a different apartment and will move him in there this afternoon. She says that all of his neighbors are Chinese and that they do love him and will protect him."

Tang Lok Hee reached for the bottle of whiskey and poured a drink for each of us. He looked at me. "There is something about this which disturbs my Younger Brother. There is a curtain over his eyes. What is it that you would hide from me?"

"There is a sorrow that comes before there is a reason for it."

"Is it because of Madame Le?" he asked.

"No. I am glad that it is possible for her to leave Saigon."

His gaze was sharp as he looked at me. "Has my Younger Brother ever met Le Chin Kuang?"

"I have not had that pleasure. I know of him only from Madame Le."

"I know him for many, many years," he said. "I have often visited him here in Saigon. He is a scholar in the old sense. His heart was broken by his grandson joining those in the North and by the stories of how he has acted since then. It is true that he has been saddened by his granddaughter's activities for the Viet Cong, but he always felt that there were other qualities in her that would eventually draw her away from them. That is why he is pleased that she is going to leave Saigon. Now, what is it that brings sorrow to you in connection with the grandfather and the granddaughter?"

I lit a cigarette and took a drink of the whiskey. "It has occurred to me that perhaps Madame Le's grandfather thinks that he is too old and will only be a burden on his granddaughter and that her chances of getting away will be threatened if he were to go with her. Therefore, he tells her that he would be happier with his friends here and prefers not to leave. I believe that you think the same."

He nodded. "It is so. But I can tell that my Younger Brother has other thoughts on the subject."

"I do," I said. "I think that Madame Le and her grandfather are doing the same thing to each other. She's trying to protect him and he's trying to protect her. Either one will insist on staying here if there is a guarantee that the other can leave. I will make my Elder Brother the judge."

"In what way? Madame Le would not listen to anything I say. She does, I believe, listen to you."

"And her grandfather listens to you."

There was a hint of a smile on his face as he nodded his head. "You suggest?"

"I thought of it this morning. I'm sure that my Elder Brother would also like to see his old friend leave Saigon before the Viet Cong take over. Perhaps you could pay him a visit this afternoon and convince him that he should leave. Once he agrees, I'm sure that you could manage to get him on your boat this afternoon. I seem to remember that there are supplies kept below the deck, and one of the rooms should have enough space so that the grandfather could remain there out of sight until the boat is well away from Saigon. By the time Madame Le discovers that he is also aboard, she will be so happy to see him that she will forget everything else. Besides, it will be too late to turn back. Incidentally, I will pay you for his passage."

"My Younger Brother is very clever, but not that clever. There is no charge for the passage of Le Chin Kuang. I will go to see him as soon as I leave here. Then a little later I will send two men—an old man and a young man—to pick up some fresh supplies. The supplies will be brought back by an old man and a young man, but it will be a different old man. Now let us discuss Madame Le, for I must leave you soon. Tell her that she must reach the boat before the dinner trade is over. Tell her there will be a boatman with his boat at the wharf. His name is Luk Foy and he is loyal to me. He will not take any passenger but her. Tell her she must disguise her clothing and wear no paint on her face. There may be people looking for her. She is to ask the boatman if he is Luk Foy and tell him that she brings a message from my Younger Brother.

He will put her aboard. Tell her to have her pedicab waiting, and in a short time a somewhat similar lady will come off the boat, carrying a bag of food, and will leave in the pedicab."

"It sounds good," I said. Switching to Chinese, I added, "May the gods reward my Elder Brother since he will not let me do so."

"It is nothing. If the gods think kindly of us, we will see each other again."

I watched him walk to the door and leave without looking back. He was a good man, and I wondered if I would ever see him again. I was still looking at the door when it opened and there was Thuy.

Again she looked entirely different. Her face was older and she was dressed like a peasant woman. The clothes were not ragged, but they did show signs of wear. To complete the picture, she carried something wrapped in newspapers. It could have been a couple of chickens or some extra clothes she had picked up from a street table. She dropped it on the floor and it made a solid thump.

"Do I please you, my lord?" she asked in a singsong voice.

"You are, indeed, a moon flower come to life. What is in the newspapers? Your dinner?"

"Many dinners. These are the possessions of an old woman, including many dollars in American money. When they are exposed to the air, they look like rays from a full moon. Shall I cage them somewhere, or do you wish to count them?"

"The temptation might be too great. After all, I am only a caretaker for a short time. How did the moving go?"

"Very well. Only the people who live in the small commune

even knew that someone was moving. My grandfather was pleased with the new apartment. He is pleased with me, but I know he will miss me, as I will miss him."

"Perhaps the gods will see that you are together again one day. In the meantime, everything is arranged for you. You will leave Saigon about midnight, but you are to be at the boat before ten while the diners are enjoying themselves."

"Who is taking me?"

"Tang Lok Hee."

"I should have guessed. I have always thought he was little more than a river pirate. But you like him and my grandfather likes him, so I must be in error. Does he know why I am going?"

"Yes. He also approves. He will not charge for taking you."

"In that case," she said with a smile, "where shall I put the money?"

"Shouldn't you take some with you?"

"I already have pinned a few bills under my shirt. No one will think of trying to assault an old peasant woman, so it will be safe."

"Okay. Open my suitcase and put it in there. You can leave the paper around it or wrap it up in some of my clothes. While you're at it, get out my full duty uniform. Also take out my ribbons, a shirt, shoes and socks, and shorts."

"Want me to help you dress?"

"I would love it," I said, "but one of the nurses would be sure to come in at the most interesting time. I do think, however, I can manage. One of the nurses can button my jacket and my shirt and tie my shoes. That should take care of it."

She pushed the package over to the suitcase and opened it. "Oh! You do have a hidden treasure in here." She held up a bottle of Canadian Club, three-quarters full.

"I'd forgotten it was there. We might as well take a break and have a drink."

"An excellent suggestion, my lord." She took the glasses into the bathroom and rinsed them out. She filled them with ice and whiskey and handed one to me.

"To your trip," I said.

"To my trip," she repeated sadly. "Did Tang Lok Hee have any other instructions for me?"

"Yes. When you arrive at the wharf, there will be a boatman there waiting to take you to the ship. His name is Luk Foy. He will warn you if there is anyone there looking for you and will get you aboard at once. How did you get here this time, Thuy?"

"Pedicab. It is one from the section where my grandfather is now. He is waiting for me downstairs."

"Isn't he liable to be spotted?"

She laughed. "No chance. There is an underground garage for the doctors and nurses. He and his pedicab are inside the garage and will stay there until I come back. They will be looking elsewhere for me."

"All right," I said. "The uniform I was wearing is hanging in that closet. Empty out the pockets and put everything on this stand. That includes the eagles for the shoulders."

She did as I asked. There was some money, cigarettes, matches, and a ring with a few keys on it. "That small key," I said, "is for my suitcase. Make sure everything else is in it, then close it and lock it." I waited while she did that. "Now look in my duffel bag. You will find a small gun there with extra bullets for it. Take it with you."

She wrapped it up in a scarf and put it away in some part of her clothes. "Anything else, Milo?"

"Yes. Did you bring your account number in Macao?"

She pulled a small piece of paper from another part of her clothes and placed it on the stand.

"I will send the money to your bank as soon as I get to New York. That will depend on when the hospital in Washington releases me, so it might take a week or two."

"I have enough money until then. Is there anything else you want, Milo?"

"Yes. Let's have another drink together."

She poured the drinks and added ice cubes. She handed me one glass and raised the other one. "To one more day, Milo."

"To one more," I repeated.

We drank and I suddenly felt very tired. I couldn't think of anything I might have forgotten. There was nothing else, and I could feel the tension leaving my muscles. "I don't know what day I'll be back in New York, but if you need to reach me, you can phone me. I have two listed numbers there. Good luck, Thuy."

"I've already had my good luck, Milo. You." She stood up and walked over to the bed. She looked down at me, then suddenly leaned over and kissed me. "Thank you for coming to Saigon and quietly drifting into my life. And thank you for drifting as quietly out of my life, as you are doing now. Will I ever see you again, Milo?"

"I can only tell you what Tang Lok Hee told me. He said, 'If the gods think kindly of us, we will see each other again.' And I tell you the same."

She smiled. "I have gambled on almost everything in my life. I have now reached a point where I will gamble on the ancient gods. Good night, Milo." She turned and walked with regal grace from the room. In some ways, I thought, she *was* a princess.

The night nurse came in and gave me my medicine. "They'll be coming for you early in the morning, Colonel March. You've had a busy little day. Now go to sleep."

I outranked her, but I obeyed....

SIXTEEN

The nurse awakened me at five-thirty in the morning. While I was getting the sleep out of my eyes, she brought my breakfast. She warned me that there wasn't too much time.

I felt that there must have been a peephole in the door because the minute I'd finished the last bite, she came back to pick up the tray. "You need help in getting dressed, Colonel?"

"I don't know," I admitted, "but it's time I find out. If I haven't learned by this time, I'm in trouble. I'll ring if I need help."

When she was gone, I sat up on the edge of the bed. So far, so good. I stood up. My legs were a little wobbly, but I won that argument. And the one with the shorts and socks. I even managed to put my pants on, but that was a little harder. The shirt was easy, but I couldn't button it. I gave up and rang for the nurse.

She buttoned my shirt while I tucked my tails in. She did most of the work with my jacket, my tie, and my shoes. Then she pinned on my silver eagles and fruit salad.

"Well," she said, stepping back and looking at me, "you survived that, so you must be practically recovered. Don't try to overdo the standing up. You've lost a lot of blood and you're bound to be weak for a few days. Sit down and rest until they get here." She reached over and tapped the fruit salad. "You'll get another ribbon to add to those."

"I'd rather have a raise in pay."

"You'd be unhappy if you were given one. It wouldn't help the way you talk to the underprivileged of the Army. Who could you browbeat?"

"Generals," I said happily. "I already do."

She laughed. "I'll bet you do. Sit down and rest. Would you like a drink?"

"I thought you'd never ask, Lieutenant. I'll predict that you go far in the Army."

She dropped ice cubes into the glass and poured the drink. "To a quick return, Colonel. How will you feel when you come down in Washington?"

"Good, but not as good as I will when I reach New York."

"Is that where you're stationed?"

"I'm not stationed anywhere. I'm in the Reserves, but I get recalled whenever there's dirty work to be done. How long since you've been home, Lieutenant?"

"Too long. But the scoop is that we may all be shipped out within the next two or three days. It must mean that everybody's healthier."

"That's one way of looking at it," I said dryly. I lifted the drink. "To you, Lieutenant. Happy landings." I finished the drink and put the glass down.

The door opened and they came in. They consisted of a colonel, a major, a captain, and three noncoms. The colonel was a medical officer. That meant the noncoms were along to do the work. Dante was looking at them as if he wasn't sure whether to charge or hide.

"It's all right, Dante," I said. "They are merely the *nibo-*

nicho." There was a questioning look on the face of the nurse, so I explained. "That is Russian for 'nonbelievers.' Dante understands the language. You've heard of drug-sniffing dogs? Well, Dante is a language-sniffer."

The nurse put a hand over her smile and the Colonel stared at me as if he were wondering if he should have brought a straitjacket. The rest of the soldiers looked as if they did this every day.

"The suitcase is mine," I told them. "There's nothing in it except clothing and a handgun. It's locked, and it and the duffel bag go wherever I go in the plane. I'm ready."

"All right, men," the Colonel ordered. Two of the noncoms picked up the two pieces of luggage and followed the officers from the room. The third noncom looked around the room and shrugged. "May I sit down, sir?"

"Help yourself, Sergeant," I said. I crossed to the stand next to the bed and opened the drawer. I took out most of my money and stuffed it into my pocket. I also took a lone package of cigarettes, which left two partially filled bottles of whiskey. I motioned to the nurse to come over. She did and looked into the drawer.

"The spoils of war," I said.

"Thank you, Colonel," she said with a smile. Her gaze fixed on the two ten-dollar bills partly hidden under one bottle. "What is all this?"

"The two more solid objects are for toasts to the day you return home. The fragile items are for at least more toasts. Call it, if you like, an oversight on my part." I closed the drawer and glanced out the window. Down below, I could make out an ambulance, a big limousine, and several other cars.

"It looks more like a parade than a military escort," I said. "The condemned man doesn't even get to enjoy walking that last mile. Instead, I have the honor of being bounced over it."

As I turned back, another sergeant entered the room carrying a stretcher. He saluted me. "Whenever you're ready, sir."

"Anytime. How do you want me? Sunny side up or scrambled?"

He looked puzzled, then glanced at the nurse as if seeking a clue. She came forward to stand beside me. "He wants you to lie down on the stretcher, face up. The best way to make it is for you to first sit down on it. I'll help you get down and then help you stretch out. Put as much weight on your right arm as you feel you need." She put her hands under my shoulders and I made it down in good shape. Then she shifted her hands to support my back. "Down we go." She eased me down, and I didn't feel any pain, so my shoulder must have been getting better.

She walked around in front of me. "I used to have a friend," she said, "who was in the same part of the service as I think you are. He had a favorite expression that he used as a toast. It was 'One more day.' I wish the same to you, Colonel March."

"Thank you, Lieutenant. I also want to thank you and Lieutenant Summers for putting up with Dante and me. Please do one more favor for me. Pick up Dante and put him on my lap where I can hold him." I raised my voice. "Dante, it's all right. She's a friend. She's going to bring you to me."

A moment later, the nurse reappeared with Dante. "Did he

really understand you?" she asked as she put him on my lap. He made a soft sound in his throat as he looked at me.

"He says it was his pleasure," I said. "He understands almost everything. Well, good-bye, Lieutenant."

"Happy landings," she said, and stepped back. The two soldiers picked up the stretcher and we left.

It was a fairly short ride to the airport. The ambulance came to a stop and the back doors opened. I could barely believe what I saw. The usual crowd of Vietnamese was on hand, but between the crowd and us there were enough soldiers to look like an army. All Americans. Part of them were Military Police and the rest Infantrymen, all of them armed with automatic rifles. Somebody must have decided they didn't want me to be greeted by another hand grenade. The big limousine was there, an American flag flying from one front fender and a red rectangle with white star insignia indicating this was a general's personal transport from the other, and General Lawson and his aide were getting out. They walked toward some point behind me. I twisted my head to take a look. There was a big jet on the field, and near it a small group of men.

My attention was attracted by hearing my name shouted. I looked around until I spotted a man struggling to get through a line of Military Police who were trying to keep the crowd from spilling over on the field.

"Hold it," I said to the men who were carrying me. "Can you get an officer over here? If not, then carry me over to where that sergeant is trying to get through the line of military fuzz. And I mean today."

The corporal waved wildly in the direction of the plane.

His arm dropped and he looked at me with surprise. "There's an officer coming, sir. On the run."

Well, I thought, that had brought somebody to life. He was soon beside the stretcher. It was Colonel Blake.

"Where the hell is the damned band? That's about the only thing that's missing."

"Quite a show, isn't it?" he asked dryly. "You're suddenly a brand-new hero and might last ten minutes before they change their minds. What can I do for you?"

"See that man over there trying to get through the line? That's Sergeant Dan Farrow, who isn't trying to get my autograph. He was my driver while I was here. I want to see him."

"Consider it done." He strode toward the line. When he was near enough to be sure they saw his silver eagles, he stopped and yelled. The struggling stopped and Dan broke through the line. He came running across the field.

"I never saw such a crazy bunch," he said as he reached me. "What the hell's wrong with them?"

"It's known as grenade phobia," I said. "Maybe a little brass blindness too. Where's your wife?"

"She couldn't even get to the line, but she said if I didn't get through, she'd never speak to me again. We brought you a present." His hand came into view with a package, which he placed beside me on the stretcher. I didn't have to examine it. I knew it would gurgle if it was shaken. "Thank you, Dan. Are you sure she's safe there?"

"A couple of my buddies are guarding her. We just wanted to say thanks for everything. My wife is crazy over that necklace you gave her, and we're both crazy over your present to me. The order came through and we're leaving Saigon tomorrow."

"I'm glad, Dan," I said. "Don't forget to call me when you get settled. I forgot to tell you something. Do you still have the wrapping from the present to your wife?"

"She never throws anything away. Why?"

"My address and phone number are written on the outside of the paper. When you get settled and have that bar opened, call me. I'll come out to have a drink at your bar."

"That'll be great. But you should know something else. That call of yours to the general in Washington must have done more good than you know. My whole company is being shipped back in three or four days. And that's not all. The scuttlebutt is that hundreds of guys are going to be shipped out for home within the next week. Maybe ten days."

"It's about time," I said. "Happy landing. ... All right, fellows, let's go. The General looks like he is getting nervous."

The next stop was beside the group of officers standing near the plane. They marched by the stretcher one by one, saying nice things to me, which didn't conceal the fact that they were glad to get rid of me. The last one to reach me was Colonel Blake.

"Never saw anything like it," he said. "They shower presents or ribbons or nice words with one hand, and with the other one they give you a little push toward the back door. Happy landings, Colonel."

"Thanks," I said. "Will you do me one more favor, Colonel?"

"Well, I don't think I can have Madame Le arrested and put on board the plane, but I'll do almost anything else."

"Just make sure that my suitcase and duffel bag are put right next to me on the plane."

"That's the easiest job I've had since I've been in the Army. Will do." He strode toward the plane.

The two noncoms carried me into the elevator at the side of the plane and we were lifted to a door that led into it. They carried me inside, where there was already a bed prepared for me. I was placed on it and the stretcher was removed. Another noncom appeared with my luggage and put it down next to me. A few minutes later I felt the plane moving down the takeoff strip. When we were finally airborne and leveled off, the Colonel came back from the cockpit to see me.

"The natives are restless today," he said with a smile. "We'll soon reach our ceiling, but we'll probably have to run through some flak to make it. Anything I can get for you in the meantime?"

"Yes. A glass and some ice cubes, if you have any."

He nodded and went forward. He brought back the glass and some ice in a plastic bag. I had just unwrapped Dan's present for me. It was a bottle of Canadian Club.

"Care to join me?" I asked.

"Maybe later," he said. "Keep an eye on your glass. Sometimes we have to do a little sneaky dodging. There's one more precaution against the danger of things rolling on the floor. Here, I'll fix it." He leaned over and picked up the two ends of a strap and buckled it across me. "What about your dog?"

"He'll stay with me and I'll hold him."

He stepped across the plane where there was another hospital bed and sat down. "Where'd you get the newest Purple Heart?"

"In the air over North Vietnam."

"What were you doing there? You're not in the Air Force."

"No. I was in Hanoi on a mission, and there was a Russian general there who recognized me and used his influence to get them to turn me over to him for a visit to Moscow. There was another American there in prison, and he became part of the passenger list. After we were on our way, I managed to take over the plane and headed it for Saigon. They sent two fighter planes after us. One of them hit me in the shoulder. That's all there was to it. How long have you been nursing this invalid plane?"

"Not long. I was flying bombers most of the time. Those B-52s are really something, especially after the 29s we used in Korea. In one way, that wasn't too bad. Their anti-aircraft gunners weren't too accurate, but we were bombing almost around the clock, so none of us got much sleep."

"A shortage of pilots?"

He shook his head. "More a shortage of time. Bombers were going out to drop their bombs and coming back to load up again like they were on conveyor belts."

"That sounds like a lot of bombs."

"You'd better believe it," he said. "If you like figures, here's something for you to think about. We dropped two million tons of bombs during World War Two. And we dropped a half million tons more than that from 1968 to March of 1971.

It eased off somewhat after that, but not a hell of a lot."* He stood up. "Well, back to the salt mines. See you later."

I put ice cubes in the glass and poured Canadian Club over it and lit a cigarette. The first drink tasted fine. I relaxed and thought back over the last few days. Everything seemed to have worked out fine—maybe too fine. It was, however, too late to change anything. I finished the drink and went to sleep.

Three hours later, I was awake. The scenery was the same and so was the sound. I solved it by pouring a fresh drink and lighting a cigarette. Just then the Colonel came strolling back. "We have some cold cuts if you're hungry. I'm afraid that is about all on the menu."

"I'm not hungry," I said, "but I'll accept for Dante. I think he'd like some water, too, if it's not too much trouble."

"No trouble at all." He went forward and returned with two bowls and a glass. He put the bowls down. I lifted Dante and placed him in front of the bowl with the meat. He went right to work.

"Help yourself," I told the Colonel, gesturing at the bottle and ice.

"Don't mind if I do. Just a short one while I try to forget that I'm on duty."

"Don't think of it. I doubt if there are any traffic cops up here, but you can always explain that you were drinking while under the influence of flying."

He laughed. "I'll remember that. Well, back to the salt mines."

---

* According to *A People's History of the United States* (1980) by Howard Zinn, "By the end of the Vietnam war, 7 million tons of bombs had been dropped on Vietnam, more than twice the total bombs dropped on Europe and Asia in World War II."

He picked up the bowls, which were already empty, and left. I picked up Dante and deposited him next to me. He curled up and went to sleep. I did the same thing a few minutes later.

That was the story of our flight. I would sleep two or three hours, then have a long, slow drink and go to back to sleep. The naps merged into a blur of time, and I lost count of the periods of wakefulness and sleep.

Finally I awakened and saw the Colonel standing outside the cockpit and looking at me. "Good morning, Colonel March," he said. "Welcome to the city of Washington. We'll be on the ground within a few minutes. There's an ambulance waiting for you there."

It worked out like he said. My luggage, Dante, and I were taken to the ground in the elevator. Two soldiers came to pick up the stretcher and carried me off in the direction of the ambulance. One of them opened the doors, and they slid the stretcher inside. A moment later they put my luggage inside and the doors slammed shut. There was a shout from outside and the ambulance began to move.

"Hello, Bamboo Tiger," she said.

It took a few seconds for it to penetrate. It was too dark to see anything. "Marya," I said, "where are you?"

"About two feet from you. Don't you remember that I told you I would meet you at the field when you returned? Well, you're here and so am I. How do you feel?"

"Everybody asks the same damn question. I feel a little out of focus, probably from too much sleep, and I'm a little tender in one shoulder. Otherwise, I'm fine. When we reach the hospital, we'll talk about anything except how I feel. Okay?"

"Okay, but not convenient, Milo. I have a hundred questions I want to ask you. I want to hear the whole story. But it will have to wait. The hospital says absolutely no visitors today. When we arrive, I shall get into the car and drive home. You will go upstairs and do whatever they tell you to do. We'll talk when they say it's all right. Those are orders from General Baxter."

I muttered a few words about General Baxter, but she ignored them. "Where's Dante?" she asked.

Dante must have understood, for there was a soft sound in his throat. She laughed at the sound. "He's smarter than you are, Milo."

The ambulance braked to a stop. The back doors opened. Marya was out before anyone realized she was there. "I'll call you in the morning, Milo," she said, and disappeared around the side of the ambulance.

Two privates were there to carry me into the hospital and up to a room. There were three doctors waiting there. As soon as I was in bed, they started getting my clothes off and looking me over. They spent most of the time on my shoulder.

"You're doing all right, Colonel," one of the medics said. "The team in Saigon did a fine job on the operation. Everything else seems to be in good shape. We'll run a few tests on you in the morning, but we're pretty certain you're making a good recovery. We'll get you on your feet in a very short time. Good night." They left.

I looked around the room and spotted my luggage. I remembered that Dan's present of the bottle of Canadian Club had been in a box on the stretcher with me. I looked around. It was on the stand next to the bed, so I left it there for the moment.

A nurse came bustling in. She took my temperature, gave me medicine, and left. I had intended to ask her for some ice, but I was already feeling so sleepy that I let it pass.

The same three doctors were in early the next morning. They didn't waste much time. They x-rayed me, drew blood for the lab, and probed and prodded until I almost imagined they were checking to see if I was fat enough for slaughter. Then two of them left and the third lingered.

"You're in good shape, Colonel," he said. "The shoulder has started healing nicely. The surgeon in Saigon did a fine job on repairing the bone damage. The lab tests also came out fine. There was, however, one strange thing about the test of your blood. It showed a rather high content of alcohol. How do you account for that?"

"By taking a drink when I feel like it. That's the easiest way."

"Well, you've survived pretty well. You must have pretty regular habits about eating. Mostly high protein, I suspect. You should be out in a few days."

"I'll be out as soon as I can walk down and get into a car. And as soon as I'm in New York City, I'll be out of the Army. As you leave, please ask the nurse to bring me some ice cubes."

He laughed. "All right, Colonel, but I don't know about leaving so soon. We'll see." He left.

The door opened and the nurse came in. She was carrying a tall paper cup with ice cubes in it. She plunked it down beside the Canadian Club. "You have a visitor, Colonel March. General Baxter has approved of the visit."

"Show her in."

She walked back and held the door open while Marya Cooper walked in, then left and closed the door. Marya walked over to the bed and saluted. "Sergeant Cooper reporting for duty, sir."

"Reporting for duty, hell! What kind of duty?"

She leaned over and kissed me. "That, for one thing. General Baxter told me that I was responsible for your complete recovery and that I was to get on the job."

"What the hell is wrong with all of you? I went on a simple mission, took a scratch on the shoulder, and everyone acts as if I'd just led the Charge of the Light Brigade. Pour me a drink."

"Yes, sir." She poured the drink and handed it to me. "Anything else, sir?"

"Yes. Get me out of here as soon as I finish this drink."

"General Baxter says you'll be able to leave within a few days."

"To hell with that. Get on the phone and tell General Baxter I want to talk to him. Now!"

"All right, Milo." She walked around the bed to the phone and asked the operator to get General Baxter. She waited, smiling at me. "This is Sergeant Cooper," she said finally. "Let me speak to General Baxter." There was another short wait. "Yes, sir. I'm with him now. He wants to speak to you. ... Yes, sir." She handed the phone to me.

I took it. "Good morning, General Baxter."

"Good morning, Colonel March. How are you feeling?"

"Fine. Get me out of here."

"The doctors think you should stay for several days more."

"General Baxter," I said, "I am leaving this hospital today. This morning, in fact. If necessary, I will tear up a sheet and tie Sergeant Cooper up, knock a nurse down, and walk out. I have finished my tour of duty and am going to become a civilian as soon as I reach New York City. Do you read me?"

"Loud and clear, Colonel. If I was sure you couldn't make it, I'd put you under room arrest."

"I was in prison in Hanoi and I got out. I was in the custody of the Russians and I got away. There's no way you can keep me in here. Now, tell me about Sergeant Dan Farrow. Is he on his way home?"

"He left today. I think his whole company will be leaving Saigon this week or next."

"A strategic withdrawal?"

"I am told that it is planned to get all of our servicemen out of the area in the near future. The Defense Department has already announced that there will be less than twenty thousand Americans there by the end of the month."

"That's a lot of advisors," I said dryly. "Okay, General, I'll see you the next trip around."

"I expect so, Colonel. I'll let the hospital know that you're leaving today." He hung up.

"He's going to order the hospital to release you today? I don't know how you get away with it."

"It's my natural charm."

"Well, it fits in with one thing," Marya said. "Colonel Locke said he would be over this morning to get Dante. In fact, he should be here soon. In the meantime, I'll go downstairs and see if I can grab one or two privates to come up and get your luggage."

"Ask the nurse to come in while you're passing through."

She nodded and left. I poured myself another drink and sipped it as I waited. But the nurse was there almost at once.

"Would you like me to bring you some breakfast?" she asked.

"I'm already having it. But I will get some solid food when I get out. General Baxter is probably already on the phone, ordering the hospital to discharge me at once. Sergeant Cooper has gone to try to get a couple of soldiers to come up and carry my luggage. Do you have a place where you can keep the dog for a short time? A Colonel Locke will come to pick him up. Please tell him that I'm not allowed any visitors. The dog belongs to him. I'm not in the mood to see Colonel Locke."

"All right," she said uncertainly. "You've already broken so many rules, I don't suppose one more will mean anything. Will he follow me?"

"Sure." I let my arm hang over the side of the bed and called softly to Dante. He came over next to my hand and looked up at me. I rubbed his head with affection. "Dante, old boy," I said, "I'm glad that you went with me. You were a help and a pleasure."

He tilted his head and licked my hand. Each of us had said good-bye in his own way, so Dante went to the middle of the room and stretched out.

"Stand up and say hello to the lady. She's a friend." He stood up and wagged his tail. "Go with her, Dante. She will take good care of you. And I'll see you around, old buddy."

She moved toward the door and he followed. He looked back once, and then they were gone. I poured a big drink and went to work on it. I wasn't so tired, so it must have been the sight of Dante going out of the room that had left the lump in my throat.

ENVOI

There was a light knock on the door and it opened. It was one of my doctors. He came in and closed the door. He looked at me and smiled. "I would like to know something. How can a colonel pull enough rank on a general so that we get a call ordering us to discharge the colonel from the hospital at once?"

"It's simple. I carried out an order which came from him. I told the Army how to get out of a difficult situation with the Soviet Union—and he may need me some other time."

"It seems to work, so it must be a sound approach. Since you are leaving this morning, I want to put a fresh bandage on your shoulder. You can probably remove it in two or three days."

"Okay," I said. He went to work and soon finished.

"Happy landings, Colonel," he said. He turned and left.

I sat up on the edge of the bed and lit a cigarette. I finished the drink and waited impatiently, but the door soon opened and Marya came in. "I found one private, and he'll be here in a few minutes. He's big enough to carry both pieces. In the meantime, I'll help you get dressed and we'll be able to leave as soon as he takes then down. Where's Dante?"

"I sent him out with the nurse, who will turn him over to Kim Locke."

"The transfer must have already taken place, because he's not with the nurse. Where are your clothes?"

"In the closet. I can put most of them on myself, but you'll have to help with things like buttons."

She picked up the bottle and put it in the small bag, then went to the closet and got out my uniform, shirt, socks, and shoes. I dressed as far as I could go, then she took over. It was soon finished and she stepped back to look at me. "There," she said. "The perfect picture of a handsome officer."

"Flattery will get you nowhere, Sergeant."

There was a knock on the door and Marya went over and opened it. A private was standing there. He looked at me and saluted. "Are those the two bags, sir?"

"Yes," Marya said. "Put them in the General's car, right in front of the hospital. Put them in the back seat. Thank you, Private."

He saluted me again, picked up the two bags, and left.

"Let's go, Milo," Marya said.

"The sooner the better. After you, Sergeant."

We went downstairs and got into the car. The bags were already in the rear, but the private was no longer in sight. She started the car and pulled away from the curb.

"I have an indefinite leave of absence from General Baxter," she said. "Are you still going to help me?"

"I said so, didn't I? When we get to your apartment, I want you to phone an airlines office and get two seats for us to New York for this afternoon."

"Yes, sir."

She drove straight to her apartment. "I'm already packed.

All I have to do is get out of this uniform and put on a dress. We can leave your luggage in the car."

"No. I will carry the larger piece upstairs myself." I got out, opened the rear door, and got the suitcase. "The duffel bag can stay in the car. Let's go."

We went up to the apartment. With some assistance from Marya, I got the suitcase on top of the table and then sat down. "First, I'll have a very dry martini. The most exciting drink I had while I was gone was the blood of a freshly killed pig mixed with warm wine. It almost made me join Alcoholics Anonymous, but my sanity returned in time."

She went into the kitchen and mixed a martini. She brought it in and put it down in front of me. "Is there anything else the Colonel wishes?"

"Yes. Do you have any fairly large manila envelopes?"

"I'll get what I have." She went into the bedroom and came back with a number of them and put them on the table. "Is there anything else my lord desires?"

"Yes. Just because I'm fresh from Vietnam doesn't mean that you have to talk like an Oriental stereotype. Call the airlines office." I lit a cigarette and took a drink of the martini. She was dialing the phone as I opened the suitcase and took out the bundle of money.

"Milo," she called. "We can get a plane to New York in about two hours."

"Make the reservation."

I started unwrapping the money and putting it in stacks. It was a little difficult with only one arm, but I started counting it.

"We have the reservation," Marya said.

"Good. Get dressed."

"Stop pulling rank on me," she said as she headed for the bedroom.

I started counting the money. I had reached almost sixty thousand dollars by the time she had returned. She was wearing a red dress that almost made me forget the money. Almost, but not completely.

"What is that?" she asked.

"Money. Lovely, isn't it? Sit down and start stuffing the money from that pile into the envelopes. Try to get as much as you can into each envelope but not enough to make them look suspicious. I don't want to be held up before I get it into the bank."

"Whose money is it?"

"A citizen of Saigon. Both South and North Vietnam take a dim view of anyone removing money from the country. I am therefore the temporary custodian of it until I can get to my bank and have them send a bank draft to another bank in Macao."

"Is it legal?"

"Depends on your point of view. I consider it legal. And no one can make a more legal claim on it than the person who will receive it. Enough of that. Let's go get the plane. Maybe there'll even be an earlier plane and we can transfer to it."

"I have to get my bag from the bedroom."

"Okay," I packed the envelopes into the suitcase, then went to the bathroom. When I came out, she was on the phone but put the receiver down as I entered the living room.

"What was that?" I asked.

"I called the Pentagon. We're taking General Baxter's car to the airport, and I was calling Corporal Wild, telling her when she could pick it up. Let's go."

We went down and got into the car. I took my suitcase into the front seat with me and placed it on my lap. I opened it and took out the manila envelopes. I closed the suitcase and put it down by my feet. The envelopes were on my lap.

"Stop at a store," I told her, "and buy something that will hold these. A big briefcase, a small suitcase, anything."

She spotted a store within a few blocks and stopped. I gave her some money. It didn't take her long to come out with something that looked just the right size. I began to transfer the envelopes to the new case. By the time I'd finished, we were at the airport. We turned everything except the case with the envelopes over to a porter and boarded the plane.

When we were airborne, a stewardess came down the aisle. We ordered two martinis, and when they came, we settled back in the seats.

"Milo," she said, "I want to hear everything, and I have a million questions to ask. But when we get there, I don't want to stay at a hotel."

"Where do you want to stay?"

"At your apartment. My orders are to take care of you."

"All right. Just relax."

It's a short flight from Washington to New York, and we were soon coming in for a landing. We waited for our luggage, then got a taxi. I gave the driver the address of my apartment on Perry Street. Marya was busy looking out the window, so there was little conversation.

"Leave the meter running," I told the driver as he stopped in front of the building. "I can only use one arm, so I'll appreciate it if you'll help us upstairs with the luggage. Then I want you to drive me to another address."

We all got out. I carried the case with the money, Marya took the duffel bag, and the driver carried the other two bags. When we reached my floor I unlocked the door. Marya entered and the driver stepped inside and put down the bags.

"Where are you going?" Marya asked.

"I have to go to the bank, then I'll stop by the office and pick up my mail. I won't be long." I followed the driver down the stairs and into the taxi. I gave him the address of my bank on Madison Avenue. It was a short ride. I paid him off and went in.

After talking to two people, I was finally shown into an office and greeted by three men. I dumped the money on a desk. They turned their full attention to the money, reminding me of a hen rushing to protect her chicks. They were all three counting money, stopping frequently to feel a bill or hold it to the light and also to examine the serial number. I lit a cigarette and waited.

When they finished, they compared notes with each other. Finally they stopped and one of them looked at me. "Our figures show that there is fifty-nine thousand, eight hundred dollars here. Did you wish this deposited to your account, Mr. March?"

"No," I said. "I wish to exchange it for a bank check to be sent to this account number at this bank in Macao. You may deduct the cost of transferring it there and make the bank check for the amount of the balance."

"It will be more simple than that, Mr. March. We do business with a bank in Macao, and it will only be necessary to send them a cablegram and the money will be immediately deposited in the account there."

A few more minutes were spent in going over everything again, and then I left. It was less than two blocks to my office, so I walked it. There was a lot of mail scattered over the floor. I picked it up and glanced through it quickly. Most of it was obviously junk mail, but a few pieces looked like they might be of some value. I dumped them all into the case that I had used to carry the money. I picked up the phone and called my answering service. There had been only two calls for me that had any meaning. One had been from Martin Raymond at Intercontinental Insurance, asking me to call him as soon as I got back. That probably meant he had a job for me. The other call had been from Macao. The only message was a phone number and the name Le Thuy Duong. I picked up the phone and put in the call. The operator told me to hang up and she'd call me as soon as she had the party on the line.

I put the receiver down and opened the top drawer of my desk. There was a bottle of bourbon there. I took it out and poured myself a drink and sipped it while I waited. I had just about finished it when the phone rang. I picked it up and said hello.

"Milo," she said. "Is it really you?"

"I think so, but I'm not really sure. I haven't looked in a mirror yet. How are you, Thuy?"

"You recognized my voice," she said with delight.

"I recognized your voice, but I also put in the call to you. I didn't think the call would be answered by Ngoc Dinh Binh."

She laughed. "How are you feeling?"

"My shoulder is still a little sore, but that's all. I am also sick and tired of hospitals and sick and tired of the Army. I got back to New York a little more than an hour ago, so I'm slightly tired. How are you, Thuy?"

"Very happy. You have given me the best surprise present possible."

"The money can't have arrived there yet. I made arrangements for it to be sent only a few minutes ago."

"I wasn't talking about money," she said. "I mean my grandfather. I had been certain I would never see him again. And he is also happy. He's already met several old friends whom he last saw many years ago. And I have found a wonderful restaurant that I can buy. It is in a large building which also includes large and attractive living quarters above the restaurant. My grandfather can live there with me and I can look after him. I am grateful."

"The money should be there today. Tomorrow at the latest. The amount is almost sixty thousand dollars. The bank will send it directly to your bank. Actually, my bank here does business with your bank and has funds there. They are sending a cablegram to your bank telling them to transfer that amount of money to your account."

"The building is being held for me. I already have plans for the restaurant, both inside and out. I even have a name for it, which I think will please you. The Yuan Mei Restaurant."

"After the poet-gastronome?" I thought for a moment. "It

might sound good to name it after his book of recipes, 'The Garden of Contentment.' "

"Milo, you are brilliant. How can I thank you?"

"Just do one thing for me, Thuy. Remember that today—every day—is the first day of the rest of your life and the first day of a new year. And you are starting a new life and a new year. *Gung hay fat choy.*"*

"To you, too, Milo. Perhaps even the ancient gods will bless both of us and we will see each other again. ... Good-bye, Milo." There was a click as she hung up.

I went downstairs and took a taxi back to Perry Street. Marya was sitting on the couch, looking frustrated. "What's wrong?" I asked.

"I tidied up, and I wanted to have a nice lunch ready for us by the time you got here. But there's no food in the house, and I couldn't go shopping because I didn't have a key to get back into the apartment."

"Naturally, there isn't any food in the house, except for a few canned things. The food would only spoil, silly. We're going out for lunch as soon as I can change out of these military rags. We're going to go out for dinner tonight too. Tomorrow we'll worry about shopping."

"What should I wear?"

"What you have on. We're going to a small place very near

---

* The saying "Today is the first day of the rest of your life," popularized in the 1960s and '70s, is attributed to the founder of Syanon, Charles Dederich. *Gung hay fat choy* is the greeting for the Chinese New Year in the Cantonese dialect (which predominated both in Hong Kong and among the Chinese Vietnamese); it is literally a wish for happiness and prosperity. In 1975 the Chinese New Year fell in February; the fall of Saigon was on April 30. So Milo's new year wishes refer figuratively to a fresh start in life.

here, but the food is good. Let me get changed. I've always hated uniforms." I went into the bedroom and changed. I felt better at once. "Ready?" I asked as I returned to the living room.

She looked me up and down. "It's the first time I've ever seen you in civilian clothes. Mmmmm! Not bad."

"Flattery will get you nowhere. Let's go."

We went downstairs and walked down to Barrow Street and over to the Blue Mill on Commerce. We stopped at the bar long enough for me to introduce Marya to the owner, Alcino, and say a few words. I told him to send us two martinis and we went back to a table. The martinis were there almost as soon as we were.

"I want to make a toast," I said. "Remember what I said to you about one more day?" She nodded. "Well, another way of saying it is: Today is the first day of the rest of your life. It's like the first day of a new year. You're starting a new year and a new life. So, to you, Marya Cooper: *Gung hay fat choy!*"

"What does that mean?"

"Happy New Year." I lifted my glass. "Happy New Year, Marya."

AFTERWORD

Editing the Final Novel

Among the papers left behind after Ken Crossen's death in 1981 is a plot synopsis for a novel to be titled *The Bamboo Jail*. The three-page typescript (see pages 320-322) has essentially the same storyline as the completed *Death to the Brides*, except for the nationality of Milo's antagonist. The synopsis is spare: it does not include the role of the military dog Dante, lent to Milo by a character from another series, Kim Locke of the CIA; Marya, the stateside girlfriend who is a budding women's-libber; or the lengths that Milo goes to in ensuring a happy ending for Thuy, his lover in Vietnam, and Sergeant Dan Farrow, his loyal driver in Saigon. Milo's relationships with these characters give greater depth to the formulaic plot. To gather intelligence and rescue or kidnap a man are the typical missions of the six spy novels in the series of primarily detective adventures.* It is also typical for Milo to have affairs with at least two women and to bond with at least one male character, who is usually an assistant on the case.

The character named Thuy is referred to simply as a Chinese woman in the synopsis, but Thuy's ethnicity is ambiguous in

---

* *No Grave for March* (#2), *The Splintered Man* (#5), *So Dead the Rose* (#9), *Wanted: Dead Men* (#14), *Wild Midnight Falls* (#17), and *Death to the Brides* (#22).

the book manuscript. Despite having a Chinese grandfather, she has a Vietnamese name, and her brother's allegiance is to his Vietnamese identity. Though Chinese people were not a large percentage of the population of Vietnam, they had been a strong presence in commerce there since the French colonial period. As I wrote in a footnote to the novel, many Chinese took Vietnamese names and married Vietnamese spouses. It seems to me that Thuy is one of this minority, called variously Chinese Vietnamese, Sino-Vietnamese, or Hoa.

The synopsis says that Thuy falls in love with Milo and that he initially encourages her to think he will stay with her, because he needs her help to get to Hanoi. However, he seems to genuinely like her, while being aware that she could betray him. In one passage he lets her down easy. She says:

> "... I confess that I have had a few thoughts about us spending the rest of our lives in companionship. I have never felt that way about any man before. It may even be a childish fantasy. I do not dwell on it for long."
>
> "I understand," I said gently.

Milo cares enough about Thuy to go to considerable trouble to ensure her safety, but he has no problem parting from her. The departure of the little dog Dante, on the other hand, brings a lump to his throat.

There has never been a dog before in the Milo March books. Nor has a character from one of Crossen's other series ever stumbled into a Milo March novel. Kim Locke seems to enter the story only to lend Milo his dog. And here I must reveal a major bit of editing I did to this book.*

Throughout this series, I have done mostly minor copy editing. Being a professional book editor, I did a number of things that I felt Ken's editors at Holt should have done, such as correcting errors and changing character names that were too repetitive (Henri, Heinrich, Henry, Hank...). I made a few politically correct decisions about phrases that seemed too jarring to today's sensibility, such as deleting "His skin was so dark that I suspected it indicated an Indian ancestor somewhere" from *Six Who Ran*. (Although there are stereotypes in the series—notably the Italian hoods—two books feature positive African-American characters during the Jim Crow and Black Power periods: *A Hearse of Another Color* and *The Flaming Man*.) Normally it would be inappropriate for me to change much about a character. Dante, however, was a problem.

I discussed the problem with the writer Richard Lupoff, who contributed valuable editing to *Death to the Brides*, described in his foreword. In the Kim Locke books, Dante is a Hungarian puli, a breed weighing about twenty-five pounds and having long dreadlocks. He makes a unique companion to Major Locke in one story and two novels. But the first Kim Locke work—the story "The Red Candle" (written as by Christopher Monig)—was published in 1953. That would make Dante almost twenty-five years old in 1975, if we estimate his age at about age two in 1953. The puli's lifespan

---

* The digital manuscript, with tracked editing visible, is on file with the Howard Gotlieb Archival Research Center at Boston University, where researchers can also view a copy of the original hardcopy.

is twelve to sixteen years. We might expect such a working dog to retire by age ten in real life. The last Kim Locke novel, *The Gentle Assassin* (as by Clay Richards), was published in 1964, making Dante already thirteen then. Aside from the age problem, Dante's weight and coat would make him unsuitable to be carried through the jungle. After conferring with Dick Lupoff, I settled on the miniature pinscher as the best breed for a younger military working dog, to be named after the original Dante. I was happy to learn that the U.S. military actually uses miniature breeds for some missions.

No changes were made to Marya, though I would have liked her to stop jumping in and out of her red robe so many times. In fact, I did remove one of her requests to Milo: "Don't you want to get into your robe?" Marya is a nurturing woman who enjoys plying Milo with his favorite drinks and meals. There were so many drinks that I deleted two of them.* I thought she was rather pushy about asking Milo to facilitate her career ambitions (he's barely out of the hospital when she is once more making him promise to help).

But Milo likes intelligent, independent women. Marya is the one to whose arms he returns at the end. Yet there's no hint that he will stay with her any longer than it would take to get to the next Milo March book—if there had been one. At the end they drink a toast to the Chinese New Year, not because that holiday is actually upon them (it's not), but as a way of heralding a new start in life. For Marya that means pursuing her aspiration to be an Intelligence agent. And for

---

* See the afterword to *A Man in the Middle,* #16 in the series, in which I comment on Milo's drinking.

Milo? What might have been ahead for him? After reading about him marching through the jungle for many miles with a dog inside his jacket, I have to remind myself that he's now (in 1975) fifty-seven years old, given that he was thirty-four in the opening book of the series, *Hangman's Harvest* (1952). Yet he shows no signs of slowing down.

In letters to Elaine Greene, his foreign-rights agent in London, Ken Crossen spoke of working on a new Milo March novel, after *Death to the Brides* failed to get published. As explained in Dick Lupoff's foreword to this edition, Holt, Rinehart & Winston had declined to publish the book primarily because of the scene in which Milo treats President Nixon with disrespect and rejects the promotion that the president is giving him. Maybe there were other objections; I don't know, because none of that correspondence has survived, nor have previous versions of the manuscript. But Ken refused to make any changes to the book, and so it remained unpublished.

Here is how he described the situation to his friend Nick "Wooda" Carr in a letter of February 11, 1975:

Sorry to be so long in answering your letter but I was on the last leg of a new novel on which I had been working for four months. I finally finished it and put it in the mail yesterday, then I came home and collapsed. Actually, I could say I'd been writing it for ten years. I was then doing it for a specific editor who died the week I finished it. Some time later, I reread it and never submitted it anywhere. About five years ago, I decided I still liked the idea so I threw away the original and wrote it for the second tine. That I also didn't like. I then happened on some new research (the subject was Vietnam) and

THE N BAMBOO JAIL
A New Milo March Adventure
By M. E. Chaber

     Milo March is recalled into the Army and "loaned" to the
CIA for another mission. This time he is to go to Saigon, in full
uniform ostensibly as a military attache to the Embassy. Actually,
his real mission is two-fold. He's to try to find a Viet Cong center
in or near Saigon which Intelligence knows exists but hasn't been
able to find. They also want him to rescue an Intelligence man who
was Captured and is a prisoner in Hanoi.

     Milo shows up in Saigon with full dress uniform, plus all
the ribbons, and someone tries to blow him up almost the minute he
lands. Within the first two days there are two more attempts to kill
jim. Obviously there is some kind of leak.

     From a former Chinese friend, Milo learns that information
may be going through a popular Chinese restaurant in Saigon which
is frequented by American military and civilian personnel. He
starts going to the restaurant and meets the owner, a beautiful and
fairly young Chinese woman. He kax becomes friendly, and intimate,
with her and manages to drop the information that he had asked
for this assignment in order to undertake a mission which is
personal. He says that the American prisoner in Hanoi is a friend
of his and that he believes the man is being held because he is
suspected of being an Intellugenuo man. But Milo adds that he
knows the man is not and that if he can only reach Hanoi and talk
to government officials he is sure that he can convince them and
so negotiate the man's release.

tackled it with a brand new picture four months ago. This time I liked it and
sent it to my regular publisher. It may, however, blow up there because the
editor is afraid of timely subjects and this one is as timely as they come.*

---

* Letter reproduced in *The Pulp Magazine Scrapbook* by Wooda N. Carr (Ron
Hanna, Wild Cat Books, 2007).

The Chinese woman finally tells him that she can help him reach Hanoi. He accepts her offer. He also gets a certain amount of help from American military men in Vietnam although they don't know who he is or what he wants to do.

He goes with the woman north to an area where they are met by Viet Cong soldiers. The leader of the group is the brother of the woman and is very hostile. The woman, however, is already in love with Milo although this will not make her turn traitor to her own people. She hopes that once he is in Hanoi he will see that they're
~~thair~~ right and will stay with her. He encourages this.

Marching only at night, they finally reach a small air field in the north and then are flown to Hanoi. Milo is at first received on friendly terms and he is permitted a short visit with his "friend" in prison and manages to tip off the other man so that no one suspects anything. But that night he runs into a Chinese Army officer who once saw him, or met him, in Hong Kong and is suspicious. The Chinese officer vanishes for a day or two and then returns with full information about Milo -- partly derived from Soviet files on him.

Milo is exposed to the North Vietnamese and is thrown into the cell with the American he came to rescue. They are both to be flown the following morning to Red China to go on trial. They are loaded into a Chinese plane the next morning with two Chinese pilots and a guard. Once they are up in the air, Milo frees himself and the other American and overcomes the three Chinese. He knows enough about planes to manage to keep it ~~m~~ in the air but that is about all. He points the plane southward and hopes for the best.

Ken told a couple of correspondents that he had begun a new Milo March, to be titled *The Ides of March*. But in a letter of January 29, 1976, to Virginia Kidd, his American agent, Ken said, "After much soul searching, I think that I will start the complete rewrite on the new March story. Not because it

The Bamboo Jail - 3
R Outline

The North Vietnamese soon discover the plane is off course.
They send two flighter planes after him. He manages to shoot both
of them down, but is badly wounded himself. He continues to fly
the plane southwadd, avoiding further pursuit, until he thinks
he's nearing American installations. Then he begind to send radio
messages to the one air base for which he knows the code word. He
finally gets a response. They send planes out to meet him and he
is "talked" down to the landing.

He recovers consciousness in a military hospital in Saigon.
He calls Washington and makes his report. He has the American with
him and then gives the information on the Chinese Restaurant to
local American officer. Against the doctor's wishes, he is then
taken by ambulance to an American plane and heads back for the
States.

####

has any politics in it, but the beginning is just wrong." That
is the last reference to it that I can locate, and unfortunately
no trace of this project was found.

Of *Brides,* Ken wrote to Virginia on April 11, 1976: "I think
I should put it in mothballs for a couple of years and then

maybe we can sell it as a historical novel!" But on February 14, 1977, he wrote to her: "I do think that with the proper cuts and a new title BRIDES might make the grade." I wonder what other title Ken had in mind. *The Bamboo Jail*?

Kendra Crossen Burroughs

ABOUT THE AUTHOR

Kendell Foster Crossen (1910–1981), the only child of Samuel Richard Crossen and Clo Foster Crossen, was born on a farm outside Albany in Athens County, Ohio—a village of some 550 souls in the year of this birth. His ancestors on his mother's side include the 19th-century songwriter Stephen Collins Foster ("Oh! Susanna"); William Allen, founder of Allentown, Pennsylvania; and Ebenezer Foster, one of the Minute Men who sprang to arms at the Lexington alarm in April 1775.

Ken went to Rio Grande College on a football scholarship but stayed only one year. "When I was fairly young, I developed the disgusting habit of reading," says Milo March, and it seems Ken Crossen, too, preferred self-education. He loved literature and poetry; favorite authors included Christopher Marlowe and Robert Service. He also enjoyed participant sports and was a semi-pro fighter in the heavyweight class. He became a practicing magician and had a passion for chess.

After college Ken wrote several one-act plays that were produced in a small Cleveland theater. He worked in steel mills and Fisher Body plants. Then he was employed as an insurance investigator, or "claims adjuster," in Cleveland. But he left the job and returned to the theater, now as a performer: a tumbling clown in the Tom Mix Circus; a comic and carnival barker for a tent show, and an actor in a medicine show.

In 1935, Ken hitchhiked to New York City with a typewriter under his arm, and found work with the WPA Writers' Project, covering cricket for the *New York City Guidebook*. In 1936, he was hired by the Munsey Publishing Company as associate editor of the popular *Detective Fiction Weekly*. The company asked him to come up with a character to compete with The Shadow, and thus was born a unique superhero of pulps, comic books, and radio—The Green Lama, an American mystic trained in Tibetan Buddhism.

Crossen sold his first story, "The Aaron Burr Murder Case," to *Detective Fiction Weekly* in September 1939, but says he didn't begin to make a living from writing till 1941. He tried his hand at publishing true crime magazines, comics, and a picture magazine, without great success, so he set out for Hollywood. From his typewriter flowed hundreds of stories, short novels for magazines, scripts radio, television, and film, nonfiction articles. He delved into science fiction in the 1950s, starting with "Restricted Clientele" (February 1951). His dystopian novels *Year of Consent* and *The Rest Must Die* also appeared in this decade.

In the course of his career Ken Crossen acquired six pseudonyms: Richard Foster, Bennett Barlay, Kent Richards, Clay Richards, Christopher Monig, and M.E. Chaber. The variety was necessary because different publishers wanted to reserve specific bylines for their own publications. Ken based "M.E. Chaber" on the Hebrew word for "author," *mechaber.*

In the early '50s, as M.E. Chaber, Crossen began to write a series of full-length mystery/espionage novels featuring Milo March, an insurance investigator. The first, *Hangman's Harvest,* was published in 1952. In all, there are twenty-two Milo March novels. One, *The Man Inside,* was made into a British film starring Jack Palance.

Most of Ken's characters were private detectives, and Milo was the most popular. Paperback Library reissued twenty-five Crossen titles in 1970–1971, with covers by Robert McGinnis. Twenty were Milo March novels, four featured an insurance investigator named Brian Brett, and one was about CIA agent Kim Locke.

Crossen excelled at producing well-plotted entertainment with fast-moving action. His research skills were a strong asset, back when research meant long hours searching library microfilms and poring over street maps and hotel floorplans. His imagination took him to many international hot spots, although he himself never traveled abroad. Like Milo March, he hated flying ("When you've seen one cloud, you've seen them all").

Ken Crossen was married four times. With his first wife he had three children (Stephen, Karen, Kendra) and with his second a son (David). He lived in New York, Florida, Southern California, Nevada, and other parts of the country. Milo March moves from Denver to New York City after five books of the series, with an apartment on Perry Street in Greenwich Village; that's where Ken lived, too. His and Milo's favorite watering hole was the Blue Mill Tavern, a short walk from the apartment.

Ken Crossen was a combination of many of the traits of his different male characters: tough, adventuresome, with a taste for gin and shapely women. But perhaps the best observation was made in an obituary written by sci-fi writer Avram Davidson, who described Ken as a fundamentally gentle person who had been buffeted by many winds.